Love Moves Forward

Learning to Love - Book Two

Kaitlyn Calicott

Emma's life was going great.

Then one moment changed everything. The great life she had worked so hard for was suddenly taken away.

Now Emma has given up. No one can penetrate the fog that surrounds her: not her family, her best friend, or even the love of her life.

No one, that is, but a solitary voice that finally breaks through. From a person she least expected she would ever listen to let alone be friends with.

Emma faces tough choices in order to move forward in all aspects of her life.

Will she make the right decisions in swimming, her career, and her love life? Or will she be left wondering if she should have chosen differently?

Contents

Prologue

"Ma'am, can you hear me?"

I blink my eyes open. A bright light shines back and I immediately shut them.

Where am I? My head hurts.

I open my eyes again and try to move. Pain shoots through my right leg.

I grab it. I don't know why. Maybe hoping grabbing it will stop the pain.

That voice once again says, "Ma'am, do you know your name?"

My name? Why is he asking my name?

"Emma Anderson."

I take in my surroundings and it clicks. The accident.

Logan!

I look to my right and he isn't there. Where is he?

Last I looked, there was so much blood. The seat still glistens with red.

I try to move again, doing my best to ignore the pain. "Logan?" I turn to the voice I heard. It's a paramedic. "Where's Logan?"

"You need to stop moving. We're going to have to cut you out."

"Logan? Where is he?" I start to panic. He was right next to me. I yank on the seatbelt, pushing through the pain I feel everywhere. I need to get out and get to Logan.

"Ma'am, he was taken into the hospital." He puts his hand on me but I yank it off. Why is he holding me down? I need to get out of here. Now.

"We have to cut you out. Your leg is crushed and we need to get it checked as soon as possible. How many fingers am I holding up?"

I stare at his hand trying to focus on the fingers. It looks like a lot. My head is pounding. I try to focus again and slowly four fingers come into focus.

"Four," I say with no confidence.

"Good. We are going to cut you out now. You need to be still."

A loud grinding starts up and a screech pierces the air. I squeeze my eyes shut. I see a bright light of a truck coming towards me.

No. No. Not again.

My whole body starts shaking and my arm feels like it is being pulled out of its socket. Another light shines in my eyes. I blink to make it go away.

Slowly I open them to see a face in front of me. This time a woman. She has a glow around her.

Is she an angel? Am I in Heaven?

She immediately turns off the light and her face comes into focus. "Hi sweetie. I want you to focus on my voice. We're going to get you out of here but we need you to stay still, and stay awake."

She starts talking but all I can hear is the grinding and screeching. I shut my eyes again and it stops. I open them back up to see the windshield being lifted off the front. Next, two guys with a giant pry bar looking tool come towards me. I wiggle trying to get away.

The voice of the angel says, "Look at me. I want you to count backwards from twenty. We are going to get you out of here." She pulls my face back towards her and I feel pressure on my shoulder as she holds me down.

I can't breathe. I wiggle more. Please let this stop.

The pressure on my shoulder releases and then something lifts me under my back and my thighs.

It is quickly replaced with something soft. The stars above me shine bright. Wait, stars?

That must have been an angel taking me up to heaven.

Something is put over my face, and my last thought as my eyes close are, "Logan, please don't leave me."

I must have passed out, because the next time I wake up to a bright light above me. My head pounds as I look around, and I realize I'm in the hospital.

There is a curtain around my bed.

I hear someone talking on the other side.

"...never walk again." I hear an unknown voice say.

I lean up and pain shoots through my entire body.

My head is pounding so much, I don't know what to think. The drugs are making everything foggy.

Okay, so someone said something. Oh right...never walk again. Did I hear that correctly?

I realize I can't feel my right leg. Were they talking about me? I may never walk. Do I still have a leg?

I look down at my body to make sure I still have a leg. It is there but completely bandaged up with a massive brace and metal rods sticking out here and there. It is hanging in straps, elevated slightly.

The talking stops but then whispering immediately follows.

"Should we tell her about..." the voice hesitates.

Tell me what? Finish the sentence. I will whoever is out there to finish what they were going to say. Too many things come to mind.

Another voice answers. "No, it's too soon with everything else. We should wait."

The voices sound familiar but I can't place them. I try to focus on the rest of the conversation, but the voices become muffled. I struggle to fight against the fog in my head. Why can't I focus? Panic rises up again. I look around for something to stop it. My eyes land on the machines next to my bed and the many tubes.

Drugs. That's what's making my head foggy.

Pre-med has taught me that much. They must have given me something to help with the pain.

I close my eyes, hoping the pounding will stop and the fog will clear.

A voice rings out.

"...is dead."

Dead? Who died? Logan? No, no, no. He can't die. Did my... No, I can't think about that.

My heart starts to race. A scream pierces the air.

The screaming continues until a warm hand slides into mine and I realize the screaming is coming from me. I squint, seeing my mom next to me.

The curtain is pulled back. I see Logan's mom, Victoria, standing just beyond the now open curtain.

"Sweetie, calm down. You're safe," my mom says.

My heart is still racing and I can barely breathe but I manage to get out the question I need an answer to, "where's Logan?"

My mom glances back to Victoria. No. Why is she looking at her?

An alarm sounds.

Before she can answer, nurses rush in.

"You both need to leave. We need to calm her down."

One nurse starts fiddling with the tube and another tries to usher my mom and Logan's out.

"I am staying with my daughter." My mom doesn't move, still grasping my hand.

"Once we get her to calm down, you can come back in. If her blood pressure gets too high, she could give herself a stroke from her concussion."

My mom nods and slowly gives my hand a kiss before releasing it and following the nurse with Victoria out the door.

No. She needs to come back. I need an answer. I look to my left at the nurse.

She has a needle in her hands. I thrash around, trying to get away but I'm stuck with my leg in the sling. "Stop. Don't. Please, I need to know about my--" I feel a prick and my brain becomes foggy once again until I can't think at all.

I slowly blink but feel my mind wandering. I feel like I'm watching myself in the hospital bed in a dream.

I see my mom next to me, talking to me.

I shout, "Let me see. I don't believe you. He can't be dead. I want to see him."

"Sweetie, you can't see him. It's been two weeks. You were in a medically induced coma to let your body heal. They already took his body." My mom says gently touching my arm.

Flashbacks of the accident race before my eyes. I scream.

I lightly touch my stomach, feeling completely sick and I look at my mom. She has tears running down her face as she subtly shakes her head.

"No!" I scream.

I don't remember what happened next but I wake up later.

I have no idea how much time has passed but I remember my mom saying two weeks and something about a coma.

Was that real or a dream?

I don't know what is real anymore.

As I open my eyes, everything is foggy. It's always foggy. I am sure I am on some very heavy drugs right now.

I glance at the window and notice a figure sitting in the chair. The figure looks up at me and I gasp, "Logan."

He gives me a look I could only describe as confusion but it quickly turns to a smile.

He immediately stands and walks towards the bed.

He reaches for my hand. Shocks shoot through my arm. My hand feels perfect in his, just like it always does. I close my eyes, enjoying the warmth from his hand and the fact that he is alive.

"Emma, look at me."

I wait a few seconds in case I am imagining this. I still have a terrible headache and my brain feels cloudy.

I slowly open my eyes and he's still there. I smile. He's really here. He's alive.

"Logan," I say again.

"Emma, you need to listen to me."

"Umm hmm..." I'm barely listening because we have all the time. He's here and that's all that matters. Something is nagging at me that he should be recovering in his own hospital bed. Maybe more time has passed than I thought.

"You're here," I say in my delirious state.

"I am but I wanted to say goodbye. I have to leave...." I don't hear much else after that. Why is he leaving? I grasp his hand tighter, afraid to let go. Now that I see Logan, I know that scene with my mom was a dream.

But what if it wasn't?

What if *this,* is also a dream?

No, he is alive. He is standing right here in front of me. I feel his hand holding mine. My leg is still hanging from the sling. The hospital room looks the same. I think.

Logan is still talking. "You have your family, my family, Ashley. My brother would go to the ends of the earth for you, so lean on him. I love you, Emma. Always have. Always will."

He lets go of my hand and gently takes my face in his hands, kissing my forehead. He turns to leave.

Again, why is he leaving?

"Logan, don't go. I'm not ready."

"Yes you are, Emma."

I don't hear anything else as I watch him walk to the door.

Right before he leaves, he looks back to me and once again says, "Don't stop fighting," before he disappears out the door.

"Wait. Come back. I need you!" I yell. The monitors once again come to life as the alarms blare but all I can hear are my sobs and shouts for him to come back. I don't want to be alone.

I blink away the tears that fall. What is happening right now?

The nurse comes into my room and adds something to one of the tubes in my arm.

My last thoughts as I drift off once again is Logan left me. He walked out of my room and left. Hopefully I will wake up from this nightmare and we can continue our lives... happy... and together.

Chapter One

8 months after the accident

"Why can't I take a semester off?" I ask Ashley.

"Because you don't take semesters off. You are Emma, queen of kicking butt, not procrastination. Look at your leg after almost six months of rehab. Most people wouldn't be standing, let alone running like you are. Not taking classes this fall will put you behind with your master's."

I grab a pillow off the couch of the apartment we share, put it over my head and groan. After the accident I almost gave everything up, but a friend pushed me to keep going. A friend I should probably text.

"I just don't know if I can continue my plan of being a physical therapist. It was his idea. How can I move forward when every class reminds me of Lo...Log... of him."

"You can say his name."

"I can't..."

"Why not?"

Before I can answer, there's a knock at the door. I glance at Ashley to find her on her phone sitting on the recliner. Guess I'll be getting the door. I hop off the bed and open the door to find, "Jeremy?"

That's weird. I was just thinking that I needed to text him.

"Emma, my favorite girl." He pulls me in for a hug but not before I see him wink at Ashley.

Is something going on with them? She hasn't mentioned anything.

We separate and I ask, "What are you doing here?"

"I was in the neighborhood." He walks in and plops down onto the couch, immediately making himself at home. He always had a way with doing that and making me feel at ease. I close the door and walk over to sit across from him.

"Somehow I don't think Nashville is anywhere near here."

"Okay you caught me. I hadn't heard from you in a few months and I wanted to make sure you were still moving forward. Now where is a good place to get food around here?" Jeremy asks.

"We love grabbing burgers from a place around the corner and then eating it at the park," Ashley adds. "You all go. I have some work I need to do for the fall semester."

I look at her confused. What prep work does she have to do? I know all the classes she is signed up for, and none of them require work beforehand.

"Let's go!" Jeremy hops up from the couch and extends an arm to me. "Emma and I are due for some friend bonding since she ignores my texts now."

I knew I should have texted him back. Now he's here and I'll never get away with taking a semester or more off. Unless I don't tell him. Yeah, I just won't tell him.

"Fine." I get up before he can pull me up. I grab my purse from my room. Back in the living room, I spot Jeremy and Ashley whispering to each other. Jeremy sees me and walks over but not before I see him wink at Ashley again. I need to ask Ash what is going on with them later. I notice a duffel by the door.

"Are you staying here?"

"I could. If you don't mind me crashing for a few nights?"

"Uh sure."

"I can make up the couch when we get back. I'm hungry," Jeremy says.

"I figured you'd want to stay in Ashley's bed."

Jeremy looks at me confused. "Why would I want to stay in Ashley's bed?"

I shrug. Jeremy still looks confused but doesn't say anything else.

A black car is waiting in the parking lot for us. Instead of renting a car like a normal person, he orders car service to take him wherever he needs to go. I guess when you are one of the top quarterbacks in the country, you can afford it.

Jeremy asks me for the name of the burger place and then tells the driver. He then pulls out his phone to put an order in online. I'm starving so I tell him to order me a cheeseburger with all the toppings, a large tater tots, and a large sweet tea. The best thing about not training anymore is that I don't have to worry about what I eat–although I probably should start watching my weight.

I dropped significantly after the accident, but I've started to gain it back.

We get to the burger place and Jeremy runs inside to grab our orders. I wait in the car. He gets back and the driver takes us to the park nearby.

We find a picnic table under a tree to give us some shade and relief from the heat. Summer in North Carolina is hot and humid, and we are barely into the hottest part.

We eat in silence for a little while before Jeremy breaks the ice with the question I was dreading. I will be having a serious talk with Ashley later about spilling the beans.

"Why aren't you signed up for classes? School starts in two weeks, Emma."

"I'm going to kill Ashley."

"She's worried about you. And so am I."

"Is that why you came here? To make sure I am a good little girl and go to school?"

"That's part of it. The other part is that I missed my best friend. You stopped texting me, and you never answered my calls. I know I was hard on you at the beginning of the year, but would you be doing half the things you are now if I hadn't?"

I sigh because I know he is right. Other than my family, his family and Ashley, he was one of the few people allowed in my room after the accident. Without him, I wouldn't have finished my first year of my master's, let alone be walking. If not for him, I would probably still be laying in a hospital or at least home in bed and barely getting out of it.

I owe him so much and that is part of the reason I stopped responding to him. He was always there looking like a doppelgänger of his brother. The same brother that was the love of my life, the one who left me after the accident. My last foggy memory of him was when he walked out of my hospital room telling me goodbye.

I couldn't take seeing Jeremy and having that constant reminder.

"No, but every day in class is a reminder that he was the one that came up with the idea of me being a physical therapist. How can I move forward when this was part of our dream?"

"Emma, this was never his dream. He recommended physical therapy because he knew you better than anyone. He knew what would make you happy. Getting a degree in sports medicine is the perfect path for you. Anyone who knows you well enough would agree." He pauses for me to say something. When I don't he continues, "Tell me this, would Logan want you to give up on your dream just because he is no longer in the picture?"

I wince at Logan's name. It's been almost eight months since the accident and I still can't bring myself to say his name. Instead of the happy memories I have with him, all I can think about is our fight in the car. The fight where he told me he wanted to go to school in California and I said no. I didn't really hear him out. I just pushed it off thinking we'd talk about it later. Now I can't help but wonder where we would be if the accident hadn't happened. Would he have persuaded me to move to California?

Or would we have stayed on this coast? I'll never know because he left me and didn't fight for me.

I shake my head. "No, he wouldn't."

"Then continue school and follow your dream. It may have started out as his idea, but it turned into your dream. You're going to help so many athletes. Look at how much you've learned already and how it helped you with your rehab."

"You're right. It just gets hard sometimes."

"That's why you have me and Ashley and your parents. Even my parents. They ask about you all the time."

I think about all the times I've thought about calling them but didn't because I was too afraid that they blamed me for the accident. I don't say this to Jeremy because he'll think it's ridiculous.

We gather our trash and toss it into the nearby trash can. Jeremy pulls out his phone, I assume to call the driver to come pick us up when he opens the camera and aims it at me.

"Now can you say that part about me being right again?"

I playfully shove him to the side. "I don't know what you're talking about."

"Please?" He gives me a pout that most girls would fall for in an instance. I know because Logan had the same one that I fell for more often than not.

"Still don't know what you're talking about." I skip away before he can say more.

"I will get it on camera one day. How about we get some ice cream and walk around the park. I saw an ice cream stand when we first came in."

"Sure, but you're not allowed to steal mine. You get your own." He always gets his own but manages to somehow steal half of mine.

"You always pick the best flavor." He pouts again.

"Then pick the same flavor I do."

"Yeah, but then I can't try the other flavors that look good. At least if I get my own flavor, then I can also have some yours."

"Then get two!" I exclaim.

"Now that's just being greedy."

I laugh because somehow what he says makes sense and no matter what I say, he will still end up eating half of mine. He has since high school. Logan used to joke about it all the time and I always tell him to get his own. Then Jeremy would try to steal Logan's too.

I order two scoops of fudge brownie on a cone and he orders two scoops of chocolate chip cookie dough on a cone.

We enjoy our walk around the little pond and try to quickly eat our melting ice cream. The coolness of it gives relief to the hot day.

"Hey Emma." I turn my head to him, not realizing how close he was and somehow managing to get his ice cream all over my cheek.

"I was going to ask if you wanted to check out the festival they are setting up for but now I'll say you have a little something right there." He points to my cheek.

"No really, captain obvious."

"Here let me help." He chuckles, holding up a napkin like he is going to wipe it off but instead licks it off and then takes a big bite of my ice cream.

"Ewww!" I shout and find Jeremy crouched over laughing. "Why would you lick me?"

"To distract you so I could eat some of your very guarded ice cream."

"You're gross."

"I got the ice cream off your cheek and got you to smile, didn't I?" He smirks and I can't help but join in laughing.

"Now that's what I like to see. You've been sad too long. One of my goals today was to get you to smile." He turns his phone around and shows me the picture he just took. It shows me mid-laughter. My eyes are clear and show no sadness. Even though I know it's there, at least I can see what it used to be like to be happy.

How did he manage to steal my ice cream and take a picture? I'll never know.

I sigh. "I'm trying. Sometimes it just gets to be too much."

Jeremy pulls me in for a side hug. "I miss him too. Honestly, I still text him sometimes even though I know he won't respond."

"I used to do that but I'd call him instead. I know he won't answer my calls but it's nice to hear his voice in his voicemail." I just can't do it anymore because it makes me too sad.

We finish our ice cream and throw away the trash. As we walk back to the car, I ask him, "can I be honest about something?"

"Emma, you can always be honest with me."

"I thought the reason for you coming here was because you and Ashley were talking."

"We've been talking a lot." He must see something on my face because he continues.

"Not talking like that. We've been talking about you. We're both worried about you."

"I'm sorry I made you both worried. It's just been hard."

"I know, but like I said before, we're here for you. His absence affects all of us and all we can do is go day by day. You and I are both similar in the fact that keeping busy is what helps. That is why I've been pushing you because I know if you just stay still too long, you'll get inside your head."

We head back to the car. I stop Jeremy before he can get in. "Hey Jer? Thanks for coming. I know I can always count on you to have my back even when I don't want you to."

"Of course, and don't you forget it." He kisses me sweetly on the forehead and opens the door. "Let's go get you signed up for classes."

I slide in the car and Jeremy leans in. "One other thing, don't you dare ignore my texts again," he says as a massive grin spreads across his face.

I laugh. "I promise."

Chapter Two

1 year after the accident

I step off the plane and pull my coat tighter around me. "Mom, I just want some time to relax before spring semester."

I'm already dreading my next semester. Don't get me wrong, I love what I'm studying but it's still a ton of work. Not only do I have classes, but I'll also have my second clinical practicum.

"You are already on your way to Nashville. I can come pick you up. Please honey, we miss you."

"The only reason I'm going to Nashville is because I promised Jeremy I would go to one of his games. My schedule is so crazy this semester. This is the first and only one I can attend. As his best friend, it's required–or so I am told."

"I'm glad you have him. I don't think anyone else could have helped you through everything. He was the only one you would listen to."

I sigh because I know it's true. I never would be where I'm at if it weren't for him. It's the reason I made myself come back here to see his game. He supported me when I needed him so it's time I returned the favor.

"You know, your dad was always scared that you would date him."

"What?" I blurt out because I'd never heard that.

"Yes. You may not know this but all those times you came to the football practices, Jeremy got distracted more often than not staring at the bleachers. He still can't take his eyes off of you the second you walk into a room."

"You can't be serious?"

My mom laughs. "Oh, I am."

"How did I not know this?" The idea of all this is crazy to me.

"Because you always had your head in a book. And then you were dating his brother."

I know the first part is true. Ashley loved to go watch the football practices or more like stare at the guys on the team. Usually practices were closed but since my dad was the coach, we were allowed to watch. I never paid attention to what was happening on the field. I knew every rule and play by heart.

As for the second part, well Logan came into my life and I never looked at anyone else. And I don't think I will for a long time either. The pain of him leaving gets better every day but it's barely been a year.

"Well I don't know why he would be looking at me. We never talked other than the one time I spilled coffee on him. Actually that makes sense. He was probably plotting how to get revenge."

"Emma, why wouldn't he look at you? I am not just saying this because you are my daughter but you are beautiful. You turn heads wherever you go. Not only that, but you have a heart of gold and you don't flaunt it. You can see it in every video Logan ever captured of you."

A tear runs down my cheek. I sniffle before saying, "Mom, I miss him so much."

"I know sweetie. I also know that is the real reason you won't come home. I won't push this time, but eventually I hope you will."

"One day."

I hope. I don't know when that day will be. Home has too many memories and is still too raw. The one year anniversary of the accident is in a few days and I am doing my best not to think about it. I could never be anywhere near where it happened on that day.

"Just promise me this. Promise me in the future you'll open your heart again. Best friends are a perfect start for more."

Was she saying what I think she was saying? Me and Jeremy? Now that would be funny. We are seriously like brother and sister. We fight like siblings and I have always looked at him like my older brother. I was married to his younger brother after all.

Does Jeremy look at me as more than a sister? I shake away the thought.

"I'll try. Thanks Mom. I have to go because the plane is getting ready to take off."

"Bye sweetie. I'm here if you ever need to talk. Love you."

"I love you too. Bye Mom." I love my parents and I feel bad not going home but they have to understand the memories surrounding that town. Everywhere I go, I see Logan.

I hang up and see a new text.

Jeremy: *Sending a car to pick you up.*

That's weird. Normally, Jeremy picks me up from the airport and his texts are always more cheerful. Come to think of it, he has barely texted me recently. He is probably nervous about his game.

Yeah, that's it.

I pick up my bag and head to my gate.

The driver takes me to the hotel Jeremy reserved for me, despite my disagreement. It is a cute boutique hotel a few blocks from the stadium. A very nice hotel.

He better not have paid a ton of money for this place. Knowing him, he probably did. Money has never been an issue for him and certainly not now that he is a professional football player.

After putting my stuff into my room and grabbing lunch, I still haven't heard from Jeremy since his text about the driver picking me up. I head to the stadium to see if I can find him. He is probably warming up since the game is tonight.

The stadium is packed with people tailgating everywhere. The air smells like a backyard barbeque. Everything from hotdogs and hamburgers to shrimp and steak kabobs. My stomach rumbles even though I just ate lunch.

I shoot Jeremy a text.

Emma: *I'm at the stadium. Know anyone I can hang out with?"*

My seat says box on it. I am going to kill Jeremy for that once I find him and figure out where the box even is.

A guy not much older than me walks up to me. He is dressed in dark jeans, a titans t-shirt with a coat on top. Very business casual.

"Are you Emma Anderson?" I wince at the last name. I couldn't bring myself to change my name. I really should have because it hurts to hear anyone say it.

"Yes."

"Follow me."

I am not following him until I know who he is.

"Who are you?"

"I'm Connor. Jeremy sent me to bring you to your seat."

I wonder why Jeremy didn't text me back. I'm still not going with this stranger no matter what he tells me or who he says sent him. That name does sound familiar, but he could have taken a wild guess as to who I might be a fan of on the team and then take me to a dark corner and do whatever he wants. I am not taking any chances. No thank you.

As if he could read my mind, I get a text from Jeremy.

Jeremy: *Go with Connor.*

I look up at the gentleman, trying to find any hint of pretending. I don't see anything suspicious. "Lead the way."

We arrive at the box or should I say suite. My jaw drops. Inside is a good sized room with a table lining one wall and with food warmers, a large window in front with rows of chairs, and the other side is a bar.

We still have several hours before the game starts and not many people are in the suite yet. I guess you can't get into the stadium until two hours before the game, but Jeremy must have pulled some strings.

I look out the giant window and the view is amazing. I can see the entire field from here and everything going on. I can see the players warming up. I try to find Jeremy but they all look the same. Knowing how football works, I search for the quarterbacks but still come up empty. There is no number five out there.

"Looking for someone?" I jump as I hear the whisper in my ear.

I turn to find Jeremy in his uniform behind me as he pulls me into a hug. He squeezes me tight. So tight that it is almost like he needs the hug. As I hug him back, I feel him relax. He must be nervous for the game.

"Aren't you supposed to be down there?" I point to the field as I pull away.

"Yeah. I told my coach I'd be right back."

"And he just let you go?"

"Why not? He trusts me, plus I didn't go far."

"Are you ready for the game?"

Jeremy shrugs. Now that is weird. Normally before games he is bouncing off the walls and super hyped up.

"Is everything okay?"

Jeremy pauses before he speaks. "Emma, do you know what's in a few days?"

I suck in a breath. Now I get it.

I nod my head because I no longer have words.

He pulls me in for another hug. "I'm sorry. I didn't mean to bring it up. I have just been in a weird head space recently."

I glance up at him, placing my hand on his cheek. "I get it. He left us both."

"What would you say to staying a few extra days?"

"I don't know Jer. I was planning on locking myself in my room with action movies and ice cream. Ashley was already coming up with ways to entice me out."

He laughs. "I am sure she was." He wraps his arms around me tighter and rests his chin on my head. "Just think about it."

I nod again and I know he can feel it.

We stay like that embraced in each other seeking comfort from a tough time when someone clears their throat behind us.

"Mr. Anderson, I believe you are supposed to be down on the field warming up," the same guy from earlier says with a smile.

"Yes sir." He pulls away from our hug and gives the guy a salute.

Next to him is a beautiful brunette whom I instantly recognize. She is in a long sleeve Titans t-shirt and dark skinny jeans with black leather boots with the biggest heels I have ever seen.

I am about to say hi when Jer leans forward to kiss her on the cheek. "Hi Danielle."

The jealousy that fills me is not something I am ready for and it definitely shows on my face because Jeremy grabs my hand

and whispers in my ear. "I am honored that you are jealous but nothing to be jealous of. She's my publicist."

Before I can protest, he turns back to them. "Emma, you know Danielle. She's my publicist and this is my manager, Connor."

Connor reaches out his hand for me to shake and then kisses it. "Nice to meet you, officially." My jaw drops open at his boldness. I've never had someone kiss my hand before other than Logan and Jeremy.

Jeremy laughs. "Connor likes to think he has a way with the ladies."

"I most certainly do, and I'd like to keep my job too. Get your butt back on the field before I drag it down there myself."

Now I am the one laughing. I've heard plenty of stories about Connor but it is nice to finally put a face to the name.

Danielle is next and instead of shaking my hand, she enthusiastically pulls me in for a hug. "I missed you. I hate that we lost touch after college but I can't wait to catch up. I've already heard so much about your life since then."

I look back to Jeremy who shrugs.

"Don't worry, all good. Mr. Anderson here talks my ear off about you," she says in a teasing remark. When I look at her though she is looking at Connor, not Jeremy.

That is also surprising that Jeremy has been talking about me. We have always been good friends but it's weird he would talk about me all the time when he has so much going on in his life. This past year we have gotten even closer with him overseeing all of my rehab and making sure I was doing what I said I would. I am still waiting for the day when he pushes me in the pool and makes me swim again.

"On that note, I am going to head to the field. Danielle and Connor let's go."

"Didn't you hear? I get to stay up here with Emma." She locks her arm through mine.

She smirks at him. Okay, no more jealousy. I know they had a short fling in college but I remember why we were such good friends from back then. She can totally put him in his place now and I don't get any romantic vibes from either of them. If anything I can't help notice the way her and Connor have found multiple little ways to touch each other in the few minutes that we've been here.

"I'll walk you down Jeremy, but then I have a date with two hotties." He winks at us and ushers Jeremy out the door.

Jeremy pokes his head back through the door. "Emma, think about what I asked." And then he is gone.

Danielle drags me onto a couch. "Okay I want to know everything. We can start with what he asked you."

I forgot how much energy this girl has and I really like it. Normally I would be running in the opposite direction unless it was Ashley because she is the same way. But Danielle is a breath of fresh air after all these years.

I laugh. "Am I allowed to tell you that? Isn't it a conflict of interest?"

"I'm not a journalist or anything like that. I'm just his pub-licist. I post on his social media, fix any of his mess-ups before the press gets to it, and other little things."

"Now tell me because it may have been years since we last spoke but it feels like no time has passed. I basically know you already."

"Do I need to say off the record?"

"Again, not a journalist. As your old and soon-to-be best friend again, I would never use anything you said."

I laugh again. I trusted her way back then and I know Jeremy wouldn't work with someone he didn't trust.

"He asked me to stay a few extra days before I go home."

"Oh, that sounds romantic!"

"Ha, not like that. We're just friends."

"Are you sure? It was a firework show when I came in here. You two were intertwined in that hug and I was scared that if I touched either of you, I would burn."

"We are definitely just friends." What is with everyone recent-ly telling me or asking me if something is going on with Jeremy? Sure, we've been spending a ton of time together but that's just because he's been helping me.

"So why did he ask you to stay?"

"Umm..." I gulp because I do not want to talk about this. "We both had someone close to us leave almost a year ago. We...uhh ...he just wants someone around I guess." She probably already knows, but I can't bring myself to say his name.

"Logan?"

I nod. I am on the verge of tears and if I say anything, I won't be able to keep them in.

"I am so sorry. Okay topic change. Tell me about the Olympics. You were amazing. I knew back when you first swam with us at Florida State that you were going all the way."

"Thanks. It was great to be there. It sometimes feels like it was a dream."

"I bet. You were actually my inspiration for being a sports publicist."

"Really? How?" I ask.

"I was an entertainment publicist for several actors and actresses. I've always loved sports, but I thought working in the Hollywood bubble would be so glamorous. It does have its perks but it can be a lot. A few months after your accident I met Jeremy in a bar. He was super drunk, hitting on me and droning on about some girl and his brother."

She must see something in my expression because she immediately adds, "I turned down his advances. Don't get me wrong, he is super hot but I won't ever date someone that could ever become representation. I wasn't in the sports industry yet but many athletes do movies or other TV events. Plus, when we had our short fling in college, I knew there was nothing there. I slid my card into his shirt pocket with a note saying to call me if he ever needed to talk."

I'm wondering where she is going with this. If she is trying to make me jealous of her and Jeremy then it is working, which is really weird because I don't know why I would be jealous. I was only roommates with her for a year before I moved out of the dorms and then I transferred. We stayed in touch for a short while but lost touch. She was a great friend in college and I hope we can be close again.

"It didn't hit me till later that he was talking about you. He mentioned his brother, Logan, and wife, Emma. I knew who he was so I connected the dots. We ended up getting coffee a few days later. He apologized for hitting on me and we talked. Both about college and our current lives. You know we never slept together in college right?"

"Really?" I ask. I did not know that. I always thought they had a summer fling that started when I swam in the meet over spring break my Senior Year of high school.

"No. We made out but there were no sparks. We didn't see a point in trying to force anything. It was fun hanging out with him, but I knew even way back then that you had his heart."

My jaw drops. He didn't like me back then, did he? I guess there were moments when he flirted a ton or that moment when we were dancing, but he was always making sure Logan and I were happy.

"I know you never saw it but it didn't matter because you were with his brother. He knew that and would never have jeopardized it. That day we met for coffee, we clicked again right away but not romantically. More as a client and rep should click. He talked a lot about you and how he was helping you recover."

I should have been mad that Jeremy had said so much about me and my recovery but it seemed to help him. I probably would have been madder if it had been someone else besides her. I always wondered how he was so okay after the accident when I was a mess.

As if she can read my mind, she adds, "don't worry, he never went into specifics but he said he was helping with your rehab and you were having a hard time. I don't blame you at all. I'd be devastated too."

"Anyway, I have been going on and on when I was supposed to be telling you about why you inspired me. After hearing about how well you were doing and the miraculous recovery you were making, it got me thinking. I want to work with people that have stories to tell. Not that actors don't, but I love when athletes come back from an injury. Do you think you'll ever go back to the Olympics?"

I gulp because this is not a conversation I ever want to have so I give the answer I always give. "Maybe. Depends what the doctors say."

She nods probably knowing there is more to it. Thankfully she doesn't push. "Promise me, if you do decide to go back that I can represent you as your publicist. I have so many ideas."

"Sure," I say, knowing it most likely won't happen. Me going to the Olympics, not her being my publicist. That would be a ton of fun. "So how did you become Jeremy's publicist?"

"After we had coffee that day, we continued to talk. Again, it was just as friends. We really do have as much chemistry as two rocks. Anyway, where was I? Oh yes, so I was telling him how I wanted to branch out into the sports industry and he was telling me how he hated his publicist at the time."

I remember his publicist. He was always so serious and everything he posted on Jeremy's social handles was too businessy. Anyone who knows Jeremy well enough knows he's a total flirt and goofball. If I were his publicist, I'd use that in the posts but then again what do I know about publicity. Lately, his posts have been less serious and more fun and light. I guess that credit goes to Danielle.

She continues, "We decided to work together. I slowly switched over to sports and he fired his other publicist. He was coming up to the end of their contract."

"Do you like it?"

"I love it. I have always loved sports but like I said before I wanted to be part of that glamorous Hollywood world. While it was fun at times, it was filled with drama. The sports industry has its fair share of drama too, but it is more based on the actual game than 'did he have an affair with her' or 'her wild night out'."

I laugh. I could never handle that either. "That makes sense."

"So tell me about you and Jeremy."

"What about us?"

"I want all the gossip."

"Uh okay. Well you know how we met and all that. Ummm... he's been a great friend these past few years. Honestly, I don't think I would be here without him."

"So you two really aren't dating?"

"No," I laugh. "We have a very brother and sister relationship. We were in-laws."

"You'll have so much chemistry even after all these years."

Everyone always tells me that but I don't see it. I do get jealous when he goes out with other girls but that's just me being protective. Right?

"I'm not saying to date him, but you two have some serious sparks."

We talk a ton more and exchange numbers with promises to keep in touch. I tell her I'm not sure when I will be back in town but I'll let her know if I do.

Connor joins us a few minutes before kickoff and we get ready to cheer on the Titans.

Chapter Three

It's halftime and we are losing. I have never seen Jeremy play this bad. He looks miserable out there. We are only down by two touchdowns but both of those were scored from Jeremy throwing interceptions. We should be at least tied if not ahead. I'm pretty sure before this, he has only thrown two interceptions his entire football career including college.

"I'm going to go talk to him. I'd invite you ladies but no one but agents are allowed in the locker rooms."

"Hold on," I tell him. I pull out a piece of paper from my bag and jot down a note. "Give him this for me."

Connor nods and leaves the suite.

"What did the note say?" Danielle asks.

"I will only stay if you stop handing the ball to the other team and win this game."

"That's perfect," she says with a smirk.

The rest of the game goes well and we end up winning by a touchdown.

After his interviews, I meet Jeremy outside and we walk to his car. When I say car, I mean car service. We start heading in the opposite direction of my hotel.

"Aren't you dropping me off at my hotel?"

"I thought you could stay at my place."

"Oh, did you now?" I laugh at him. "I still need to get my stuff, and what about canceling the room? I don't want to take the room away from someone else if I'm not staying there."

"That was easy. I thought you would fight me more."

"I don't feel like fighting right now. The last time I had a fight in the car..." I don't need to finish my sentence. Jeremy knows what I'm talking about. The last fight I had was with Logan the night of the accident.

He grabs my hand and squeezes. "It's okay. No fighting."

I give him a small smile and pull my hand away. "You never answered my questions," I tease wanting the sad vibe to go away.

"I may have already had your stuff packed up and brought to my apartment. Before you say anything, you hadn't even unpacked anything minus your toothbrush on the bathroom counter and a pair of shoes on the floor." I sigh because it is true. I wasn't planning on being here long.

"To answer your second question, the hotel is owned by a friend of Dad's, so canceling is no problem."

We get to his apartment building and it is massive. I'm so exhausted that I don't have a chance to really take in the beauty of the building. Jeremy shows me to the guest bedroom in his two bedroom apartment. I barely say goodnight before I'm passed out.

The next morning I smell something burning. Kind of smells like bacon burning.

I throw off the covers and run out to the kitchen just as the smoke detector goes off. I see Jeremy through a cloud of smoke holding up a few strips of bacon with tongs.

"What're you doing?" I laugh.

Jeremy smiles so big. "Making breakfast."

"You mean burning breakfast?"

"That too. I did make eggs and toast though." He points to the eggs and toast on plates on the counter. "The bacon didn't make it. It was sizzling perfectly on a pan and next thing I know it's on fire."

"That is your first mistake. You tried to cook the bacon in a pan."

"Isn't that how you cook it?"

"Sure you can cook it like that, but everyone knows the best way to cook bacon is in the oven."

"What?" Jeremy looks almost horrified.

"Preheat the oven to 400 degrees and then bake the bacon for about twenty to twenty-five minutes depending on how crispy you want it."

Jeremy sets the temperature on the oven and grabs the un-cooked bacon.

I eye the eggs because they do look good but no one likes cold eggs. Jeremy must see me because he grabs the plate of eggs and the plate of toast and puts it in a warming drawer.

Yes, he actually has a warming drawer because his kitchen is that fancy. He then grabs a coffee mug, fills it with coffee, a splash of vanilla creamer, and hands it to me. I'm surprised he remembers how I take my coffee.

"Thanks." I take a sip and sit down at the breakfast bar. He takes a seat next to me with his cup and we fall into a comfortable silence.

A few minutes go by when Jeremy says, "Emma, I wanted to th..." He doesn't finish because the timer for the oven goes off. "Hold that thought." He grabs the baking tray of bacon and puts it in the oven, setting the timer for twenty minutes.

He sits back down. "I wanted to thank you for coming to my game. It meant a lot to me. Also, your note at halftime made me laugh and got my head back in the game. I just didn't expect it to feel like this."

He doesn't have to say any more. I know what he means. In a few days it will be a year from the accident and the day we both lost Logan. We talk some more until the bacon is ready and then dig into our breakfast. After we clean up Jeremy asks if I want to go for a run with him.

"No, I'll just hold you back."

"Emma, you could never hold me back. You set the pace and I'll follow."

It takes some persuading but finally I agree. We set off and my leg is stiff. I have been going to therapy for almost a year now. I've been told by multiple doctors that I'm a miracle; that most people would barely be walking at this point. I am no miracle, but rather have this annoying friend currently in front of me that wouldn't stop nagging me or pushing me to do better.

My leg is healed, but I still have a slight limp caused by the stiffness, which the doctors say will go away in time. Physical therapy and exercise are the best things I can do. I still haven't gone back in the pool, and I don't know if I ever will. I'm not scared of water. I'm scared of the memories that surface every time I get near the pool. Logan was my number one supporter other than my family. I just don't think I could do it without him at this point.

Jeremy leaves pretty soon after we get back to head to practice.

At dinner, I get a notification that my grades are available to view. I aced all my classes. Jeremy laughs at the surprised look on my face. I loved my classes and the material came easy to me but with everything that has been going on, it was a lot. One less thing to worry about, having to retake a class.

The next few days are similar and very relaxing. I actually enjoy my time here and forget about what's coming up.

A few days after the game I wake up with a pit in my stomach. I know what today is, but I don't want to admit it has been a year. I make my way out of bed and into the shower. As the hot water hits my back, the tears come pouring out. They won't stop. I sink down to the floor, my legs no longer able to support me as my sobbing takes hold of my body.

I think back to lying in the hospital and finding out that Logan didn't make it. How will I ever conquer my dreams without him when he was the one that pushed me towards them? I remember refusing to believe the truth. When the time came to say goodbye, I refused. I refused to cry. I refused to see what was right in front of me. I turned into a shell of myself.

The worst part was when it finally hit me that he wasn't coming back, I almost tried to end it all. Without my family, Jeremy, his parents, and Ashley, I would probably not be here today. Especially Jeremy, the one who pulled me out of the darkest pits and forced me to see that life was worth living. I was the distraction he needed to not fall into the dark pit with me while he was the light guiding me out.

Eventually the tears stop. I realize I'm shivering. I hadn't even noticed that the water was cold.

I stand, turn off the water, and grab a towel to dry off. I dress in leggings and a sweatshirt. All I care about is comfort. Jeremy has seen me on my worst days, so there is no need to dress up or even put on makeup.

I head to the kitchen to make coffee. While I am waiting for it to brew, I notice Jeremy isn't up yet. I slept in for a while and normally he would be up by now getting ready for practice. I venture into his room and find the door slightly ajar. I peek inside and find him still in bed. He is on his side facing the door and I can tell he's been crying.

I walk over to the bed and slide in next to him. He pulls me tight against him and we lay there in silence. No words are needed. We know what today is and right now this is perfect.

We must have fallen asleep because I wake up still wrapped in Jeremy's arms. I feel Jeremy stir and glance up to find him already awake.

He kisses the top of my head and whispers, "Thanks Emma."

He gets out of bed and stretches his arms above his head. I gulp. I hadn't noticed when I slid into his bed earlier that he was wearing nothing but boxers. His abs are toned and rock hard. How did I not feel them when I was practically laying on his chest a second ago? I shake my head.

Stop it Emma. This is Jeremy.

Jeremy smirks at me as if he knows exactly what I was thinking. He winks and heads to his bathroom.

I quickly throw the covers off and practically run to the kitchen. I grab a coffee mug and fill it to the top with coffee. I don't even care about creamer. I just need caffeine. Maybe that will clear my head of whatever thoughts were just running through it. I am not one to shy away from the human body. I'm after all going to school for physical therapy but this is Jeremy we are talking about. He is basically my brother.

I take a sip of my coffee and wince. It's still super hot. Thankfully it didn't burn my tongue but I blow on it before taking another sip.

A few minutes later Jeremy comes into the kitchen. This time he has on gym shorts and a black compression t-shirt. Better than just boxers but I still have to tear my eyes away. What is going on with me today?

"Oh you made coffee. I need that." He glances at the cup in my hand and fills a cup for himself. He grabs some creamer out of the fridge and puts a splash into my coffee.

"Thanks." He knows how I like my coffee, and the fact that he could simply look at mine and tell I didn't make it how I normally would has impressed me. He smirks like he knows I was running from his room.

"Don't you have practice today?" I ask him.

"No. Well, yes, but coach gave me the day off. He knows what today is. He said as long as I do some sort of exercise, then I didn't have to come in."

I nod. "What's your plan for today?"

"I was going to hit the gym downstairs for an hour. When I get back we can have some lunch. There is a menu in the drawer next to the fridge for the restaurant downstairs. Take a look and order something. They'll deliver it up here."

"What do you want?"

"Doesn't matter. Order a bunch of stuff. Today, I don't care about healthy or really anything." He finishes his coffee and sets it in the sink, proceeding to grab a bottle of water from the fridge and his phone and wallet from the counter. "I'll be back soon." He kisses me on the head again and leaves.

Why does he keep giving me sweet little kisses today?

I finish my coffee and find the menu he mentioned. There are so many delicious items to choose from.

I select a few options and put in the order to be delivered in an hour and a half. I make some drinks for later and settle down on the couch, turning on the television in hopes of a distraction.

Jeremy comes back a little over an hour later and goes to his room to shower. Right as he comes back into the room, there is a knock at the door. I go to stand up.

"Stay. I'll get it."

He opens the door and they wheel in a cart with tons of trays. It smells so good.

Jeremy thanks the server and pushes the cart over to the coffee table to unload the food.

Once everything is laid out, he says, "This is quite the spread."

"I thought a mix of comfort and vegging out would be perfect." I stuck with Mexican and got everything from fajitas and tacos to a giant plate of chips with tubs of queso, salsa, and guacamole. "I also made a pitcher of margaritas. It's in the fridge."

"I'll grab that. Find us something funny to watch."

The rest of the day we spent gorging ourselves on Mexican food and sharing memories and stories from before the accident. Dredging up all the memories is painful for both of us, but it's nice to have someone to share the pain.

We even talk about the funeral. Jeremy had put together a memory video using footage Logan had collected over the years. I still don't know how he was able to do that. When I asked him about it, he said it helped him sort through his feelings and remember his brother. I never would have been able to do it. I barely even remember that time let alone the funeral.

The next morning I wake up and slowly lift my head. A sharp pain shoots through it. I look around and see the cause. An empty tequila bottle and several empty wine bottles lay scattered across the coffee table.

I try to stand up but there is a heavy weight across my stomach. Jeremy's arm is wrapped around me. I'm not even sure how, since we are on the couch where we must have fallen asleep. I lay my head back down. It isn't long before I fall back asleep, more comfortable than I have been in a while even with a pounding headache.

A few hours later, I am at the airport once again to head home. I know if I stay any longer, my mom will persuade me to come home for Christmas since I am so close. I am not ready to go home yet.

The nice thing about flying private is that we can pull the car right up to the plane. Jeremy helps me out of the car and grabs my suitcases. He hands them to the flight attendant who puts them onto the plane.

"Thank you for everything, Jeremy. I don't know what I would do without you."

"I could say the same for you." I snort because that isn't true. He's a big time quarterback. He would be perfectly fine without little old me. "I'm serious. You have no idea what you do to me, do you?" I must look at him confused because he continues. "You may think you don't help me or push me like I do for you, but you do. You have since high school. You were always there to talk football or make me laugh. In college, you were my rock when I lost a game and were always there when I needed to go for a run. After college, you told me to never stop chasing my dreams and fight for what I want. Your accident showed me that, and I plan on going after what I want."

A tear falls down my cheek because his speech is one of the sweetest things he has ever said. I never knew how much I helped him. I was always just being a friend.

He looks at me intently, like he's searching for something. It's almost deja vu back at prom when I thought he was going to kiss me, only this time nothing is standing in our way. Before I can even comprehend something like that happening, he kisses me on the cheek, squeezes my hand, and then pushes me toward the plane.

I nod and walk up the stairs to the plane. As I enter the plane, I turn around and wave.

"See you soon Emma," Jeremy shouts and winks. Then the flight attendant ushers me to my seat. I am so in my own world, I don't even see them close the door.

What just happened?

Chapter Four

2 years after the accident

I used to love this time of year but now I hate it. I can't stand the decorations or the lights that are everywhere you go. Christmas is in five days and I need to hide out.

I still can't go home. Way too many memories haunt the streets, my house, store, and restaurants. Basically everything. I just can't do it. Going to Nashville to hang with Jeremy would be better, but I just don't want to deal with anyone right now.

Tomorrow is the second anniversary of Logan's death. I want to drink a bottle or several bottles of wine, curl up in front of the fireplace, and just not think about anything. My best idea? Probably not.

This is the perfect place to do that. I rented a cabin a few hours from the University. Only Ashley knows I'm here, in case something happens. I plan on staying here till the New Year and then I will drag myself back to school.

I love school and it's been going great. I'm set to graduate at the end of spring semester. I don't know what job I'll get once I graduate, but the possibilities are endless. Logan always encouraged me to do something I love.

I always thought working as a personal trainer with Olympians would be awesome, but I'm not sure if I'm ready for that just yet. Logan was one of my biggest supporters and being there would just bring back too many memories I'm not ready to face. Maybe one day. I do know I want to stay within sports.

Tonight, I plan to get lost in my text books. I know I'm on Christmas break and classes don't start till January, but I figured why not get a head start. It'll give me a distraction and I love learning.

Yes, I'm a nerd.

Most of my credits this last semester will be part of a clinical, but I'm taking a Sports Physical Therapy class that I'm very excited about.

I grab a few bottles of wine, a blanket, some pillows, and my textbook. I settle on the floor by the roaring fire. There may not be snow outside but it is still freezing. I arrange the pillows to lay against and throw the blanket across my legs.

Twisting off the cap of one of the wine bottles, I take a swig before leaning against the pillows and opening to chapter one.

Several hours later, I wake up, looking around. I must have dozed off. I have my book open on my lap and two wine bottles empty next to me. I'm too comfortable to move to the bed so I close my textbook and set it to the side before cuddling under the blanket.

"Let me see. I don't believe you. He can't be dead. I want to see him."

"*Sweetie, you can't see him. It's been two weeks. You were in a medically induced coma to let your body heal. They already took his body,*" *my mom says as she gently touches my arm.*

Flashbacks of the accident repeat in my mind. We're heading home for Christmas. Logan is singing Christmas carols with silly lyrics while working on his project. Then he brings up a different college and we are fighting about that. Then we are laughing and joking around. I stop at a stop sign and it's clear so I hit the gas. Lights come out of nowhere and we spin. Then pain. I try to wake up Logan but he won't wake up and I pass out.

I lightly touch my stomach, sick to my stomach and look to my mom. She has tears running down her face as she subtly shakes her head.

"*No!*" *I scream.* "*I can't go on. I can't. Please Mom. Make it stop. Just make it all go away.*"

I hear alarms going off. Probably has to do with my extremely high blood pressure and heart beat.

Nurses rush in and they must sedate me because I fall into a deep sleep.

I wake later. I have no idea how much time has passed but as I open my eyes, everything is foggy. I'm sure I'm on some very heavy drugs right now.

I glance at the window and notice a figure sitting in the chair. The figure looks up at me and I gasp, "*Logan.*"

He immediately stands and walks towards the bed. It can't be. I thought he was dead.

He reaches my bed and grasps my hand. "Emma. You're awake."

I feel him squeeze my hand so I know this is real. "Logan I thought you were dead."

I see a moment of confusion across his face but it quickly disappears and is replaced with sadness.

"I am, but I wanted to say goodbye. I'll miss you. Don't give up. Keep fighting and moving forward. I'll be watching over you, cheering you on when you win your next gold medal, encouraging you in your dreams, and smiling when you smile. I want you to learn to love again. I wish it was me, but please find someone that will love you as much as me and help heal your heart. Don't forget you have people to lean on. You have your family, my family, Ashley. My brother would go to the ends of the earth for you, so lean on him. I love you, Emma. Always have. Always will."

He lets go of my hand and gently takes my face in his hands, kissing my forehead. He turns to leave.

"Logan, don't go. I'm not ready."

"You are, Emma. Now wake up so everyone can see you're okay. They are all in the waiting room and have been taking turns coming in here. I have... Jeremy has refused to leave your side. They need you too." He motions to the chair by the window which is now empty. Wait, that's where Logan was. I look back to Logan but he has already turned toward the door.

Right before he leaves, he looks back to me and once again says, "Don't stop fighting." before he disappears out the door.

"Wait. Come back. I need you!" I yell. The monitors once again come to life as the alarms blare, but all I can hear are my sobs and shouts for him to come back. I don't want to be alone.

"Emma! Emma, wake up. You're having a nightmare." I open my eyes to find Logan... no Jeremy inches from my face.

"Jeremy, what are you doing here?"

"I may have bribed Ashley to give me your location so you didn't have to be alone. I knocked but there was no answer. Then I heard screaming and I busted the door down. I didn't know what was happening."

My mind is spinning. I close my hands trying to clear my head. I'm still half in my dream and half in the present. Ashley told him where I was. Jeremy broke in. Logan was visiting me.

I close my eyes, thinking back to my dream. I remembered everything that happened in the hospital room, not just bits and pieces as I went in and out of consciousness.

I open them again. Jeremy has sat back but then it clicks all at once.

"It was you."

"Me what? You're going to have to be more specific."

"It wasn't Logan in the hospital room. It was you."

Jeremy suddenly looks very uncomfortable. He stands. "Can I get you some water? I think you had a lot of wine and you're confused," glancing at the bottles on the ground.

"No, it was you. When I first came out of the coma, I thought it was Logan coming to say goodbye, but it was you."

"Emma, you have to understand, you were--"

"Get out." I point to the door.

"Emma, I just drove hours to come here so you didn't have to be alone. So I didn't have to be alone."

"Just get out. I can't look at you right now."

Jeremy throws his hands up. "Okay, I'm leaving. But I won't be far in case you need me." I walk him to the door to make sure he leaves.

Once he leaves, I close the door behind him. Thankfully he didn't break it when he "busted it down".

I take a deep breath and turn back to my mess on the floor. I gather the wine bottles and dump them in the trash. Then I fold the blanket and set the pillows on the couch.

I down some Advil and a glass of water hoping to prevent a hangover tomorrow.

I make my way up to the bedroom, quickly changing into pajamas and sliding under the covers.

I know I need to deal with Jeremy but that can wait until tomorrow.

Chapter Five

The next morning I wake to the smell of something burning. Wait burning...I turned off the gas fireplace, didn't I? I throw off the covers and race down stairs to find Jeremy in the kitchen.

Jeremy is taking out to-go containers from a brown paper bag. I eye coffee next to it and grab one, chugging it down.

"What's burning?" I ask.

Jeremy gestures to the completely charred bacon. "I tried to make some bacon and eggs, but I left the bacon on the pan way too long in the oven. It burned the one side so I decided to flip it to maybe save the other side, but it just all burned. Then I realized it would still taste bad with one burned side. All I managed was to create a bunch of smoke. I think they need to check the fire alarms in this house."

During his whole spiel, I stay quiet. Why is he even here? I glance to the living room and notice the blanket I had folded sprawled out on the couch.

"Did you stay here last night?"

"Yeah... I wanted to be here in case you had another night-mare."

I sigh. He makes this so hard. I am supposed to be mad at him but here he goes saying something sweet.

"How'd you get in?" As soon as I ask, I know the answer. I didn't lock the door last night. In my rush to get him out, I simply closed the door and went to bed forgetting to lock it.

"You left it unlocked."

"Let's eat, and then we can talk about the stunt you pulled in the hospital."

I grab the other coffee cup and take a sip, surprised to find another skinny vanilla latte. My coffee drink of choice.

"Since when do you drink vanilla lattes?" I ask Jeremy.

"Since I got you two as part of my apology."

"You're on your way to being forgiven, but you have a long way to go."

We eat in silence. I notice the bag says 'Pam's Diner." I saw it on the way to the cabin. It was a cute rustic looking diner with rocking chairs on the outside and it was packed. I told myself I needed to check it out while I was here.

After finishing breakfast, I now know why it was so packed. The food was delicious. Jeremy got a little bit of everything.

"Thanks for breakfast," I nod to him, falling silent.

Jeremy stands to start gathering the empty containers. I stand as well to help but he stops me.

"Go sit on the couch and finish your coffee. I'll clean this up and then we can talk."

I nod again. A few minutes later, Jeremy joins me on the couch. The same couch but thankfully he sits on the other side.

"So..." We both begin at the same time. I motion for him to continue.

"Emma, I owe you an apology. I never should have pretended to be my brother in the hospital. When you woke up, I was so excited. Then you called me Logan and I was disappointed but I understood. You were mourning and I wanted to help so I figured it wouldn't hurt to go along with it."

"Didn't you think about how I would feel if I realized the truth?"

"I wasn't thinking about it at the time. I did plan on telling you one day, but it just never came up. After a while, I figured you didn't remember. You had just come out of a coma and were on tons of drugs."

"That doesn't make it right."

Jeremy moves closer to me. "I know that. But I didn't know what to do. It killed me to see you laying there helpless. I just lost my brother. We were all grieving. I wanted to give you the goodbye you didn't get."

Jeremy plays with my hand. For some reason I find it soothing. I'm quiet for a few minutes.

"Did you mean everything you said?"

"Every word," Jeremy turns my face toward him. "Logan is watching over you, but I think he would want you to be happy again. How many times since the accident have you truly smiled?"

I shrug because I probably couldn't even fill one hand.

As if reading my mind. "I could probably count on one hand and half of those were fake. You forget I know you, Emma."

"How am I ever going to be happy again? Am I just supposed to move on? With who? You?"

Jeremy replies, "You could."

"I'm serious Jeremy. Do you really think Logan wants us to be together? I don't think half of what he said–I mean you said–is true. I highly doubt you would go to the ends of the Earth for me."

"I woul..." Jeremy starts but I hold up a hand to stop him. I don't want to hear his excuses. He takes my hand I held up and links his fingers with mine. "What I was going to say is I would. You've become my best friend, Emma. I'd do anything for you. I thought I showed you that when I brought you back from the hole you were in after his death."

He wipes the tears running down my face. "I know this is hard to hear, and I'm sorry for bringing it up. But I want you to know how much I care for you. I know you aren't ready but I'm not going anywhere."

We are quiet for a while. I'm glad he left it at that because I'm not ready to dig into the whole learning to love again. It's only been two years since the accident. Then again many people find love right away.

I glance at Jeremy to find him watching me. Maybe I've found love? Maybe it was always there? What am I thinking? I love Logan. I always will, I can't love anyone else.

"I can see the wheels in your head moving. No one would ever think you didn't love Logan if you decide to open your heart again."

I sigh. Part of me knows that but the other part... the stubborn part refuses to believe it. "Maybe one day." That's all I have to offer him right now.

Jeremy gets up and moves to sit next to my legs. "We can come back to the love part later. Starting now, we focus on swimming. The Olympics are a little over a year and half away. How many times have you been in the pool since?"

"Two," I say quietly.

"I can't hear you. How many?"

"Two, Jeremy. Just two."

"How do you expect to win another gold medal by only going in the pool twice?"

"Jeremy, that ship has long sailed. I just don't have the strength anymore." I made it to the Olympics the summer before the accident and it was a dream come true. I don't think it's in the cards for me to go back.

"I don't believe that for one second." He moves to my feet and takes them in each of his hands. "I want you to push against my hands as hard as you can."

He gets in a runner's stance bracing himself.

I figure I will humor him and push against his hands. I feel resistance. He is after all a professional quarterback. He isn't the biggest or even strongest guy on the team, but he still has some serious muscle.

I pull my feet back a little and then push more until he wobbles a little. Eventually, he loses his balance and falls over.

"See Emma, you have so much strength. We need to channel that into kicking in the pool. I wasn't going easy on you either."

I fall to my back. "I wasn't talking about that strength... you know what... never mind."

Jeremy lays next to me on his side. "I know. You don't have the mental strength to swim. We will fix that. Don't make me throw you in the pool again."

I actually laugh and think back to that day. It was right after I met Jeremy in Nashville for his game around the one year anniversary of the accident. I remember getting on the plane, thinking I was heading back to North Carolina. The plane landed and I was so in my own world, I didn't notice the airport we landed in or the fact that Jeremy was on the plane. He had arranged a car for me so I absentmindedly got in the car which took me to the park that Logan and I always went to. As soon as I opened the door and realized where I was, I knew Jeremy was behind this. He knew I wasn't ready to come home, but he also knew I needed a push or I never would've come home. I decided to just go with it and walked over to the gazebo...

I sit down in the gazebo looking out at the mountains. Why did Jeremy send me here? He knows I'm not ready. I pull my jacket around me tighter. There is a chill in the air coming more from sadness surrounding me than the actual weather.

I hear footsteps but I don't bother looking. I already know who it is. I always know when he's near. He sits down next to me.

"It's time Emma."

"Time for what?"

"It's time to face your fear. The fact that you got out of that car shows you're ready."

"What are you talking about? I'm not scared of coming home. I just don't want to fall into a pit of despair with all the memories coming back."

"You won't. I will make sure you don't. This is your first stop because this is the hardest. This is where your love story began. Let's go back to where the whole story began."

He takes my hand and leads me back to the car. I should be scared but Jeremy gives me a sense of calm. I may feel like I'm not ready, but I'd trust Jeremy with my life. Logan once told me to.

After a few minutes of driving, I know exactly where he's taking me.

The high school.

The car pulls up to the curb and I slowly get out.

Jeremy leads me to the hallway where I first ran into Logan.

I look around. Not much has changed. There are still rows of lockers and flyers for different events happening.

A tear slides down my cheek but I quickly brush it away. I will not cry.

He then leads me to the pool.

"You're conquering your fear of coming back to where all the memories started. Now it's time to conquer your future."

I wouldn't say I've conquered anything regarding facing the memories but I stay quiet.

"I know what you're thinking, Emma, but just coming back here is the first step. By conquering the future, you will conquer the past." He faces me towards the pool, knowing I've purposely angled myself away from it.

"This is your future." He points at the pool. "The Olympics is once again calling your name. Will you answer?"

"I'm never going back to the Olympics and will never be the swimmer I once was."

"I know you and I know that anything you put your mind to, you succeed at. You can make the next Olympics if you choose to."

I can't face him or admit what I'm really thinking. He's always had a way of seeing right through me. It's why we always fought because he calls me out. "No I can't."

Jeremy lightly squeezes my shoulders, "You haven't really been in the water at all since the accident, have you?"

I feel him right behind me but stay staring straight ahead. "I've been busy with school."

"No. You're scared, I saw it in your eyes when I mentioned the Olympics. You're scared that you won't be what you once were. Logan would want you back in the pool."

I turn around, now angry because how dare he say that. "Don't you dare use Logan against me. He was my husband and he died. I don't need another reminder. I've cried enough this past year."

His face gets very serious before saying, "He was my brother and my best friend. I lost him too, but I also know how proud of you he was. When you chose to become a Sports Physical Therapist, he couldn't stop talking about it. When you won the gold at the

Olympics, I never saw someone more excited for someone else. You don't know this, but before you all first started dating, he came home after your study date and said he met the girl he was going to marry. I just laughed at him but when he told me it was you, I told him you were a very special girl."

Annoyed at him I say, "Why are you telling me all this?"

"Because... I've only seen him cry three times. When he was about five, he fell out of the tree and broke his arm. Second time was when you walked down the aisle on your wedding day. Third was on Thanksgiving when you mentioned how thankful you were to be with him, his family and one day soon starting a family with him." He looks me right in the eyes, "You were pregnant weren't you?"

I am shocked he knew. I thought only my parents and his parents knew from the hospital. "How'd you know?"

He touches my cheek, "You had this glow about you, and when that tear came down my brother's cheek, I knew something was up. He doesn't just tear up for anything." He drops his hand. "Like I said, I've only seen him cry three times and that was one."

Not knowing what else to do, I start to pace before finally sitting down, resting my chin on my hands. I think back to the hospital room when they broke the news to me that I had lost the baby. We were going to tell everyone at Christmas dinner.

"Jeremy I thought I could keep going with school, but every day is a reminder of the short time I had with him. He gave me the idea of going into Sports Physical Therapy because of my swimming.

He said it could help train myself to become a better and faster swimmer. I said he was crazy at the time, but he was right."

Jeremy stands in front of me. "My brother was a smart man. That could be the exact answer you're looking for. PT could help you get back into swimming. Will you ever be the swimmer you once were? No, but you can still be an amazing swimmer."

"I can't."

"Why not?"

"I just can't explain it."

"Try," he practically begs.

"I'm scared okay?!" I stand up right in front of him. "Is that what you want to hear?"

"Yes."

"What?" He wants me scared?

"I mean no, I don't want to hear that, but I need you to admit it to yourself. Now I'll ask you, what are we going to do about it?"

"Every time I go near the water, I freak out. I think back to all the times Logan was cheering me on in the crowd as I swam my heart out. I think back to how I never would have made it to the Olympics without him and he made me the swimmer I was by always encouraging me. He put my dreams ahead of his. I am not afraid because of my leg. I've learned enough in this first year that can help strengthen my leg but I know that if I get in the pool, I'm going to break down and drown. I don't know how to do it without him and that scares me."

"I have an idea. Do you trust me?"

"What?"

He asks again, "Do you trust me?" I nod because I do trust him. I always have. "Good. Now, come with me."

He leads me towards the locker rooms. I feel a pit in my stomach. Why would he lead me to the locker room, other than to change? I stop. "I can't do this."

"Yes you can and you will. We will take it slow because Emma, your training officially starts now."

"I don't have a bathing suit." I purposely didn't pack one because I knew I wouldn't be going anywhere near a pool.

"Yes you do." He grabs a bag from the bench next to him and hands it to me. I look confused at the bag and he shrugs. "I have connections. Now go change and meet me back by pool. If you aren't back out here in five minutes, I'll come in there after you."

"Jeremy." He leaves before I can say anything else.

I open the bag to find a brand new, all black speedo. Thankfully it's a one piece and not a two piece. Despite our past with the spring break incident, I still wouldn't put it past him to buy me a bikini.

After changing, I take a deep breath and walk out to the pool. Jeremy is already in the pool and I walk over to the edge.

"Help me out."

I step back with my arms crossed. "I'm not falling for that."

"Fine." He lifts himself out of the pool and runs his hand through his hair. I can't help staring at his abs with the water dripping down to that perfect V. The NFL training has made his body even more toned, if that is even possible. I shake my head and look at him coming towards me.

"See something you like?" He teases me.

"No I was just... uhhh..." Of course he would catch me checking him out.

"Emma, I'm kidding. I'm not kidding about getting in the water."

Before I can react, he picks me up in a fireman carry and jumps in the pool. We hit the water and I panic, or maybe I started panicking before. I don't know but I know I don't want to be in the water.

As we come up to the surface, I start to squirm and Jeremy holds on to me.

"Emma calm down. The water isn't going to hurt you. You and water have the best connection I have ever seen. Breathe." I glance up at him and take a deep breath. Something in his eyes says he isn't going to let anything happen to me.

Once I calm down, he slowly lowers me so I am standing. "See? You're fine."

"Jeremy I appreciate you trying to help, but I really can't do this." I may trust him not to let anything happen to me but this is too soon. I start heading towards the stairs. Jeremy grabs my hand before I can get away.

"Let's try one thing first."

I take another deep breath knowing he isn't going to let me go anywhere. "Fine, you have one minute."

He picks me up again and has me float on my back.

"Now close your eyes." I look at him. "Trust me. I got you and I'm not letting you go." I close my eyes. "Now feel the water against your back." All I can think about is his hand on my lower back. I *shake it off knowing I'm just missing Logan. I listen to his words and focus on that. "Let it all go and just feel the water holding you up. Now I want you to slowly kick your legs and we're going to move." I kick slowly and concentrate on the water holding me up. I kick for what seems like forever but in reality it's probably only ten seconds.*

"You got it," I hear Jeremy shout. Wait, why is he shouting? I open my eyes to see him across the pool. He must see the fear in my eyes because he is instantly by my side the second I start to freak out.

"Shhhh, you're okay." He puts his hands back under me and takes us over to the edge. He sets me up there before lifting himself up next to me. "You told me you weren't scared because of your leg but rather because of Logan."

"Well...that's not exactly what I said."

"Let me finish, you and Logan had an epic love that most people only dream of. Like you said he was always there to cheer you on and encourage you to follow your dreams. Just like I was here in the pool holding you, that's what he was doing without you realizing it. Every time you got in the pool you knew he was there cheering for you even if he wasn't able to be in the audience. You felt his presence carry you through the water."

"Yeah okay but that doesn't explain before I met him. I was winning meets and swimming fine before."

"Yes, but you were also swimming for fun, am I right?"

"Yeah I guess. I've always wanted to go to the Olympics."

"*But it wasn't until your junior year when you really started training and swimming towards your goal, correct?*"

"*Yeah, but I'm still not getting it.*"

"*Okay, along the way you started to fall for my brother. When you seriously started training for the Olympics was right around when you started dating. He was always there to encourage you and pick you back up when you didn't do well. He was your support and you felt that when you swam. When you were apart for the semester during college he always called you or texted you before a meet, am I right?*" I nod. "*Although when he didn't show up at that one meet, you didn't swim your heart out.*"

"*How did you know about him not showing up at a meet from my junior year of high school? That was before we even started dating.*" Maybe he was paying attention to me back then more than I thought.

"*I may have been there...but that's beside the point. The point is when he wasn't at that meet you didn't feel the support and you didn't swim your best. You never got a text or call either. Without that encouragement, you feared that the water would consume you and you would drown. Since he died you equate that drowning to swimming. You lost your support system and before you will swim again, you need to find it.*"

"*But how do I do that? I am never going to stop missing him.*" There are days where I wonder if he really did take my heart with him.

"*No, you won't and that's okay. He was a huge part of all of our lives and we will never forget him. But now to move forward, you need to put that support onto someone else and let them carry you. When you do that, I bet you'll get back into this pool on your own."*

"Is that why you had me lay on my back and you held me because you wanted me to put that support on you?" I question him.

"Yes and no. I was trying to show you that you have support all around you. Me, my parents, your parents, your brother, Ashley. You have support everywhere you turn. We all loved Logan and we love you too. We want you to remember him, but also live your life. Live the life Logan would have wanted you to have."

"Thank you." What he says makes sense. He may be the stereotypical jock but he definitely has a brain. It shouldn't still surprise me when he comes up with scenarios or ideas like this.

I give him a hug and rest my head on his shoulder. "One day I'll get in the pool. I just need some time."

"We will take it one day at a time."

The memory fades as I lay on my back staring at the ceiling.

"I don't know how to find that support again Jer."

"I'll be your support. I'll be there helping you in the water and getting you on that Olympic team."

"Let's focus on getting in the pool first."

"Deal."

I think back to all the times Logan told me to lean on Jeremy if I needed to. It's almost like he knew I'd need those words one day. I then think back to what Jeremy as Logan said in the hospital and how he'd be watching over me. Even though it's Jeremy that said them, they aren't any less true. I'll always miss Logan, but I continued school because I knew he wouldn't want me to stop.

Now I need to focus on swimming. He wouldn't want me to stop swimming just because he isn't here. I'm scared to put that support somewhere else but Jeremy's always been there, so maybe he's been part of that support all along.

He has mentioned love but I am not ready for that. I need to focus on swimming and then maybe one day, I'll be ready for love...with Jeremy. I shake my head. No, that's crazy.

Swimming... focus on swimming.

Chapter Six

2 and half years after the accident

The music starts and that is my cue to start walking. I grab onto my dad's arm and begin what will become the most emotional walk of my life. I look down the aisle to the gazebo where he stands. Our eyes connect and the tears come with no warning. When I finally make my way down the aisle and grab onto my future husband's hands, I know this is till death do us part.

The gazebo we stand under is the same one he asked me to marry him that special New Year's night. It is covered with white roses and baby's breath flowers. Over to the side is a giant tent where the reception will take place.

My dress is very simple with a lace long-sleeved top and a skirt that flows out at the waist. The train extends a foot behind me. The entire dress is embroidered with a very subtle swirl design. I have on a small thin veil that cascades down the length of my dress.

I feel like a princess.

The entire ceremony goes by in a blur—except his vows which I remember clear as day. "I will never forget the day my life changed, that cold September day when I would meet the girl that forever changed everything I knew. You walked into my life at a time when everything was perfect but nothing seemed right. You taught me that life is short so we should live every moment to the fullest. You taught me that you can never smile or laugh too much. You taught me when to be serious and when to let loose. But most importantly, you taught me how to love. I promise to take care of you forever till death do us part."

Soon it's time to party with the sunset casting a glow across the mountains. There are stunning hues of red, orange and purple. We dance the night away and when it's finally time to say our goodbyes, I can barely stand. We go back to our hotel room and collapse on the bed. My hubby pops the champagne and we have our own party!

The next day we leave for our mini honeymoon to the same resort we went during our senior year. He makes good on his promise with the gorgeous hotel overlooking the mountains and our own private hot tub. The last night we are there, we drag the blankets and pillows onto the balcony and make a bed. We snuggle under the covers, enjoying each other as the sun sets and the moon rises over the mountains. Logan tells me he will love me until the last star in the universe burns up and if he's taken before that, he'll be the brightest star shining down on me. I look up at the stars.

The next morning, I don't want to leave but I open my eyes and look over at Logan in bed. All I see is red and Logan is perfectly still. I feel someone shaking me. Wait no, I have to wake up Logan. Why is there blood? Logan wake up...

I open my eyes and catch my breath. The flight attendant looks at me concerned, asking if everything is okay. I nod. It was only a dream. Our honeymoon was perfect.

The flight attendant tells me we'll be landing in a few minutes and I have to put my seat up.

As I look out the window, I see home and my smile grows thinking back to that perfect day. The real day and not the dream.

I exit the plane and as I walk through the gangway, my eyes begin to water. *I can do this*, I think to myself. I know I have some big decisions coming up. I have to remind myself to focus on the future and not the past. The past seems to creep up on me at the worst times, including my dreams.

I enter the terminal and see a very familiar figure holding a bouquet of flowers.

"What are you doing here?" He gives me a hug and a kiss on the cheek.

"I wanted to surprise my favorite girl. Plus, I couldn't be at your graduation so I thought these flowers might make up for it."

I take the flowers from him. "Yeah, yeah. Only my parents could make it but it's okay. It really wasn't that big a deal."

"Are you kidding me? You graduated from a very intensive master program while training for the Olympics. Only you would be able to do that after everything you went through."

"I have you to thank for that, you know. I never would have gotten through any of it without you." I look at him seriously.

"Oh I know! Whatever would you have done without me?" he says dramatically.

I shove him in the shoulder. "There he is."

We walk to the baggage claim and I grab my two suitcases. "By the way, thanks for the first class upgrade. You really didn't have to do that. I once only flew in economy."

"It was the least I could do when the jet was double booked." He glances down at my suitcases. "Is this it?"

I nod. "For now, I still have my whole apartment but I have to decide on jobs so I figured I would leave my stuff there till I knew."

"Okay well let's go. Everyone can't wait to see you."

"It better just be family and a few friends."

"We'll see." He starts walking faster towards his car.

"You better tell me the truth." He keeps walking until he gets to the car, throwing me the signature Anderson smirk over his shoulder.

"Jeremy Anderson, you tell me right now if there's a surprise party at home." He throws my suitcases in the trunk and winks.

We drive to my childhood home and I see balloons on the mailbox. "Are you serious?"

"It's your mom!" He laughs like there's nothing he could have done, and if we're being honest, there isn't much he could actually have done. When my mom sets her mind on something, she doesn't back down. Must be where I got it.

"Oh and your mom had nothing to do with it either?" Our moms have become best friends over the years and they're always planning things together.

We pull into my driveway and my mom comes running out. The second I open the door, she gives me a hug. "Welcome home sweetie."

I hug her back. "Thanks Mom. You know I would have come home sooner, but with everything that happened, I just couldn't."

She pulls back and looks me in the eyes. "Honey, it is okay. We all understood and no one blames you for anything."

"I know." I gulp. I blame myself for everything that happened. It's been two and half years since the accident and Logan dying. It's still hard sometimes but I'm slowly moving forward and looking to the future.

The house is filled with all my family and closest friends. Thankfully they keep it small. I walk into the kitchen where Ashley is and burst out laughing when I see the cake. I feel Jeremy's hands on my hips as he looks over my shoulder.

"What's so funny?" He asks.

The cake says, 'You made it! Congrats!' It has a picture of me when I was five years old and starting my first day of kindergarten.

Ashley tells me she helped my mom pick out the picture as they both thought it was appropriate. Jeremy still looks at us confused so I tell him the story.

In the photo, I'm holding up four fingers and I insisted on wearing my mom's college graduation hat to kindergarten. I remember telling her that morning that I was going to graduate one day. She looked at me and said she hoped so. Then I held up four fingers and said I was going to graduate four times–kindergarten, high school and twice in college. She asked why I was graduating college two times, and I told her because I never want to leave school.

To be young and naive again. I never want to go back to school now.

I smile down at the picture. "Well, I did it. Graduated college two times getting my bachelor's and master's."

Getting my master's degree was rough and I felt something missing the whole time but I managed my way through. I look around at the people in my house then I glance at Ashley. These people are my support system and I never would've been able to do it without them. Jeremy squeezes my waist. I glance back at him and hold his gaze. "I'm glad to be done with school, and I think I'm starting to move on in more ways than one."

Chapter Seven

The next day I find myself at the gazebo in the park. Winter time was always my favorite with Logan, especially at this park. It's where we shared our first kiss, got engaged, and got married, along with every talk and moment we shared in between. I haven't been able to bring myself back here since the accident, besides when Jeremy sent me here not long after the accident–which happened to occur not far from here.

This park screams Logan.

Lately, I've been coming to terms with all different aspects of my life. Recent events have opened my eyes and I know I can't stay lost in the path forever. I need to say goodbye once and for all.

I just can't help but feel like I am missing something from that night. The accident never made sense to me. That car was coming towards my side yet it hit Logan's. Maybe it is one of the crazy things that happens in movies. I will probably never know what happened that night.

A light breeze blows the leaves on the tree leaning over the gazebo. It's coming up on the end of May and the summer heat is pushing through. I want to soak up as many of these last cool mornings before the sweltering temperatures hit. Not that it'll matter since I'll be in the pool every day.

I feel him before I see him. I've always had a sixth sense for when he's around, but it's different now. It's like this flame is inside me and when he's near, it ignites into a fire that threatens to burn everything near. "Are you following me?"

"I came over to see if you and Ashley wanted to grab breakfast but she said you had left early. I figured you would come here."

Jeremy sits on the bench next to me. We both fall into silence for what seems like hours when it's really only a few minutes. Our silence is more comfortable than awkward.

Jeremy finally breaks it by asking the question I'm not ready to answer. He always knows questions that will dig deep. He says it so quietly I almost miss it. "Are you saying goodbye?"

A tear appears in the corner of my eye as I nod. I don't have to say it. He already knows. I haven't been able to come back here on my own without a push and the first time I do, it must be for a reason. More tears run down my cheeks.

Jeremy puts his arm around me and pulls me towards him. I bury my head into his chest. He doesn't say anything as I let out the tears that I have bottled up.

In the past two and half years since Logan died, I could count on one hand, the amount of times I've actually cried. Some days it feels like I never stopped crying but it was never a real cry. Most days it was a fake cry because I felt I was supposed to. Don't get me wrong I was devastated. I was so devastated that I fell into a hole of despair. I was so far deep into my sorrow that I didn't care what happened. I wanted Logan back. On the outside, it would seem like I had no emotion at all.

A short time later, the tears finally stop. I sit up wiping my cheeks. "I thought it was time to say goodbye. This is the place I was closest to him. I loved him so much and I still feel like a piece of my heart is missing. I don't think it'll ever feel whole again, but I know he wouldn't want me to be miserable for the rest of my life. I want to be happy again."

Jeremy grabs my hand and traces the lines on my palm. "I miss him too. He was not only my brother, but my best friend. Even when he was overseas at school, we never stopped talking. We had our arguments but at the end of day, I knew he was always there for me."

I give him a small smile.

"I remember this one time when we were younger and Logan had just gotten a video camera for Christmas. It was one of those ones with the mini cassette tapes. He was making a video. It was some hero saves the princess story. He was acting out the hero and he asked me to be the princess. I told him I was not a girl. He handed me a wig and wrap-around skirt. He then told me to stand over on the small platform with a hand drawn castle behind it. He wouldn't take no for an answer. Logan had this giant fake sword he swung around while I pretended to be a dramatic princess being swept off her feet. Keep in mind, I just went through a growth spurt so I was a good four inches taller than Logan. Later we all watched it. It was horrible but I've never laughed so hard in my life."

I can't help the laughter that comes out of me imagining that scene. Logan was always so serious with his films. I could totally see him bossing around his older and taller brother at that point. "How old were you all?"

"I think we were around eight and nine years old."

"I would love to see that."

"It's gone."

"What do you mean it is gone?"

"When we got older, Logan always used it to win any argument we had and teased that he would show my future girlfriends. So one day, I snuck into his room, found the tape and unraveled the whole thing. I left it on his bed in a pile."

"You didn't?"

He has a satisfied smirk on his face. "I did. I thought he would be so mad but he never mentioned it. Then I got scared thinking he somehow rewound the film into the tape, but I saw it in the trash a few days later with the film still in a complete mess."

"Wow. I wish I could've seen that." We fall into more silence. Jeremy probably is thinking of all the craziness from when they were little. I'm thinking about that video and trying to imagine Jeremy being the helpless princess. My mind goes to the funeral and the video Jeremy put together.

"That video you made for the funeral was really good."

"Logan did most of that work. I just pieced together different things he had filmed to make a montage of his life."

"I have no idea how you did that so soon after his death. I barely even remember that period of time, but putting together a video of his life would probably have killed me."

"Surprisingly it helped me grieve. It was nice to go back and find pictures and videos from when from we were younger. I spent hours going through his videos. It was hard picking the best clips because everything was so good. Everything Logan filmed was good."

"Except the princess story."

"Yes, except that one but it did make us laugh."

"You shouldn't have destroyed it. You could have added it to the video and had everyone laughing. *I know I could have used a laugh,*" I say the last part under my breath but I am pretty sure Jeremy still hears.

"You were in a rough place then. I don't think you would have even known."

As harsh as that sounds, he's probably right. I was in such a dark place. I remember watching the video and attending the funeral but I wasn't really present. There was a moment in the treehouse after the funeral where Jeremy might have been able to pull me out but I wasn't ready. My body was there but my mind was somewhere else.

Why are we here?

I ask no one in particular. I know what day it is. This shouldn't be happening. Logan should not be dead. He had so much life left to live. He was the best kind of person. I should've been the one to die.

I'm not worth the air we breathe.

I look around at all the people here for Logan. Everyone is dressed in black. I never understood that. Why does everyone wear black to funerals? I get the whole mourning thing, but shouldn't we be celebrating their life with bright colors?

I just want to go back to the night of the accident. It should've been me. The car was on my side, so why is Logan the one in a box?

People start taking their seats as the pastor makes his way toward the podium near the gravesite. Jeremy takes my hand and pulls me to the front row. I hobble over, refusing to use the crutches I was given. I sit down with Jeremy and his family to my left and Ashley, my parents and brother to my right.

I can't even look at Jeremy's parents. I killed their son. How are they even letting me be here?

I go to pull my hand away from Jeremy but he grips it tighter. I want him to let go but at the same time it gives me strength.

I feel drunk, like I'm watching time move slowly without me. I don't even hear what the pastor says.

This is too hard being here. The strength I had is gone and I look down to see my hand empty. It's then I realize that Jeremy is now giving a speech. As he finishes he moves to the side and a video starts.

As I look to the screen that was set up next to the podium, I see a photo of Logan as a small boy covered in chocolate pudding. Several minutes go by and I have no idea what I'm seeing. The screen is a blurry mess until a video of our wedding comes on. I immediately shut my eyes.

I can't watch this. Please make it stop, make it stop.

The next thing I know, I feel an arm wrapped around me as I'm pulled tight into a body. I let myself sink into him.

Jeremy holds me for an unknown amount of time. It isn't until he nudges me to stand up, that I realize the funeral is over. People are getting up ready to pay their respects to the family. Or well, us. Pay their respect to us.

A short time later, we're back at the Andersons. Everyone's smiling and reminiscing on Logan's life. I know I said funerals should be a time to remember the person while they are alive but come on, this is too much.

I go outside to the treehouse. It was a place Logan and I used to hide away anytime we were at his parents' house and wanted some quiet time.

We spent hours up here staring at the lake or looking at the stars through the small glass cutout in the roof.

Jeremy, Logan and their dad built it when they were younger and it became our place when we couldn't leave to go to the park.

I just want to feel close to him. But it feels like a mistake coming here. Everything looks like the same. I doubt anyone has been up here since he died.

Pictures line one wall, while a sleeping bag and blankets are balled up in the opposite corner. A bag of chips and a candy bar sit untouched on the small table.

I remember the last time we were here. It was a few months before the accident. We were visiting his family and we snuck away after dinner.

We curled up in the sleeping bag and enjoyed our private time together under the stars.

I reach out for the sleeping bag and bring it to my nose. It faintly still smells of him. I will the tears to come. I just want to feel something.

Anything.

A noise behind me has me jumping.

"I thought I would find you up here."

I don't respond. What's the point? What's the point of anything anymore? I don't feel anything.

Scratch that. I feel a tingle in my hand where Jeremy has linked our fingers, letting me know he is there. Maybe there is a light at the end of the tunnel.

Or maybe I will stay in my dark hole and never come out. Just kill me now. It'll make everything better. Then I can see Logan again and this will all be over.

Since then I've gone back and watched the video. I don't think about anything else from that day. I was in a dark place. Instead, I focus on the good moments from that day, like the video that was played. Jeremy did a great job capturing all of the moments in Logan's life from when they were little up to when I came into the picture.

"I want to show you something," Jeremy says pulling me away from my thoughts.

He stands, pulling me outside the gazebo. To the right of the gazebo, almost in the corner of the park is a very small tree. I give him a confused look. Why is he showing me a small tree?

"I planted this a year ago. It's an apple tree. It won't start bearing apples for a year or two but I wanted something to remember Logan by. Something that you could visit other than his grave. When it starts producing apples, every time you pick one, you can think of it as him giving it to you."

I thought the tears had let up but after hearing that, a few more slide down my cheeks.

This is one of the sweetest things I've heard Jeremy say. He must take my tears the wrong way because he says, "Emma, I can unplant it right now. I chose this spot because I know it was important to you both and it's a great spot for it to grow. I'm sorry. I should've asked."

I reach out to place my hand on his shoulder. "No, no. I was crying because the sentiment behind what you were saying is so sweet. It made me tear up. I love it, Jeremy. I can't wait to come back when it has apples and just remember Logan. Apples were his favorite."

I notice a small plaque next to the tree. It reads: Logan Anderson - when life gives you apples, take a bite and enjoy the sweet life.

I laugh because that is a Logan saying. Instead of when life gives you lemons, it was always when life gives you apples. We always made fun of him for it. Now it's here forever.

"You ready to go?"

"Give me one more minute."

I lean down so I am staring directly at the tree. I feel silly talking to the tree but whatever.

"Logan, I love you. I miss you. I'll never forget you. I know you would want me to move on and I will try. Not a day goes by that I don't think about you. You were my best friend and the love of my life. I am sorry it has taken me so long to say goodbye. I promise it won't be as long for me to come visit again. Until next time."

As I go to stand, a large gust of wind blows through the trees. The tree overhead drops a pink flower in front of me. Almost as if Logan himself was listening and sent it to me.

I pick it up and stand, bringing the flower to my face. It smells sweet, like the sweet apples of life.

"Are you okay?"

"No but I will be," I say and stare up at him. "I feel like a part of me is still missing. I think that has to do with the unknown around the accident." A guilty emotion slides across Jeremy's face. Before I can question it, it's gone. I brush it aside. "This day was good. It was a step forward in moving on and living my life again."

"Good." Jeremy wraps his arm around me as we turn to leave.

Just before we leave the park, I glance back at the small tree in the corner and whisper, "I won't forget you. I'll be back soon."

Chapter Eight

The summer is spent training and making pro/con lists to figure out what job to take. I applied to a bunch of places, but I didn't think I would get offers so soon after graduating. So far I have three offers from three different schools.

The first is Vanderbilt working part time at their medical center with the sports teams.

The second is working at the Florida State University medical center full-time but not strictly with the sports teams.

The third is where I just got my master's from, University of North Carolina.

After Logan left, I couldn't be in Boston anymore surrounded by memories. I needed a fresh start. Ashley persuaded me to join her and it turns out they have an amazing Physical Therapy Master's program.

They want me to teach a lecture on using physical therapy in the real world. I get to talk about how working out hours on end can affect your body, and how physical therapy is a great way to work through those muscles to prevent injury.

I have to make a decision by September and it is already mid-August. I just checked out the Medical Center at Vanderbilt and now I'm meeting Jeremy for coffee.

As I walk into the coffee shop, I see Jeremy already seated with two coffee cups. "That's a lot of caffeine. They must really be working you hard for you to be that tired."

I sit across from him. "Very funny. This one's for you." He pushes one of the cups towards me. "How was the tour of the medical center?"

"Amazing! I only applied to the job here because it's close to home and it's something I want to do. I'll be working first hand with the sports teams at Vanderbilt. It's my dream job."

Jeremy sips his coffee. "I feel a *but* coming."

"But... It's only part time and Nashville's cost of living is higher compared to the other places I applied. Most of my paycheck will be going towards a small apartment. It'll be like being back in college eating ramen in my dorm room." I tell him about the other offers at FSU and UNC. "Tallahassee is cheaper and UNC is giving me a housing allowance since I'll be teaching. I just don't know what to do."

He sets his coffee down. "Let me see your pro/con list." He and Logan used to make fun of me for making lists but I always said they helped. Logan...sigh. I force the tears back. Now is not the time to cry.

I pull the pro/con list out of my bag. He reads it over for a few minutes before looking back at me. "Let me ask you something—or two things, actually." I nod for him to continue.

"One. You still want to go to the Olympics next summer, right?" I nod again because I can't tell him the truth. I can barely admit it to myself. "Two. If we took out where you would live and the whole part time versus full time money situation, what job do you want the most?"

I don't pause. I know without a doubt which is my dream job. "Vanderbilt hands down. I would be working with the sports teams directly. That's why I went into Sports Physical Training in the first place."

"Then there's your answer. Vanderbilt it is! Plus the part time part will give you plenty of time to train. I know your training schedule is intense with the Olympics right around the corner."

"Okay it may seem that easy to you but even with it being the perfect job and giving me time to train, I still need a place to live. I also want to save some money and I can't do that in Nashville. North Carolina is close to the same price but they are at least giving me a housing allowance."

"Yeah, but you'll also be teaching a lecture in front of a class full of students. You and I both know how well you do with public speaking. Maybe a guest lecture, but not a whole semester. You would go crazy having to stand up in front of a room that often."

"Ugh...you're right. Florida State then. Maybe I can move into the sports department in a year." And hopefully I don't get swallowed up by the memories of Logan there.

"I love Florida State but you have the job you want right here, with time to train, and it's near your family and your favorite guy."

"Will you give me blankets and food when I'm living on the streets?"

Jeremy thinks for a moment. Just as I'm about to slap him for being mean he surprises me. "I'll do you one better. How about you move in with me?"

"Jer, I can't do that. One, I could never afford half the rent and two, wouldn't that be weird?"

"You wouldn't have to pay any of the rent, and second, why would it be weird? We lived together before."

"Jer, I have to pay for something. I don't want handouts, even from you. We did live together but I also lived with your brother who happened to be my husband at the time. We basically had our own apartment on the side of your house in Tallahassee."

"That was a pretty cool house my parents bought me. It was perfect for a guy living with newlyweds so I didn't have to hear anything." I shove him. "My condo now is in Sobro and it's a two bedroom, two bath with an amazing kitchen that never gets any love. You remember, it's huge. Plus, I'm barely there with practice for the Titans."

"That sounds great but I still don't want a handout. I'm a big girl and I can make something work." I sigh. I really want to stay here.

Jeremy scoots his chair closer to me and lifts my chin. "First of all, it isn't a handout when you're family, and second we can count all those yummy meals you will make me as payment."

I suck in a breath. Family. Logan was my husband and his family really did become my family. After the accident, I pulled away. It was my fault he died and being near them hurt. Jeremy forced his way back in and I'm eternally grateful, but it doesn't make it easier. I don't know if his parents would even consider me family anymore.

"Oh so what, now I'm your housewife? Next, you'll tell me to clean the bathrooms and your room."

"That's not a bad idea." Jeremy smirks and I look at him annoyed. "Kidding. That's what the housekeeper is for, plus she brings groceries so whatever you need you can add to the list."

"Why do I feel like I am going to regret this?"

"So is that a yes?" I sigh and finally agree. "Yes! My own sexy chef." He pulls me into a side hug. I freeze at his words. He must feel me tense because he asks, "What's wrong?"

"Nothing, that's what Logan used to call me anytime I was in the kitchen. Ugh... why is this so hard? I think all the time if he was standing right in front of me, I would ask why he didn't fight harder. He just gave up. I wanted to give up too but instead I've spent the past few years fighting."

"Emma, you know he would have fought if he could. He loved you but things happened."

"Okay, so why did he leave me?"

"Emma, you know why..."

"I just miss him so much." My head falls into my hands to hide the tears threatening to fall.

"So do I but at least you have me." He smirks again.

I try not to smile. He always seems to stop me falling into a pit of sorrow that happens anytime I think of Logan.

"Oh what a replacement. Now take me to this amazing condo of yours. I have to make sure you didn't change anything from the last time I was there. I need to make sure it still lives up to my standard of living." This time I can't help the smile that spreads across my face.

Chapter Nine

I stand with a box in my hands in the middle of the living room and take in the space surrounding me. It doesn't look much different from the last time I stayed here. Some more memorabilia hangs on the walls with some new furniture, but other than that it looks the same.

The living room, dining room, and kitchen are all a massive open concept. The kitchen still looks brand new with stainless steel appliances and gorgeous marble countertops. Jeremy rarely cooks so the appliances have probably only been used a handful of times. There's also a huge island with a breakfast bar.

The living room has two couches angled towards a massive TV that takes up the entire wall. Not really but it's huge. In the middle is a rather plain coffee table that must be new.

Jeremy sees me looking at the coffee table. "Don't be fooled." He starts pulling out hidden drawers and slides the top to reveal different storage compartments. It even has heated and cooled cup holders.

I notice a section for blankets. Currently it has one blanket in it that looks small and itchy. I'll have to fix that.

"Let me give you the tour. This is obviously the living room and kitchen. Over there is the dining room, although I mostly eat at the breakfast bar."

"You do realize that I've been here before right?" I ask him.

He leads me towards a hallway. "Yes, but this is the official tour now that you're living here. I never really gave you a tour when you stayed here before. This is your bathroom and bedroom."

I go along with his tour pretending to have never seen anything before. "My very own bedroom and bathroom? Wow. You spoil me!" I tease. He shakes his head laughing at me.

The door in front is a bathroom connected to my bedroom. The bathroom is long with a good size sink and vanity. There is a huge walk-in shower with one of those rain shower heads. It also has multiple shower heads that point in different directions. There is a fancy screen inside that controls it all. The first time I was here, Jeremy had to show me how to use the crazy shower. Now I'm excited I get to use it all the time.

I walk through the door inside the bathroom, into my bedroom. The walls are painted a light blue. It has a queen bed, two night stands, a massive long dresser, and a cute desk all made of a pretty, dark oak wood. There is a flat screen smart television above the dresser.

Even with all of the furniture in here, there is still tons of space in the room.

There is a door on the other side of the dresser leading to a walk-in closet. It's big and there will be plenty of space for my clothes.

I set the box down on the floor and walk back into the hallway through the bedroom door.

He leads me down the hallway in the opposite direction. He opens the first door. "This is the laundry room." The room is tucked in the corner and has a washer, dryer, and large folding table with cabinet storage above it.

We leave the laundry room and he points at the door at the end of the hall. "That is my bedroom."

"Don't I get a tour?" I laugh because I've already seen every part of this apartment but I'm having fun going along with his tour.

Jeremy grabs both of my hands and pulls me towards the door. He lets go of one hand to open the door. Inside the room, he tosses me on the bed and leans over me.

"Have I told you how happy I am that you're moving in?" He gazes down at me. My heart is racing. He looks like he's going to kiss me. I push him away before anything can happen.

"I hope you say that later once I move all my stuff in and add decorations."

Jeremy looks nervous.

"Don't worry, I won't make it too girly." I stick my tongue at him and go into his bathroom which is double the size as mine. It has a double sink, toilet, walk-in shower, and a jacuzzi tub. There is a door leading to a massive walk-in closet, even bigger than mine filled with clothes. More than what he used to have. I didn't know guys could have this many clothes. Maybe it's a professional football player thing.

I glance back at the tub. What I would give to soak in that tub.

I feel hands on my hips as Jeremy whispers in my ear, "If you're good, I might let you soak in there."

I lift my head to look back at him. "What's the catch? You have to be in the tub too?"

"I mean, I wouldn't say no."

"You wish," I say walking back towards the bedroom. I swear I hear him say, "I do wish," but I don't say anything more.

His room is even bigger than mine. The walls are a dark blue and he has some football inspired artwork on the walls. One wall is lined with football trophies and awards. Hopefully soon he will have something to add from the Super Bowl. Obviously, if they win, he will get a ring but I assume he'll wear it at first.

I leave his room to go back out to the living room.

"Let's get a cart for all your stuff." He wanted to show me the condo first before we brought my stuff up. I insisted on bringing at least one box up so we didn't waste a trip. He laughed but grabbed a box too which he already set on the kitchen island.

We leave the condo and go to the elevators. This building is actually a hotel but the top ten floors are all condos that range from studios to four bedrooms. The top floor has two penthouse condos. I asked Jeremy why he didn't have one of those and he said he didn't need or want that much space. He opted for a smaller condo.

The building has a ton of security which I found out when we first made our way up the elevator. It has doors on both sides, and to access any of the condo floors requires a key card and your fingerprint. The key card only works for the floor you live on and is programmed to you. That way if you lose it and get a new one, the old one is automatically deactivated. The fingerprint is the extra level of security in case someone gets a hold of a key card or you lose it. Depending on how high up you are determines how big the condos are and how many are on that floor.

Jeremy lives on the thirty-seventh floor and apparently there are seven other condos on this floor in a variety of floor plans. Half are on one side and half are on the other so that is why the elevators can open on both sides, but it will only open to whatever side your condo is on.

It is all high tech and makes me feel safe that someone isn't going to just wander to my door.

Once we are done moving in my stuff, Jeremy is giving me a tour of the rest of the building including the amenities.

We get on the elevator and Jeremy scans his key card. Not only is the key card needed for access to the floor you live on, but also several other floors that are amenities only for those that live here. A fingerprint isn't needed for the amenities as hotel guests can get access for a fee.

There is a garage for hotel guests and one for those living in the building. The garage we are going to is one of the floors that is only accessible to those that live here. The amount of parking spots is determined by how many rooms you have. You can pay for additional spots if you need them. Jeremy has been using his second spot as a guest spot but my car now claims the spot.

Once we hit the garage level, we grab a luggage cart and walk to my car. We load up the cart and head back to the elevator.

After a few more trips, I am exhausted and have never been more thankful for the cart.

Once everything is unloaded, Jeremy suggests we grab a bite to eat at one of the restaurants downstairs. We choose one of the more casual lunch places.

We both order burgers and fries. Moving makes me hungry and it's a good thing because the burger that comes out is massive. Even with my stomach rumbling, I'll probably still be taking half of it to go.

I order the buffalo bleu burger complete with buffalo sauce, blue cheese crumbles, onions, lettuce and even those crispy onions you put on a green bean casserole.

As I thought, I'm only able to eat half so we take the leftovers back up to the apartment before taking a tour of the rest of the building.

Jeremy tells me that we can order from any of the restaurants like room service. The perks of it being a hotel too, I guess.

We head down to the lobby area. We went to the condo through the garage so I didn't have a chance to see it. There are marble floors, tall pillars with gold specks, and massive sparkling chandeliers. There are flowers throughout the lobby that make it feel cheerful.

We stop by the front desk to get a key card for me and program my fingerprint.

Anytime guests come, they're either escorted up or are given a guest key card that only lasts a certain amount of time. It's all so fancy and makes me feel very safe.

A few floors up, Jeremy said they have a ballroom that is decorated similarly to the lobby as well as an event center and offices you can rent out.

On the same floor as the lobby is the main pool and gym. There's a large outdoor pool for when it's warm and a smaller pool inside for winter time. There's a good size gym with all your typical workout machines.

He leads me to an area that's for those that live here only. This is one of the amenities hotel guests can get access to for a fee.

Inside is a lap pool, sauna, steam room, and massive gym. It has everything from treadmills and ellipticals to weight machines and a running track. The running track is suspended above the gym which is pretty cool.

There's a small yoga and pilates studio off to the side.

The spa for the hotel is right above the gym. It has access directly from the gym or the main entrance on the other side that most people use. Jeremy said since we live in the building we get a discount at the spa.

Next, he shows me the other restaurants in the building. There's a sushi bar, a sandwich and salad place, an Italian steakhouse, a breakfast diner, and the burger place we went to.

We take the elevator to the roof where the Italian steakhouse is. Jeremy said you have to make reservations for dinner, but lunch is open for everyone. The view is gorgeous and I can almost see the whole city from here.

I can't wait to try it at some point.

We head back down to the condo where the unpacking begins.

Unpacking soothes me. I like organizing all my clothes in the closet and toiletries in the bathroom.

Jeremy didn't have many small kitchen appliances other than a toaster, a coffee maker, a blender, a waffle maker, and a chocolate fondue pot. I will have to ask him about that last one.

I brought all my small appliances and filled the cabinets. If he wants me to cook, I need my supplies.

By the time I'm done unpacking it's late and I'm exhausted. I'm thankful for my leftover burger as all I have to do is reheat it.

Jeremy went out with some guys from the team. I told him he didn't need to stick around to help me unpack. It would just be boring.

As if on cue, I hear the door open.

"Honey, I'm home and I come bearing dessert."

I take my empty plate to the kitchen to rinse off and put in the dishwasher. "Dessert for me?"

"Yes, for you gorgeous." I blush. We may just be friends but that doesn't stop his constant flirting. Over the years, I've grown used to it. Logan always laughed because he knew his brother never had a chance and he would joke that the only way Jeremy would have a chance is if he wasn't in the picture. Oh well.

Lately, Jeremy's flirting has started affecting me more. I know it's because of those feelings that are bubbling on the surface, but I'm not ready to face them. It's been over two and half years since the accident but I keep hoping that it'll all be a dream. I know it wasn't and I've moved on, but a part of me will always wonder: what if Logan hadn't died?

I look in the bag and there's a slice of chocolate cheesecake with a strawberry on top.

I grab two forks and take it to the breakfast bar. I sit down and open the container.

I take a bite. It's so rich and yummy. "This is so good. Thank you."

Jeremy comes around behind me as I get another piece. He leans over me and eats the piece right off my fork.

"Hey!" I smack him playfully and point to the other fork I grabbed. "I got you your own fork."

"Yours is better." He winks at me and sits down. He picks up his fork and gets a piece.

Not surprisingly, we finish off the slice pretty quickly. Jeremy throws the container away and rinses our forks off before putting them in the dishwasher.

I yawn. "I'm worn out and ready to head to bed. Thanks for your help today, and for letting me stay here."

"This is your home now too. Enjoy it."

I nod and walk towards my bedroom but stop when Jeremy asks, "don't I get a good night kiss?" I stay facing the bedroom so he can't see the blush creeping up my neck.

"Um."

"I'm just kidding. Good night Emma," he says into my ear. How did he get over here so fast? I didn't even hear him walk over. I guess it's those quick quarterback feet.

I face him. I quickly kiss him on the cheek and race to my bedroom. I close the door and take a breath. Why did I just do that?

I can hear him chuckling from here. He knows exactly what he does to me.

I'm so excited to have moved into this amazing condo, but resisting his charms is going to be a whole different story.

Chapter Ten

I've been getting settled in the condo. Jeremy is on his way home. He's depressed because he threw an interception that almost lost them the game. If the other team hadn't fumbled the ball, they probably would have lost.

In college, anytime Jeremy lost a game I'd go over to his house or his side of the house when Logan and I moved in. Sometimes Logan would join me. I would try to cheer him up with different things like board games or silly movies. Just something to get him out of his head to stop thinking about the game. He could go look at the tapes later and figure out what to do for the next game.

I remember one night when the game got crazy.

"You have sunk my battleship."

"Yes!" I shout. He only has one left while I manage to still have three on the board. He has guessed one peg in two of them but the last one he still has no idea.

Logan had left earlier when we pulled out Battleship. He knows things get heated. We are both competitive. Logan had to finish editing a film for class, anyway.

Logan was right. Things are heating up and I'm confident I'll win.

"C2," Jeremy says.

Oh no. He figured out the second peg in my three peg ship.

"Hit. Submarine."

"F7," I say.

"Miss."

Several rounds later, I miss every single one. Meanwhile, he has sunk two of my ships. We are both down to our destroyers, the only ship with two pegs. Neither of us have been able to find the others yet.

"E4," Jeremy says.

No! Now he has figured out where mine is and there are only four spots where the second one could be. I need to figure out where his is fast.

"Hit. Destroyer."

Jeremy cheers loudly.

"B9," I say.

"Miss."

"E3."

"Miss." I sigh in relief.

I look at my board trying to figure out where his destroyer could be. I notice the position of where my destroyer is. I haven't guessed anything around there for his ships. I wonder...

"E4."

"Hit. Destroyer." No way. Did we put it in the same spot? I cross my fingers hoping he doesn't come to the same conclusion.

I glance up at him and he must see something on my face because he smirks.

"E5."

"How did you know?"

Jeremy smirks even bigger. "Is it a hit?"

"Yes," I say angry, but more in a shocked way. He does this every time. Gives me hope I can win and somehow comes back.

"Say it."

"Hit. Destroyer."

"And?"

I grit my teeth. "You sunk my battleship."

"I win!"

"I hate you."

"No, you love me!"

"Only a little. I don't know how you do that every time." I do love him like a brother but I also hate him like a brother when he does this.

"You have no poker face. With games like this, you're super easy to read. You basically give away anytime I'm really close to one of your ships or really far away."

"Ughh. I'm going to bed."

I help him clean up and he gives me a friendly hug. As I pull away, he whispers in my ear. "Thanks for playing with me every time I have a bad game or lose. It really does cheer me up."

I pull away and smile at him. "I'm always here for you Jeremy."

"Good night Emma."

Good night Jeremy."

Something tickles my ear as I come out of my daydream and hear a whisper, "What are you thinking so hard about?"

I was so lost in the memory, I didn't even hear Jeremy come in.

"I was remembering the time we played Battleship and I almost beat you."

"Oh yes. You were one move away from beating me. You never did manage to get that close again."

"Hence why I banned it."

"Logan was so mad at you. He loved playing that game unless it was you and me playing. Then he didn't stick around."

"He was also super easy to beat." I think Logan only ever beat me twice.

"You realize he was letting you win, right?"

"What? No he wasn't. I beat him fair and square."

"Emma, he was better than me at Battleship. I could probably count on one hand the number of times I beat him."

"No way."

"I'd ask him if he were here."

"Yeah..." I say quietly. "I miss him."

Jeremy pulls me into a hug. "I miss him too."

"Will it ever not hurt anymore to think about him?"

"No, but I think having people that loved him around you makes it a little better. We can miss him together, but also remember all the great times we had."

I sink into his hug a little more, enjoying the calm it gives me. Logan was always my protective calm, but Jeremy is the calm when things get rough and I need a little push.

"I have a good idea."

"What's that?"

Jeremy pulls away and walks to the hall closet. He pulls something out from the very top shelf.

"Is that...?" I ask and Jeremy smiles. It is. It's Battleship.

I cross my arms and shake my head.

"Please." Jeremy gives me his best puppy dog face complete with a pouty mouth and squinty eyes.

"No." I back away before he can convince me. He knows that puppy dog face always works. His brother knew it too and they both used it on me plenty. I swear it's an Anderson thing because I've seen their dad, Blake, use it on his wife. "I have a better idea. What if we watch a movie and play guess the line?"

Jeremy reluctantly agrees, putting Battleship back and grabbing the remote. "I'll find the movie if you'll make the popcorn."

"Deal. Parmesan or salt and butter?"

"A bowl of each."

I nod and head to the cabinets with the popcorn maker. As professional athletes we both have to watch what we eat. As much as we love bagged popcorn, all that butter is not good. Instead we pop our own and add toppings that we can control. Parmesan is a favorite along with good old butter and salt. We use this amazing everything salt that has other seasonings in it too. You don't need much of either and it's delicious.

As the popcorn begins popping, I check out what movie Jeremy picked.

"I'm deciding between these two."

We always pick a one or two star movie and play "Guess the next line." Logan actually came up with the game when he was researching for a film class. He was trying to figure out why some movies do better than others. Is it the actors or directors? Is it the plot? Is it the writing? Maybe a mix of both. He started watching different one and two star movies to see if he could figure it out. It honestly varied. To make it more fun and the awful movies more enjoyable to watch, he turned it into a game.

The rules are simple. At any point, someone can yell freeze, the movie is paused and whoever yelled freeze must say someone else's name. Whoever they call must say whatever they think the next line is. It's actually really fun.

We agree on some thriller comedy. I didn't even know there was such a thing.

The popcorn is done popping so I split it into two bowls, add the toppings and then bring it over to the coffee table. I grab us drinks and settle on the couch next to Jeremy with a few feet in between us.

Being in a condo with him all the time is tempting enough.

We sit through the movie laughing and constantly yelling freeze. I couldn't even tell you what the story was about. Some girl with bad luck who goes to a haunted house and gets stuck in it. I really don't know but when the spooky creatures come to life, we come up with some great lines.

When the movie ends and the popcorn is gone I can't help but smile. It's nice to play a simple game like this again. It helped cheer Jeremy up and reminded me of the fun times with Logan.

I glance at Jeremy to find him watching me. He smiles and I smile back. Being here with him has been nice. Other than Ashley and my family, Jeremy has been one of the closest people to me. He truly is my best friend and I don't know where I'd be without him. I feel the sparks between us but I'm afraid to give in. What would that mean? Would it be weird?

For now, I'll push them aside and enjoy moments like this. I stand before I give in to those sparks.

"Goodnight Jeremy."

Jeremy stands, gives me a kiss on the cheek and says, "Goodnight Emma."

He walks towards his bedroom and I can't help watching him walk away.

I shake my head, clearing my mind of any thoughts.

As I fall asleep that night, my dreams are filled with weird memories where Jeremy and I were together but Logan was still alive.

I wake to find sunshine spilling through my window.

What did I just dream about?

I shake my head. Breathe Emma, it was a dream. I turn over, closing my eyes, wondering what comes next.

Chapter Eleven

I officially accepted the job at Vanderbilt and I love it. Three days a week, I work the morning shift at the Medical Center and the other two days, I work the afternoon/early evening shift. When I'm not working, I'm in the pool training.

I work with all the sports teams but my favorite is definitely swimming and football. They've always been my favorite sports but then again I'm a little biased.

The swim meets are fun and I have the chance to show them some tricks they can use to improve their times.

Every other Saturday, I work with the football team and even get to travel to some away games. It's a great experience and something I wouldn't mind doing more of.

I still swim a few hours on Sundays to keep up with my training since it's my only official day off. Well, kind of. It's my day off of work but I'm still super busy since my best friend/roommate is the starting quarterback for the Titans. He tells me I'm required to be at all home games. I don't mind and love attending his games. Plus I get to spend time with Danielle and Connor.

His parents even drive over for the games whenever they can. It's always nice seeing them after everything that happened even though I feel they still blame me. We never talk much. I know I created the distance but I don't know how to get back what we had before Logan passed away. I need to talk to them, but I'm just not ready yet.

It's the last game before the Christmas break. Both Jeremy and I have a week off. The nice thing about living in Nashville is that it's only a three hour drive home.

The Titans win and when Jeremy is done with all his interviews, we head home. His truck is already packed with our stuff. I can't wait to get home to see my parents.

My phone rings and I recognize the number as The University of North Carolina Physical Therapy admissions. They had offered me a job as a guest lecturer for the semester but I turned them down since I wasn't big on speaking in public.

I answer, "Hello, this is Emma."

"Hey Emma, this is Karl with the UNC PT department. We're calling to see if you would like to be part of our Physical Training workshop next semester?" I think back to the job they offered me at the beginning of the semester teaching a lecture centered on Physical Training in the real world.

"What part would I play in the workshop?" I ask him, hoping I won't have to speak.

"We're bringing back a few of our top students to talk about their current jobs and how they have used Physical Therapy in their own lives. We are hoping you could talk about the Olympics and your accident. We know it's very forward to ask you, but your story is incredible and we think it would help our current students see the value in what they're doing."

I think back to the accident and I wipe away a tear. I've finally gotten over what happened but it still hurts when I think back to that night. "I'll think about it and let you know."

"Thanks Emma. We would love to see you again. When you first denied your acceptance for your bachelors, I'll admit we were bummed. We saw a ton of potential in you as a student. Then you called and asked about spots in the master's program. We knew you from the Olympics and your original application. When Mr. Anderson called after and filled us in about the accident..."

"I'm sorry, you said Mr. Anderson?"

"Yes, the dean is always talking about the Andersons after we did the program with Andertainment. We were surprised to hear from his son, Jeremy. I hear he's in the NFL these days."

"Yes he is but why did you say he called?"

"He called letting us know about your accident and how you needed a fresh start that was still close to home, so if there was any way we could accept you in the master's program for the spring semester. We were able to add another spot and were ecstatic to have you. We definitely made the right choice."

"I was very thankful for the opportunity. Thanks also for letting me know about Jeremy." I hadn't applied to their master's program because Logan and I wanted to go to a school together that catered to both our majors. Ashley went there and tried to get me to apply but I didn't see a point when Boston College had the best programs, film for Logan and a physical therapy master's program for me.

Yet, after the accident, Jeremy somehow knew that having my family close by and my best friend even closer would be the push I needed. I only had a semester of the Physical Training program under my belt so transferring wouldn't be too hard since I wasn't too deep in the program.

"Of course. We would have been happy to accept you regardless of that phone call, although it did help the admissions board. Anyway, I'll email you all the workshop details and please let us know your decision."

"Thanks, Karl." We hang up and I'm shocked. Jeremy must've talked to them after the accident when I was still in the hospital. I think back to that night I was ready to give it all up.

"How're you feeling, Emma?"

"Like I got hit by a car and then had my heart ripped out."

Jeremy takes my hand and draws circles on my palm. "I was thinking you need a fresh start when you get out of this hospital room. Have you thought about what you're going to do?"

I give him the most disgusted look and yank my hand away from him. I was most definitely not thinking about the future.

"Do I look like someone that cares about the future? I just found out I may never walk again and my husband died. The last thing I am thinking about is school or swimming or whatever fresh start you're thinking about. I don't care about any of it."

"I get that your world has just been turned upside down but you need to fight. Fight for your career. Your hard work at school.

Fight for that next gold medal." He pauses, making eye contact and I already know what he is going to say next. "Fight for lo..."

"Don't say it. I can't, Jeremy. He left me. He didn't care. You know we had a fight in the car. He wanted to go out to California for his master's program and wanted me to transfer. I said I'd think about it but deep down he knew I didn't want to."

"Then fight for him. Don't let your fight, or the accident, or fear stop you from living. The nurses said you haven't even tried to do anything and have barely eaten. It's been several weeks since the accident. School is starting next week."

"I can't go back there." I think about the time we had at Boston College. Logan and I had so much fun. I just can't go back to Boston now without him. There're too many memories. My heart has already been ripped out and it'll feel like it's being ripped out over and over if I go back. I don't even care about finishing school.

"Then we'll find somewhere else. I'm sure Ashley would love you with her at UNC, and they have an amazing PT program. My dad knows the dean and I could call--"

"Don't you dare call, Jeremy. I'm done with school, swimming, and everything. I don't want it."

"Emma, you're the strongest person I know. And I'm the most stubborn. Since my brother isn't here, it's now up to me to push you until you get out of this bed and start walking. Until you win another gold medal. Until your heart is no longer broken."

"Jer... That's the thing. I don't care about any of it. You heard the doctors, my injuries were bad. It'll be a struggle to even stand, let alone walk or swim again. What's the point of school? Oh and

I no longer have a heart since Logan took it with him. Just go. I don't want to talk anymore."

I can tell he is frustrated and his shoulders sag like he has given up. Maybe he will leave it alone–but knowing him he won't. "This conversation isn't over Emma. I promise you all those things will come true. We'll start with school. Then we can focus on swimming and your heart. Will you please give UNC a call?"

"Fine. Whatever. I'll call them. Leave the number on my table. I highly doubt they'll accept me when classes start next week. Plus, I can't even walk so I don't know how getting to classes is going to work."

"I'm sure we can work with them. Maybe if you explain your situation."

"Jeremy, enough. I'll call, okay? Please, just go. Oh and can you tell the nurses I need some more pain medicine on your way out?" As I close my eyes, I see Jeremy pull out his phone and walk out of the room. I don't care enough to stop him. I'm tired and done with it all.

My thoughts are interrupted when the driver's side door opens and Jeremy gets in. "Are you ready to go?"

"Yep." I buckle my seatbelt and look out the window ignoring him.

"Well okay then." He starts the truck and turns on music. I don't try to change it to my music.

Halfway through the car ride, Jeremy turns down the music and says, "So what happened to put you in a bad mood? You couldn't wait to go home this morning."

"Oh I'm still excited to go home, just not about this car ride."

"Okay so what did I do?"

"Do you remember our conversation right after my accident? We were in the hospital and I was ready to give everything up and you told me not to. You said you were going to be your stubborn self and make me go to school. You suggested the University of NC and I basically told you it was never going to happen. You mentioned calling them for me and I said no. Well you did."

"You're mad about that now?" He laughs like it's old news.

"Well I may have just found out about it. They called to ask if I could speak at a workshop they're holding next semester."

"Emma, that's great. You should do it."

"That isn't the point. The point is you betrayed my trust."

"I was trying to help. With how upset you were, I knew you couldn't go back to Boston College. You and Logan decided to go there together when you got accepted into their master's program. I knew you needed a change and UNC seemed to be a good choice between Ashley being there and it having a great program. Logan had told me you didn't apply for your master's there because you wanted a school that had a great film program for him."

"That doesn't explain why you called after I told you not to. I said I would call and I did." I look out the front windshield.

"Like I said, I wanted to help you and I thought giving the admissions board a little push couldn't hurt. Emma, you were ready to give it all up and I knew a little good news might help you get back on track. The call didn't matter anyway."

I'm surprised by his last comment. "What do you mean it didn't matter anyway?"

"When I called them they said they were checking to make sure they could fit you in the program. Emma, you were already in when I made that call a few days after our conversation. They just hadn't called you back yet. I tried to call that day but couldn't get through."

"But you still called."

"Okay yes I called, but answer me this - would you be working your dream job right now?" I shake my head. "I may have made that call but you did everything on your own. You only needed a push in a few directions. I just explained your situation and helped with arrangements." I cross my arms. "You know I'm right. I also know you can't stay mad at me for long."

I try to continue being mad but he knows me too well. I can't stay mad at him for long. He has a way of getting me outside my comfort zone and making me see more than what is happening in the present. Soon my frown is turning into a smile.

"Okay fine, but to make it up to me we get to listen to my music." I turn to my favorite Pop radio station and Jeremy groans. I smile again. Maybe I should get mad at him more often.

Chapter Twelve

We walk up the stairs of the Anderson house for the annual New Year's Eve Ball. "I can't do this. I can't go into that house with all those memories." I have avoided coming back to this house since everything happened. Ashley and Jeremy somehow persuaded me to come back this year. I was perfectly happy to sit in my room at my parent's house with Ashley and eat junk food while watching the ball drop.

Ashley grabs my hand and squeezes. "I'll be by your side the entire night. You want to leave, you tell me. Your parents are right behind us and so is your brother. You won't be alone. Plus Jeremy and his parents are always here for you."

Behind her, my brother gives me a reassuring nod.

I feel a little better. Victoria Anderson's there to greet us and give me a hug. Seeing them almost every week at Jeremy's games has helped but things still feel awkward between us. I miss them but I still don't know how to get back to where we were before the accident. "Emma, we've missed you around here."

"I'm sorry I haven't been around much. Too many memories but it gets easier every day."

"We miss him too. Now let's get inside and find something to drink."

Most of the night, I stand on the edge of the dance floor and watch Ashley dance with Ty. It wasn't long ago I'd be right there next to them.

People are chatting, dancing, eating, and having a great time. I wish I could be in the moment and enjoy the New Year. I glance at the clock in the corner and the time reads just after 11 p.m. Only about an hour left and I can leave.

The ballroom is decorated with several disco balls on the ceilings that cast sparkles across the room. They reflect off the strings of lights, silver balloons, and other decor hung across the ceiling and draped across the walls. Usually it would be tacky but with the New Year's vibe and the way the lights are dimmed, it feels like everything glitters and swirls around you.

The tables off to the side are filled with champagne towers, charcuterie boards, light appetizers, and mini desserts all surrounded by purple and gold ornament balls.

There's a photo booth in the corner with all sorts of fun costume pieces and silly signs.

I look back out to the dance floor and will myself to dance and have fun.

As if he can sense I need a push to get out there, Jeremy grabs my hand and pulls me onto the dance floor. "Jer, I really don't feel like dancing right now."

He wraps his arm around my waist. "I know this is hard, but we need to turn that frown upside down. I requested something special." I attempt to follow his steps and remember back to my Junior Prom when Logan couldn't go so he insisted I go with Jeremy. The same waltz that comes through the speakers now was playing that night. He did all these crazy lifts and moves that I later found out was a thing he did with all the girls. "Your moves didn't work on me during Junior Prom and they won't work now."

"Oh honey, those were never just moves with you." I look at him confused. "Those moves may have worked with other girls but you were always too smart for that. You still are."

The song ends as he dips me, but I turn my head not wanting to look in his eyes. I'm afraid of what I might see. We've been getting close since living together and he's never been far since the accident. I can't seem to get away from him. It used to annoy me but he's been creeping his way in. I don't know what it means and I don't want to know either.

He lifts me back up as another faster song comes on. I shake off all my thoughts and try to enjoy my time. Ashley and Ty shimmy their way over to us. It isn't long before I'm jumping and finally letting myself be in the moment.

A slow song comes on and Jeremy pulls me into his chest. A few seconds into the song, I realize what song it is, and I pull away from Jeremy. "I need some air."

I grab my coat before stepping outside into the back yard.

I stop at the foot of the ladder of the tree house Logan built when he was younger with his dad and Jeremy. Logan used to tell me that he'd come here to think. I found him up here plenty of times and it turned into our hideout.

Tonight, I thought it might give me some clarity. I know Logan isn't coming back and I need to move on. I thought these feelings for Jeremy were friendly but lately I'm starting to feel more.

I start to climb but immediately step down. The closer I get to the top, the more the pain seeps in.

Instead, I run down to the boat house and step on the dock. I peer out at the lake.

A few minutes later, I hear footsteps behind me, already knowing who it is. I can sense anytime he is near and it confuses me even more.

"I thought I'd find you in the treehouse but when I went up there, I saw you down here. Logan always went there to think and I figured you'd do the same."

"Yeah I couldn't bring myself to climb the ladder. I needed somewhere new to think after that song. That song was…"

"Your wedding song, I know. I had no idea they were going to play that tonight. I'm sorry Emma." He stands next to me. I can feel electricity pulsing off both of us even with him still being a few feet away.

"What did you mean when you said those were never just moves with me?"

"You should know by now," he says, like it is the most obvious thing in the world.

"Know what?"

"Emma, I've always had a thing for you. Ever since freshman year when you spilled your coffee on me."

"Why didn't you ever say anything?" I glance over at him to find him already staring back at me.

"I always thought you were too good for me. I was dumb and never talked to you but always admired you from afar. Then my brother came back and won your heart so I set aside my feelings. You two were perfect, and I wasn't about to get in the way of that."

"Jer. I had no idea." I look down to my hands because I can't risk him seeing the raging war that is going on in my head.

"I figured. I kept them buried and felt so bad about what happened after spring break. I knew I had to keep my distance but I figured the best thing was to go back to my flirty ways. I did my best to never put us in that situation again, and I continued to fight for you and Logan."

"Jer..." I wondered if I knew back then how he felt. My relationship with Jeremy has always been confusing. We never seemed to like each other at the same time. Although hearing what he just said, maybe he did like me back in my freshman year. And ignoring me was such a great way of letting me know. Not.

When Logan showed up, I never looked back. Jeremy was my friend and nothing more. Logan was the love of my life and I would've fought to the ends of the Earth for him. Now the time has passed for that and I can't go back.

Jeremy has helped me through my entire recovery and I wouldn't be where I'm right now if it weren't for him. Maybe that's what these feelings are. It's like in those stories where the girl falls for her rescuer. Jeremy in this case rescued me from myself. He saved me from falling into a downward spiral after the accident. We've always had chemistry but I chalked it up to our friendly relationship.

He looks out at the lake. A few minutes pass before he speaks again. "The year I got to take you to prom, I had to do everything in my power not to kiss you. The waltz was something fun and I knew I could write it off as something I did with every other girl." He turns to me. "I know Ashley told you that was my signature move and so did my brother, but it was never that with you. I felt like I was flying the whole time I was dancing with you."

He moves closer to me and grabs my hand. I faintly hear the sounds of a countdown. It must almost be midnight. I know I should pull away and go back to join the party but I feel frozen. I can't move away. Or maybe I don't want to. What is happening?

I slowly glance up to Jeremy's face and find it filled with an almost loving expression. "When I grabbed your hand I felt the electricity." He grabs my waist. "When I pulled you close, I was scared you'd feel my heart beating fast." He dips me. "When I dipped you all I could think about was if I bent down just a little bit, I'd kiss you."

Before I can do anything he does just that. He leans down, pressing his lips to mine. It doesn't last very long, but I feel my entire body explode. Or maybe it's the fireworks that go off at the same moment.

He pulls me back up so I'm standing.

"Wow," is all I manage to say.

"I know." Jeremy gazes into my eyes.

I take a step back. "We can't do this." Now I'm even more confused. Logan took my heart with him and I've felt empty ever since, but Jeremy keeps worming his way in and I feel it beating once again.

He tucks a strand of hair behind my ear. "Even though I've been waiting forever to do that."

I glance at him. "It's just what would he think if he saw us? I can't do this to him."

"Emma, he's gone and not coming back."

I take a few more steps back and a tear slides down my cheek. "You think I don't know that Jer? I'm the reason he left. I'm the reason he's never coming back."

Jeremy reaches for my hand.

I pull away from him and turn back to the lake. The fireworks are still going off but they fade away as the memory of that cold icy night slips into my mind.

"I thought you liked it at Boston College?" I glance at Logan.

"I do, but I think this would be an amazing opportunity for both of us."

I sigh because I don't want to transfer. I love my master's program and the swim center I'm training at is amazing. "We would be so far away from our family and friends. Plus my coach is here and if I want to go to the Olympics again, I need him."

"Em, I'm sure there are other coaches out there. Or maybe he could even follow us out there. He came up here, but if he doesn't he'll probably know someone. I put out feelers for coaches in the area just in case."

"Logan, it sounds great but the Olympics were this past summer and I'm settled here with my program and training. I don't want to go. If you really want to go then go without me."

"Remember that time I transferred from NYU to FSU for you? Then I transferred again when you got accepted into Boston College for your master's this past fall. I'm asking you to do the same."

I pull up to a red light trying not to get mad. "You decided to transfer. I was more than happy to have you close when we were engaged and I've been super happy to have you nearby while we're married." I start to raise my voice. "Don't you dare use that against me."

"I'm not using it against you, but why can't you ever make a sacrifice for me? I transferred both times so you could stay on the East Coast."

The light turns green and I hit the gas pedal. "I make sacrifices for you all the time. Can we please stop talking about this until we get to my house? I'll think about transferring schools. Now let's just get home. It's been a long day, there's tons of ice on the roads, and we're almost there."

"Fine, but we'll talk about this."

I can't help raising my voice, fed up with him for not being able to drop it. This isn't the first time the conversation has been brought up about going to the West Coast. He wanted to go there before I started my master's at Boston College. He's hinted at it a few times since then. I'd think he'd be sick of transferring at this point.

"LOGAN, yes we will talk about it. Please drop it." I pull up to a stop sign just outside Logan's parents' neighborhood.

"You know I love you when you get all angry at me. It's so cute. The last thing I'll say is we'll figure out the right next step for school, but this is an amazing chance. You should see the list of things they offer. I just wanted to tell you about it. I don't like fighting but as long as I have you by my side, it'll be perfect. I love you Emma."

I can't help but smile at his words. Even when I'm angry at him, he still knows how to make me calm down. "I love you too." He entwines his fingers with mine and kisses my hand.

The road is clear and I hit the gas once again. "I will look at it and maybe--" I see the lights as the car spins and I feel the impact only seconds later. I feel the car spin again and I hear my screams pierce the air. I feel pressure on my right leg before excruciating pain shoots up it. Glass shatters and I feel warmth trickle down my cheek. I touch my forehead and when I pull back my hand, there's red. I look over at Logan and see red everywhere. "Logan!" I yell.

I lunge toward him to feel for a pulse but my seatbelt is in the way. I try to undo it but it's stuck. I can't breathe. This can't be happening. Why now? Is this the end? I feel my lungs start to give out as I look over at Logan once more.

"Logan, don't leave me," I whisper as everything goes black.

The memory shifts to the day they told me about Logan, not long after I'd woken up from my coma. I'm in the hospital hooked up to multiple machines. I sit up and a sharp pain runs through my leg. I scream in pain. The nurse runs into my room closely followed by my entire family and Logan's.

My mom rushes to my bedside. "Emma sweetie, are you okay?"

"Logan..." I swallow, struggling to get the words out. "Where is Logan?"

My mom glances at the others in the room. Logan's mom, Victoria steps forward and takes my hand. I can see her cheeks are wet. "Logan...Emma, Logan didn't make it." She chokes back her sobs. Logan's dad, Blake puts his arm around her and pulls her close.

I feel the air leaving my lungs once again. "He...he can't... he can't be..." My eyesight blurs and I can't think. My body is shutting off.

I don't know how much time passes, but I slowly feel my consciousness returning. My eyelids are so heavy, I can't open my eyes. I hear whispers next to my bed.

"We have to tell her," I hear my mom whisper.

"Can't it wait?" My dad sounds torn.

"No, she's going to ask sooner or later, once the shock of losing Logan wears off."

I try to open my eyes. When I finally do, I see my parents and Logan's parents come into focus.

"Hi sweetie. We need to tell you something."

The memory fades and I sit down on the edge of the dock, keeping my feet crossed on the dock so my boots don't get wet. I've always loved it down here, watching the lake at sunrise or sunset. This is one of my new favorites. Watching the moon cast a glow across the entire lake. The fireworks have ended so it's quiet and calm.

"I was driving the car. I killed my own husband," I whisper so quietly that I'm not sure Jeremy even hears me till I feel him sit beside me and wrap his arms around me. He holds me for a few minutes as I sob before he turns my face toward him.

He wipes my tears and lifts my chin. "You did not kill him. You may have been driving but that drunk driver was the one that hit you. It was his mistake, not yours."

"Yeah but it was snowing and there was ice everywhere."

"Yeah, there was. But he was the one that didn't stop like he was supposed to and hit you. There was nothing you could have done."

I shuffle my feet, still not believing him. "It's still my fault. It should have been me that died. The car was on my side. It should have hit me."

"Emma, look at me."

I slowly raise my head. I see something flash in his eyes like he knows something, but it's gone as quick as it comes.

"Have you been carrying this around with you for three years?" I don't answer and he takes that as a yes. "You didn't kill him, Emma and no one blames you for what happened."

"It's just... we were supposed to have forever and he left me too early. I feel like I need to be punished for what happened."

"Oh and breaking your tibia and twisting your knee wasn't punishment enough? If you were anyone else, you would not be walking right now, let alone training to make the Olympic swim team again. I've said this before and I'll say it again. You're one of the strongest people I know, and you succeed in anything you put your mind to."

"Are you sure your parents don't blame me?"

Jeremy looks at me shocked. "Are you kidding me? It's the opposite. Yes, it hurts that he's gone and they're sad about it, but they are so happy to have a daughter that made their son happier than they've ever seen him. All I have heard when I came back these past few years is, "Where is Emma?" or "How is Emma doing?" They've been so worried about you."

"I guess I should apologize for keeping my distance and explain to them why."

"They already understand, but if it'll make you feel better, I'm sure they would love to reassure you of what I've been saying."

"Thanks Jeremy." I give him a hug. "Thanks for being an amazing friend these past few years. I never would have moved on without you or accomplished the things I have."

Jeremy kisses the tip of my nose. "Of course. I am always here for you."

I bite my lip. "Umm about that kiss. I still can't help thinking that Logan is watching us. I know he isn't, but I just need more time. I need time to process what I'm feeling and figure it out. It's been an emotional night."

"I get it. Tonight was your first time back here since the accident and I shouldn't have kissed you, but I'm not going anywhere. We do live together after all."

"Oh yeah," I laugh, somewhat nervously.

"I just wanted to remind you that you have a life worth living for so live it!" He searches my eyes for a few moments. I'm not sure what he is searching for or whether he finds it before he continues, "Now let's go inside and warm up. This dock isn't very warm."

I already feel like the weight I have been carrying around since Logan's death has been lifted. Yet I still have this nagging feeling. The driver that hit us was coming at us from my side. I still don't know how it hit Logan's side.

Ashley runs up to me. "Everything okay?"

I nod and look at Jeremy. "Everything's better. Go back to dancing." She accepts my answer for now and heads back to where she left Tyler.

The ballroom has cleared out and only a few people are still dancing. I didn't realize how long we'd been outside.

Jeremy tells me he is going to find a few people to say goodbye to and then we can leave. I watch Ashley and my brother on the dance floor. They're having a blast doing some crazy dance moves. As a slow song starts, Ashley wraps her arms around his shoulders as he wraps his around her waist. I notice the look in both their eyes and wonder if they'll ever tell each other how they feel. They're both too stubborn though. Tyler says something to her and I see her blush. It takes a lot for Ashley to blush. I wonder if something happened at midnight between them.

It's almost an hour later when Jeremy comes back over to me. Before we leave for the night, I find Mr. and Mrs. Anderson.

"Hey, I owe you both an apology for the past three years. I blamed myself and I figured you blamed me too. I've been struggling these past few years to come to terms with what happened. I put everything into finishing school and therapy for my leg. I never thought about what you all were going through."

Victoria comes up to me and gives me a hug. She pulls back with a serious look. "Emma, we never blamed you for anything. It was the drunk driver's fault, and even with that being said we forgave him a long time ago. What happened was a tragedy, but we're so thankful you survived."

Blake joins her side. "Yes Emma, Logan lives inside all of us. We still see him in all the films he made and we see him in you. You changed his life and we never saw him happier than when he was with you."

Victoria looks at Blake and he nods. "Emma, I'll be honest with you. After we had Jeremy, the doctors told us that was it. I wouldn't be able to get pregnant again. Then several months later, I found out I was pregnant. Logan was the miracle child we never thought possible. I believe that even in his short life, he was born for a reason, and that reason was you."

"Me?"

"I've never been more proud of him. Sure, he made an impact with his films while he was alive. Just look at the achievements he received. But that night he sacrificed himself for you. He wanted you to have a full life and leave your impact on this world.

"What are you talking about?" Sacrificed himself for me? I think back to the accident. Did he do something? The accident never made sense to me. How Logan's side got hit when the driver was coming at us on my side. I remember seeing the lights.

Victoria looks to my side at Jeremy who shakes his head. She takes my hand in hers.

"Why don't you come over tomorrow for lunch and we can talk. We can catch up and help fill in the blanks for you," Mrs. Anderson suggests.

As much as I want to demand that she tell me what she knows, I agree. It has been a long night and it's already late. I'm ready to crawl into bed.

She pulls me in for another hug. "I've missed you my sweet girl."

I hold back the tears that threaten to fall. Mrs. Anderson was my second mom and I truly have missed her.

"I've missed you too."

She pulls away. "We'll see you tomorrow."

Jeremy wraps his arm around me as we head to the car. I don't think I'll get much sleep tonight wondering what the Andersons were talking about. It's been an emotional night and I have a feeling tomorrow is only going to add to it.

Jeremy opens the passenger door for me and I get in. Ashley and Tyler slide in the backseat as Jeremy goes around to the driver's side.

We head back to my parents' house and I gaze out the window at the darkened sky. So much has happened since that fateful night. I've been getting by but have I really been living? Tonight seemed to wake me up. Maybe it's time to really start living my life. I feel Jeremy thread his fingers through mine. He gives my hand a squeeze. I glance over at him and squeeze back. He continues to stare at the road in front of him but I can see a slight smile on his face.

My life since the accident has been almost robotic. I have times when I'm ecstatic like at my job. I love it! Then there are times like late at night when the grief overtakes me and pushes me towards the darkness. Through it all, Jeremy has been the constant push I've needed to keep moving. But maybe, just maybe Jeremy is the key to helping me actually want to live again.

Chapter Thirteen

"Come sit down." Victoria leads me to a chair. Jeremy, Ashley, my parents, and I are at the Anderson house the next day. Tyler had to go back to work but I guess Jeremy filled him in because as he hugged me goodbye, he told me he was there if I ever needed to talk. We are close but it was always more about the happy moments and less of the heavy topics. We just never needed to talk about the heavy moments because there weren't many.

I sit down at the table with Ashley on one side and Victoria on the other. Blake and my parents are standing off to the side. Jeremy stands behind my chair. There's a laptop on the table in front of me. I recognize the laptop. This is Logan's laptop. I brace myself because whatever they're about to tell me is going to hit hard.

Mrs. Anderson says, "I know you have questions about the accident. Emma, he saved your life. He grabbed the wheel right before the car hit you, causing the car to spin and hit his side instead."

"It never made sense to me, but how do you know this?"

"No one could explain it either until we found his laptop in the back. It must have been recording, because it filmed the entire accident." I glance at the laptop. She looks at me, subtly willing me not to watch.

"Let me see." They had to know I'd want to watch it. Out of the corner of my eye, I see my mom and dad move to stand behind Ashley.

Jeremy leans over to wake the computer up. The video is already queued up, paused at what looks to be an angle from the back seat.

Before Jeremy hits play, he whispers to me, "You don't have to watch this."

"I do."

He nods, knowing he can't change my mind. I know it's going to be bad but I have to watch it. I think everyone knows this. It's the reason they have the video ready.

Jeremy hits play and stands up straight, resting his hands on my shoulders.

As the video starts, I see I was correct. It was taken from the backseat angled over the center console, angled more so at the driver's side and the steering wheel. You can also see partly out my window. I briefly remember him working on a film and wedging it in the backseat.

Logan's words fill the silence.

"You know I love you when you get all angry at me. It's so cute. The last thing I will say is that we will figure out the right next step for school but this is an amazing chance. You should see the

list of things they offer. I just wanted to tell you about it. I don't like fighting but as long as I have you by my side, it'll be perfect. I love you Emma."

I hear my reply. "I love you too." I see him kiss my hand and then the car moves forward as I say my next words. "I will look at it and maybe--" There's a flash of light, I'm assuming from the car that hit us, before I see Logan reach out to yank on the steering wheel. I see my own body whip around as the world outside the car window spins. Logan is thrown back into his side and I hear my screams pierce the car. Glass shatters and I see red trickle down my cheek as I lunge toward Logan. He's out of frame but I know what I was doing, trying to get to him. I hear myself whisper, "Logan, don't leave me," before I flop over the center console not moving.

Tears stream down my face. He literally threw himself in front of that car to save me when he grabbed the steering wheel. The man I loved more than anything. I look up to see a tear fall from Victoria's eye. This is so much worse than I thought.

"How do you not hate me? This is proof I killed him."

She squeezes my hand. "Emma, you didn't kill him. This is proof of how much he loved you. All I ever wanted for both of my boys is for them to be happy. This shows right here how happy he was with you, that he sacrificed himself for you. We don't hate you because it was not your fault, and we are so thankful you're alive. Of course, we want more than anything for him to be alive too but having one of you is better than having neither."

Mr. Anderson places his hand on my shoulder. I hadn't noticed him come up behind his wife. "Jeremy, show her the other video."

"The other video?" I ask.

Jeremy leans over to pull up another video on the computer. "I believe this was going to be part of your Christmas present that year, or maybe an anniversary gift."

Logan's face fills the screen. The tears start again and I don't know if they will ever stop at this point.

"Emma, I wanted to show you just how much you mean to me. Here's a montage of our life so far." The video continues with clips of our entire relationship from our very first English project bloopers to us dancing at prom and everything in between. Then comes our college years with us celebrating acceptances, cheering at Football games, me receiving gold medals at the Olympics, our engagement, and finally our wedding.

There are so many moments throughout the video where I didn't even know he was filming, like when I was cooking dinner in the kitchen and he caught me dancing around. Then there was the time when my class took a field trip to the hospital to help with physical training for the kids. One little girl I was helping thought some of the exercises were so funny that she had me cracking up too. Soon all the kids had smiles on their faces despite the pain they were in. He includes scenes of me studying and jumping up and down when I got a good grade.

Logan intertwined his voice throughout the video to add commentary to different scenes describing it from his memory or offering something he thought about me. The video cuts back to Logan.

"These are only some of the many memories we have. I can't wait to make so many more with you and watch you impact those around you. I can't wait to be by your side as you win another gold medal at the next Olympics and see your smile up on that stand infecting everyone in the audience. One of my favorite scenes was the one in the hospital. Watching you with those kids and the joy you brought to their lives in the short time you were there was inspiring. I can't wait to see what you will do with your degree, helping people like those kids and making the world around you a better place. I can't wait to start our family. We have big changes coming and I know you're scared but you're so strong. You can do anything you put your mind to. Never give up on your dreams because they're what keep you propelling forward. As we enter this new chapter, I can't wait to see what's next. I love you so much, Emma!"

The video fades to black. I know what he was talking about when he said changes were coming. That has a fresh set of tears streaming down my face.

Ashley pulls me into a hug as if she knows what I'm thinking about. Even though he was talking about our future in this video, somehow everything he said pertains to right now.

I glance up at the Andersons. "I'm so sorry. He should've had a longer life. I miss him every day."

"So do we, Emma. But like Victoria said, he would want us all to move forward."

Mrs. Anderson nods in agreement. "We're always here if you want to watch old movies of him, reminisce on memories, or just talk. You're like a daughter to us. So please, if there's ever anything we can do, let us know."

"Thank you, both of you. You're like my second set of parents and I will try to do better to not blame myself. As hard as this video was to watch, it helps me understand."

Victoria gives me one last squeeze and then gets up. Jeremy takes her seat.

"Emma, we had an ulterior motive in showing you that video."

I lower my eyes knowing that they will see right through me although I have a feeling Jeremy already does. I raise my eyes to find him staring back at me with a look that says he does in fact know my secret.

"I've asked you this before, but do you want to go to the Olympics?" I nod. "Have you been training?" I nod again. He gives me a stern look.

"Not really."

"You forget I swim with you all the time. You're going through the motions but I can tell your heart isn't in it any-more. We wanted to show you the second video because Logan believed in you and wouldn't want you to give up."

My mom moves behind me where Jeremy was just standing. I assume she wanted to give the Andersons some space to share everything with me since Logan was their son. She crouches down next to Jeremy.

"Sweetie, we'll support whatever you want to do. We just want to see that smile on your face again. These past few years have been hard. You went through a pretty dark period right after the accident, and then you took way more credits than was healthy each semester but we get you were trying to bury yourself in it. Now you have your master's and a great job. You have a great training routine, but as Jeremy said we see you going through the motions. You smile and act happy, but you forget we know you, sweetie."

"I just miss him so much. I love my job and it does make me happy and I love swimming, but I feel like something is still missing. It feels like no matter what I do, I can't fill that space where my heart was."

"I know it feels like that, sweetie but I also know that that hole is slowly filling back up. You just have to let it in." She smiles down at Jeremy knowing I'm watching them. Of course she knows about these feelings that have been creeping in. I just don't know what they mean.

My mom takes my hand and pulls me out of the chair. "I think that once you find your heart again, everything will be so much more joyful. Swimming will be fun again, your job will have a whole new outlook, and we'll get to see that smile that lights up the whole room again, just like Logan mentioned." She pulls me into a hug and whispers in my ear so only I can hear, "And don't be afraid to love again. He's trying so hard to give you space. I've seen the looks from both of you. It's okay to let him in."

I don't have to ask her to know who she's talking about. Jeremy has been so patient with me while still pushing me in other areas of my life. I'd probably still be in the hospital if it weren't for him. But I don't know if I can give him my heart though. He's Logan's brother, after all. I don't think that's what Logan meant when he talked about what's next. I mean I know that wasn't what he was talking about because he was talking about our future together. What would he have to say about my feelings for his brother if he were alive? Wait scratch that, he wouldn't say anything because we would be happily together. I just want to scream. I don't know what to think or even how to feel. It's all too confusing.

My eyes start to water again as my mom pulls away. "Okay," I tell her. She doesn't need to say anything more. She knows I'm just saying words right now, and that I need to get there in my own time just like everything else.

My dad joins us. "We love you so much Emma. Let me know if I need to have a talk with that one." He tosses his head over to Jeremy. I give him a small smile.

"I will Dad." I give him a hug and they head out of the living room towards the front entryway.

I say goodbye to Mr. and Mrs. Anderson, thanking them for not hating me and sharing the video. It wasn't easy watching but it helped. Logan would want me to move forward and not backwards.

Victoria hands me the laptop telling me to keep it. I know it's filled with all of the videos and films he made. Maybe, one day I'll have the courage to go through them all.

Ashley and I walk out to the car. She excuses herself and gets in the driver's seat knowing I'm too much of a mess to drive right now.

Jeremy is behind me and I slowly turn to face him. "Thanks for urging me to talk to your parents. I hate that I've been distant these past several years. You were right; they don't blame me but it's nice to hear. I think it's time to move forward. He would want me to. I will always love him but I'm still alive and I need to remember that."

The talk with everyone and the video helped find the closure I know I needed but have never been able to get. Like I told Jeremy, I will always love his brother, but Logan would not want me to wallow the rest of my life. I can do this. I can move forward and finally start to live.

"I won't say I told you so, but I'm glad to hear it." I playfully punch him in the shoulder after his remark. "I'll pick you up tomorrow and we can head back to Nashville."

I watch as he heads back inside his parents' house. I'm so confused with what to do next. Everyone told me to find my heart and Logan told me to move forward. Is it possible when Logan died that he gave my heart to someone else to hold since he can't be here?

Would he give it to his own brother? I guess only time will tell.

Chapter Fourteen

In the New Year, every moment I'm not working or sleeping, I'm at the pool. I'm no longer as fast as I once was, and I have to rework my training. I've officially become a sprinter and am no longer a long distance swimmer. My leg is fully healed but grows weak after 150 meters of serious swimming. Practice is one thing, but when competition comes around and I give it my all, I just can't make the long distances anymore. It makes me sad because I lived for those long swims.

The trials are in two months and I'm freaking out. My times are down and I need to get out of my head. Vanderbilt has given me the summer off to train for the Olympics and even offered me a full time position afterward.

Jeremy has a break and is headed home. He asks if I want to join and I agree to go. Maybe going home where things are familiar will help me get my head back in the game.

I have Jeremy drop me off at the gazebo, telling him I will get my bags from him later.

I stand at the railing gazing out at the mountains. I have so many memories here with Logan and it's one of my favorite places to think.

I hear footsteps behind me. I know it's Jeremy. That feeling I get when he's near washes over me. I could always sense him before but it's more now. It's almost like a sense of relief when he's nearby. I'm still trying to figure out what it means.

"What are you doing? I just needed you to drop me off."

"Yeah, but I also know you only come here now to think, so what's on your mind?"

I sit on the bench. "I just don't know how to do this without him. My times are down and I'm never going to make the Olympic team. I don't know why I ever thought this was a good idea. I thought coming here would make me feel closer to him since we got married in this very spot. It was perfect."

"It was, and you were the most beautiful bride. I'm pretty sure you had all the guys falling at your feet that day."

"Yeah, yeah." I did feel like a princess that day. Logan always had a way of making me feel like a princess. "Coming from the NFL quarterback. You have plenty of ladies falling for you all the time."

"Never the right ones," he says so quietly that I almost don't hear him.

"Huh?" I wonder who he's talking about. He mentioned liking me back on New Year's but hasn't said anything since. Could he still be talking about me? I shake those thoughts from my head. Olympics first. Love later. Love? I mean boys, men, relationships...ugh...none of it.

He puts his finger to his chin thinking, "I think I remember my brother mentioning a certain crush that someone had on me once," he says jokingly. I stay silent, not ready for that conversation. Okay so maybe he is talking about the past. Either way, I can't focus on any of that right now.

He sits next to me. "Look, I'm sorry. I miss him too." He pauses. "Do you remember what I told you right after the accident? You were scared to get back in the pool then. Now that may not be the case this time, but you need to feel that support again."

I think back to the few times I came back here after the accident. One of those Jeremy took me to the pool and made me get in the water. "I know. It's just hard without him here."

"I want to show you something." He pulls out his phone and scrolls through his videos till he finds one. He hands me the phone and pushes play.

It shows the Olympic pool and I recognize myself getting ready to dive. The horn rings and I dive in, starting my first lap. Logan's voice comes through. "My beautiful wife is off. She's been training her whole life for this moment here. I'm so proud of her. She's coming back this way. Wow look at that flip. You know I once tried to flip like that and I ended up twisting around and bonked my head on the wall."

I laugh, recalling how I tried to teach him a flip turn.

"Whoa, she's already headed this way again. She has several more laps for this 800-meter. She's currently in fourth but I'm not worried. I know she tries not to burn all her energy in the beginning."

The video cuts over from the pool to Logan sitting on the edge of his seat with his phone in one hand filming. This must be Jeremy filming on his phone. "She's in second now about to flip for her last lap. Come on Emma." His smile is so bright and carefree. "She's coming back. She's now in first. Almost here. She did it!" He screams and leaps off his seat. "Go Emma. You got the gold!" He continues to scream along with all the rest of my family and his. The video pans across my parents, brother, Ashley, and his parents. They're all jumping up and down. I faintly hear them announcing that I beat the world record.

I hear my voice and see my face a second later. "Would you put that thing down so I can kiss my husband?"

Jeremy filmed our kiss and whoa, I didn't mean to give him such a heated kiss in public. It still makes me smile. The camera angle flips to Jeremy's face. "Congratulations Emma. We're so proud of you." The video goes black but I hear shuffling, then a voice.

Jeremy tries to get the phone back from me but I stand up so I can hear the rest.

"Man little bro, do you know what you have there? An amazing girl who just won four gold medals, one silver medal and beat a world record. Think she'll switch brothers?" Jeremy says. I remember hearing this as I was walking away. I hear the "oww" from Logan punching Jeremy and then Logan saying, "Get your own wife. Emma is all mine forever!"

I am about to hand the phone back to Jeremy, thinking it's over, when I hear something else that makes me stop. "Jer, if anything ever does happen to me, will you take care of her?"

Jeremy replies, "Always."

The video ends. I wish I could have seen their faces at the end.

Jeremy is silent as I hand his phone back. He gives me a minute to think about what I just saw and heard before he puts a hand on my shoulder and the present comes back into focus. "Do I need to take you to the pool again?"

"No," I sigh. "I just need to find that support again. That video helped me see what Logan saw. I just needed a reminder, and you're always there to give it. Thank you." Maybe while I'm here, I can find my heart that is missing too. I pause thinking again about the end of the video. "Did you mean it?"

"Yes. I never thought I'd get this chance and I hate that I am, but I'm always here for you. I didn't mean for you to hear that last part. I just wanted to show you that video to see what you looked like through Logan's eyes. He was so proud of you. I wanted you to see that support from the other side. From all of us. Emma..." He starts to inch forward and I see that look in his eyes. It is getting harder and harder to resist him but I have to.

I turn my head before he can kiss me. "Sorry, I just can't think about that with everything going on and training for the Olympics. Maybe after I win that gold medal we can talk."

He wraps his arm around my shoulders. "It's my fault. I didn't mean to push you. I'm not going anywhere. After all, what would you do without me?"

I look over at him to see him wink. I groan as I drag him off the bench back to the car. He just can't help himself sometimes and I wouldn't change a single thing.

Chapter Fifteen

The Olympics are here. I made the team a month ago. I wasn't sure I'd make the top two in the trials but I managed to in the 50-meter and 100-meter. I still don't know how I did it. Logan had to have been looking down on me.

The few weeks before the Olympics are filled with training and meetings. I have an interview scheduled for this afternoon and I'm preparing myself. I still hate speaking in front of crowds and this is no different. We will be on a stage with a live audience.

The studio has a stage with two comfy looking chairs and a table in between. The seating area has enough seats for a few hundred people. I gulp.

"There's the Olympic star. Are you ready for your interview?" Jeremy comes up behind me giving my shoulders a massage. I lean in to his touch more so for the massage. At least, that's what I tell myself.

"I hate this part. Can't I just swim?" I look at myself in the mirror all dolled up. I have on a summery blue halter dress and more makeup than I've ever worn in my life. Apparently it's for all the lights and cameras. That did not help my nerves.

Thankfully they have a makeup person on set and Ashley was on FaceTime with me.

I don't remember it being like this last time. I think I was just in shock the whole time that I was actually going to the Olympics. Now that I've been, there seems to be a ton more pressure this time around. More makeup, more dressing up, and way more interviews.

"You will, but this is part of it. I never like this part either but I have to do it in the NFL." He takes my hand to help me out of my seat. "You look beautiful and you're going to kill it. I'll be right here on the side waiting for you." He kisses my hand. "If at any point you need a confidence boost, just look over at me."

Before I can comprehend what he just said, he pushes me towards where the interview is set up.

I shake hands with the lady giving the interview and we take our seats. I look out to the audience only to be blinded by light. I can see the first row and that's about it. The heat from the lights is intense.

How do people do this every day?

"So when did you first dream of being an Olympic swimmer?" She asks.

"I think since the first time I got in the pool when I was three I wanted to be a swimmer, although maybe not the Olympics that early. It was my mom's dream when she was my age but then she had me. She never pushed me, but she showed me how fun swimming could be. When I got to high school, I had a great coach that told me I had potential to go all the way. I pushed myself and worked hard throughout the years and made it for the first time four years ago."

"What would you tell those looking to make the next Olympics?"

"I would tell them to never give up and make sure you have support. I never would have gotten anywhere without my family and friends. They supported me in the pool with training and out of the pool with my food plans and sleep schedules. It definitely takes over your life, but you need to not give up and push through because the end result is very rewarding. Standing up on the platform with a gold medal in my hand is something I'll never forget."

She asks a few other questions before it gets personal. Jeremy told me to expect this.

She starts with the question I'm most dreading. "So your accident, can you tell us a little about that?"

I glance over at Jeremy and he nods. "Yes, a little over three and half years ago a drunk driver hit my husband and me. I twisted my knee and broke my leg in three places including my tibia." I pause collecting myself. "My husband didn't make it." I pause again, swallowing back the tears that are threatening to come. "The doctors told me I may never walk again and if I did, I would probably need some sort of crutch."

"That must have been hard to hear, but it seems that's not the case. You're on the Olympic team again this year so what did you do?"

"I had support from my friends and family who helped with my rehab. I was going to school to get my master's in Sports Physical Therapy which turned out to help a lot. I learned how to get my leg to basically work again. It took me nearly a year after the accident before I even went near a pool again, but only after a ton of urging from a good friend." I smile trying not to look over at Jeremy knowing that my interviewer is watching me closely.

"Can you tell us a little bit about switching from the longer distance races–200-meter, 400-meter and 800-meter, to the shorter ones–50-meter and 100-meter?"

"Yes, I've always preferred the long distance races but after the accident my leg wasn't holding up for those distances anymore. In practice, I pushed myself but anytime I did long distance speed runs, I wouldn't come close to my previous times. My coach had me try sprinting instead and focus on 50-meter and 100-meter distances. It definitely took some getting used to the shorter distances, but I'm happy it got me on the team."

"We have time for one more question. We understand your husband died in the accident and you have been busy training but I know your fans are dying to know, are you currently dating anyone?"

Jeremy mentioned this might be one of the personal questions so I have an answer prepared. "Like you said I've been very busy with training and haven't had time for a relationship." I avoid looking at Jeremy but I can feel him smirking at me. Oh how I'd love to wipe that smirk right off his face so I add, "Maybe once these Olympic Games are over, I'll consider it."

"Well thank you so much for your time and we look forward to watching you next week. Good luck and we'll be rooting for the gold." She smiles and waves to the audience as they applaud.

"Thank you." I wave to the audience and go off stage where I finally exhale. I felt like I had been holding my breath the whole time I was on the stage.

Jeremy gives me a hug. "You did great."

"I'm just glad it is over. They definitely like to pry and get personal."

"You handled the questions perfectly. I especially like your answer to her "Are you dating anyone?" question."

I blush and punch him in the arm. Apparently the part I added on affected me more than him.

"Yeah, yeah. I could feel you smirking at me from all the way over here. Anyway, thanks for coming to the interview. I can always count on you."

"I told you I would be. Now let's get some dinner before we have to catch our flight." He puts his arm around my shoulders and steers me out of the studio.

Chapter Sixteen

I'm on a plane headed overseas for the Olympics, once again. Ashley, Jeremy and my family are meeting me there, flying with Jeremy's parents on their jet in a few days.

We spend a few days before the actual Olympics doing light training. When the day finally comes, I'm so nervous. Last time, I had Logan with me every step of the way. I think back to four years ago when I was here.

"Emma, no matter what happens I'm so proud of you! Not many people can say they made it to the Olympics."

"Thanks Logan! Thanks for always encouraging me at every meet."

"I always want you to follow your dreams. Now go win that gold medal." He gives me a quick kiss before heading to his seat with our families. I wave over at all of them.

I head to my coach and he gives us a speech. I'm part of the 200-meter, 400-meter, 800-meter freestyle, 200-meter individual medley, and 200-meter relay Race.

Michael Phelps walks over to our team. "Good luck ladies." He passes by me and I can't help but swoon. I mean come on, it's Michael Phelps. "Emma, I'm glad to be swimming with you this year. I knew there was something special about you when we talked at the museum a few years ago. Remember to swim fast." He pats me on the shoulder.

Was Michael Phelps just kind of flirting with me? I never thought that would happen. Cue more swooning. I love Logan with all my heart but it's not every day you meet your celebrity crush.

I warm up and get ready for my first finals race - the 400-meter freestyle. I adjust my swim cap and put my goggles on my head. I take my place on the starting block and pull down my goggles. The buzzer goes off and I dive in. I feel myself glide through the water and I know this is where I belong.

There's nothing like feeling the water surrounding me and my muscles straining as I stroke my arms.

In the last lap, I overtake the leader to hit the wall first and win the gold.

The next day, I have heats and semifinals in which I qualify for the finals in both 200-meter freestyle and the 200-meter individual medley.

In the finals, I receive the gold in the 200-meter and the silver in the 200-meter individual medley. The backstroke gets me every time in the individual medley.

Later in the week, we qualify for the 200-meter freestyle relay in which we end up getting the gold in the finals.

My last race is the 800-meter freestyle, my favorite. This is where I shine because while everyone is speeding ahead I'm taking my time to not get winded. In the last few laps, I pull ahead.

As I do my last flip turn, I know I'm a ways ahead of everyone else. I swim as fast as I can and hit the wall. I look up at the times and I've beaten the World Record. I jump out of the water and the rest of my team cheers.

I hear the announcer, "Emma Collins Anderson on the United States team has not only won the gold but has beaten the world record for the 800-meter freestyle." I can't help but smile.

After getting congratulations from my team and coach, I head towards my family. They all give me hugs.

"My sister is the world record holder," my brother says as he pats me on the back.

I stand in front of my Logan who, of course, has his phone filming the whole thing. I don't know if that's actually allowed but I try stopping him. "Would you put that thing down so I can kiss my husband?"

He laughs and hands the phone to Jeremy. "Yes, come here my gold medal winning and record breaking wife." He gives me a kiss that I'm sure will have all the news stations talking.

When we pull away, I blush in embarrassment about our public display. "Okay, well I should get back. Dinner tonight?" They all agree.

As I walk away, I hear behind me. "Man little bro, do you know what you have there? An amazing girl who just won four gold medals, one silver medal and beat a world record. Think she will switch brothers?"

I hear "oww" so I'm assuming Logan just punched Jeremy in the arm.

"Get your own wife. Emma is all mine forever!" I continue to walk without looking back but can't help laughing at brothers being brothers.

Logan always was my support and we thought we had forever. That forever only lasted a few years. My family is a great support system but it isn't the same. Thankfully, they're able to be down at pool level with me again. My mom and dad walk over to me as I'm stretching for my 50-meter race. "We're so proud of you and want you to know that no matter what happens, the fact that you got here after your injury is outstanding."

"Thanks Mom." She kisses me on the head.

My dad gives me a side hug. "Now go win another gold."

I laugh. I definitely get my competitive spirit from him. "I'll try."

They sit with the other families where Jeremy's parents and Ashley already are. They give me a thumbs up as I wave. They really have been great since Logan's death and I am glad we cleared the air even though there was never anything wrong in the first place.

Speaking of Jeremy, he walks over giving my shoulders a squeeze. "Are you ready to win another gold?" I shrug. Everyone keeps asking me that and I'd love to but like my mom said, I'm just happy to be here.

He pulls out a small box and very slowly hands it to me to open. I take it with shaking hands. I'm not sure what he could possibly be giving me right now.

Seeing the question in my eyes, he helps me open it. I gasp at what's inside.

It's a heart locket and as I open it a tear slides down my cheek. There are two pictures, one of me standing on the podium with the gold medal from the last Olympics, and the other from my wedding day. On the back is an inscription that reads, "Forever, my favorite Olympian."

"Logan was planning on giving it to you when you won your next gold medal. He showed it to me right after he bought it. He had faith you would make it here again, and he'd be so proud to see what you have overcome to be here today. Now go swim and know he's supporting you from heaven." I hug him because this means everything.

"Thank you for everything." I hand him the box with the locket. "Hold that for me, will you? I need to know my support is in the right hands." He nods, knowing what I just said but not saying anything further. He squeezes my arm one more time before making his way back to our families.

I do a few more stretches before my coach comes over. "How's the leg?"

"It's feeling good." I've been swimming a lot the past few days with the heats and preliminaries for the 100-meter, and both relays. After swimming the 100-meter prelim, my leg has been very stiff. Pending how my leg feels today, my coach is ready to have a sub step in. "I want to do this."

"Okay I want it checked out first but if all is well then you are good to swim." I head over to the Physical Therapists. I've gotten to know the team really well and would love to work with them some day. They check out my leg and tell me I'm good to go. I do some more stretches to relieve the stiffness and get ready to take my place.

This is the race I'm most nervous for with it being the 50-meter. I'm ready though.

I glance at Ashley, Jeremy, his parents and my family. Ever since Jeremy helped me get back in the water and reminded me of Logan being my support, I imagined him holding me as I swam. Just the thought of Logan supporting me from above puts a smile on my face and the confidence to give it all I have.

I head to the starting block and I take my position, adjusting my goggles. The second the horn sounds, I dive in. This is the quickest race with it being one lap. I swim as fast as I can once again feeling myself being held through the water.

My leg feels great. I was born to be in the water.

One thought crosses my mind; one person, and I keep swimming with that thought. I touch the wall and look up at my time.

My jaw drops when I see I not only received the gold but have beaten the world record once again. Last Olympics was the 800-meter and this year is the 50-meter.

I get out of the pool and realize it wasn't Logan I was thinking about holding me as I swam just now, but Jeremy. Somehow amongst everything he creeped into my mind. Things are changing between us and have been since he kissed me on the dock. If I'm honest with myself, probably even before that. Before I can change my mind, I know what I have to do.

I walk right past my coach and my teammates who are wishing me congratulations. I head straight towards my family who are all jumping in excitement. I stop right in front of Jeremy. I reach up, grab his face, pull him down to me, and kiss him. It's a kiss full of so much emotion and thanks all wrapped up together. When I pull away, I look up into his eyes and he looks right back.

"Not that I'm complaining, but what was that for?"

"Thank you for believing in me and for pushing me when I was ready to give up. Without you I never would have gotten back in the pool or done anything else for that matter. You told me I needed someone to carry me through the water like Logan did. You were the one carrying me this time and supporting me as I swam. I wanted to say thanks."

As I turn, I see out of the corner of my eyes, Jeremy's dumbfounded look that slowly morphs into his typical cocky smirk.

I walk back over to my coach and teammates who look at me confused and then start congratulating me once again. I accept my gold medal and we spend the rest of the day celebrating all our accomplishments.

By the end of this year's Olympics, I receive three gold medals in 50-meter freestyle, 100-meter freestyle, 200-meter relay and one silver in the 400-meter relay. I was more than happy because after everything I'd overcome, I've done the impossible.

At the closing ceremony, we make our way out as a team celebrating with the rest of the US teams. That night we're headed home and I fly back with my family, Ashley, Jeremy, and his parents.

When I get home to my parents' house, I go into my room and hang up my new medals next to the ones from the Olympics four years before. I have a total of seven gold medals and two silver medals. I admire all of them and think about how much I wish Logan was there with me, because he was always my support.

When he died, that support transferred over to his brother without me realizing it.

As I look at the medals, the photo below catches my eye. It's from the first Anderson New Year's Ball I had attended with Logan, right after we started dating.

My parents have taken a ton of pictures of all of us and I've always just looked at Logan and I, but this is the first time I really look at the picture. Logan and I are laughing looking right at the camera. What catches my eye in the picture is that Jeremy is looking over at me with so much love, I hadn't noticed until now.

I know my once brotherly feelings towards Jeremy have been changing and I kept on pushing them away. I love Logan with all my heart but he'd want me to move on to the next chapter in my life. I'm not sure if that includes his brother but only time and some serious heart searching will tell.

I need to move forward, not just with my relationships but my career too. I accomplished my dream of winning a gold medal, or multiple, and I know my time at the Olympics has come to an end. These past few years were tough and while I could continue training for the next four years, I'm happy with what I've accomplished. I don't need more. I'm ready to move on, and I have some important decisions to make.

Chapter Seventeen

Now that the Olympic part of my life is over, I need to decide what's next. I have some time to research but a part of me wants to just be there, at a job. I have several job openings pulled up along with some offers. I'm going back and forth making a pro/con list when the smoke detector goes off. I run out to the kitchen to find smoke everywhere. I open the window in the kitchen.

Jeremy is pulling out a very burned something.

Is that meatloaf?

The top is completely black. I notice equally burned potatoes cooling on the counter. How do you burn potatoes? They take forever to cook.

It's then I notice the carrots and honey next to the stove and a skillet sitting on the stove ready to go.

No, no, no. Why is he making this?

I feel myself spiraling. Jeremy turns my way with the meatloaf in his hands. He immediately drops it on the counter and rushes to me.

I can't breathe.

I thought these were over. Why am I having another panic attack? It's been over a year.

"Breathe, Emma. Just breathe." I hear his voice but it sounds like I'm underwater. I feel pressure on my lips for a brief second.

Is Jeremy kissing me?

I instantly perk up and go to slap him. He catches my hand before I can.

"There she is!"

"Did you just kiss me?"

"Yes. It was the easiest way I could think of bringing you back to the present. I saw you about to spiral." He drops my hand and steps back.

"And kissing me is okay?"

"We've kissed before."

"Yeah like twice, and they were after emotional moments."

"Those are the best kisses."

"Jer."

"Em."

"No more kisses. Even if I'm spiraling. Although it did seem to help," I say the last part under my breath.

"It did help." He agrees. And clearly it wasn't as quiet as I thought. "What triggered this attack?"

"I saw what you were making."

"Very burned meatloaf and potatoes?" He questions, clearly confused. He pokes the meatloaf but it doesn't move. It looks as hard as a rock.

"And the carrots," I add, pointing to the bowl of carrots next to the stove.

"I'm not following."

"It's the combination of the foods."

"Still not following. You've been in your head since the Olympics. I know you have a bunch of decisions about what to do next and I wanted to make something that might help."

"But, why meatloaf?"

"It was Logan's favorite. He always talked about how good yours was and I thought a good memory might get you out of your head."

My eyes well up with tears.

"Hey, I wasn't trying to make you cry." He moves towards me.

"Stop. Don't come any closer."

"Em, I was trying--"

"I just can't deal with this right now. How dare you use my dead husband to get me to make a decision?" I shove past him, running to my room and slamming the door. I fall onto my bed and let the tears come.

I don't want to cry about Logan anymore but anytime his name is brought up or some memory with him, I can't help myself.

I cry for what feels like hours when I hear a knock on my door. "Come in." I know it's Jeremy. There is no use in telling him to go away. He won't. It's not his style.

The bed dips as he sits on the edge. "I'm sorry," he says.

I sit up. Why is he apologizing? I should be the one apologizing.

"Why are you apologizing?"

"Because I clearly did something wrong for you to run in here and be crying for the last hour." That answers that question. An hour, not a few hours. That is beside the point. I need to tell him the truth.

"Jer, you don't need to apologize. I do. I shouldn't have raced out of there after you were trying to do something nice for me."

He looks at me defeated. "Apparently it wasn't that nice if I sent you to your room crying."

I reach for his hand. Thankfully, he accepts it and intertwines our fingers. "It wasn't the gesture but the combination of food."

"I'm still confused about that. I thought you loved those foods. I know..." he pauses like saying his name will set me off again. "Someone else did too."

"It's okay, you can say his name. I need to stop freaking out anytime anyone says his name. You're right. It was Logan's favorite." I gulp, trying to gain the confidence for this next part. "It was one of my favorite things to make for him. It was also the last meal I made for him, the night before the accident." If I thought I couldn't cry anymore, I was wrong. Several tears fall down my cheek.

"Come here." Jeremy pulls me into his side and hugs me. I don't know how long we sit there, me wrapped in his arms with my head tucked into his shoulder.

Eventually, he pulls away. I feel cold, like he took away that comfort and heat. He tips my chin toward him. "You okay?" He questions, looking into my eyes.

"I will be."

"Good." He kisses my forehead. "I have an idea. There's this new Thai restaurant that opened up near the lake. Let's go eat. On the roof, they have a dance club where they play different music each night."

"What's tonight?"

"No idea. But let's go find out. If it's horrible then we can leave."

I nod.

"Get dressed and we can meet in the living room in thirty minutes." He leaves the room.

Slowly, I get out of bed and walk into the bathroom, turning on the shower. I want to rinse off the sadness. Sounds weird but a hot shower sounds perfect to rinse it off and down the drain.

After my shower, I add light makeup and brush my hair. In my closet, I find a purple, blue, and black flowery skirt with a purple blouse to match. I grab sandals to finish off the outfit. I also grab a small over the shoulder purse that fits my phone and wallet.

On my way out, I grab a jacket. It has been warm but as fall time approaches, the nights are cooler.

I meet Jeremy in the living room. He is dressed in black jeans and a blue polo. I can't help looking at the way the polo fits his perfectly defined muscles.

I shake my head as Jeremy smirks at me.

"Let's go," I say punching his shoulder as I walk by. He laughs following me out the door.

The food is delicious and the atmosphere is fun. The restaurant has a romantic, down to earth aura about it. The walls are all covered in wooden panels while the lighting is dim with red chandeliers hanging from the ceilings.

This would be a great place for a date. Not that this is a date. We're just friends even if Jeremy keeps kissing me. Then again I've kissed him too.

No! We're just friends.

We finish our food and head to the rooftop dance floor. The dance floor is a mirage of black and white swirls with a giant pergola covering it. There are gold Chinese lanterns hanging from the pergola and a bar tucked into the corner. We grab drinks and sit down at the tables lining the edge. You can see Nashville from here as well as the lake. The sun has already set, but I can only imagine the view. I sit back and relax.

Jeremy and I cracked up when we read the sign coming in saying tonight's music is 90s.

When Bye, Bye, Bye by NSYNC comes on, Jeremy pulls me to my feet and towards the dance floor.

Jeremy makes me laugh when he sings the lyrics and has some moves that could rival any boy band from the 90s. We dance to more old school songs from Britney Spears, Backstreet Boys, Christina Aguilera, and more NSYNC.

All my thoughts of sadness are gone from before.

When I'll Never Break Your Heart from Backstreet Boys comes on, Jeremy pulls me close for a slow dance.

As I rest my head on his chest, I listen to the lyrics. I already know them but this is the first time I've really listened to them. Maybe it's because the words have meaning now.

Logan never purposely hurt me, but when he died that did hurt me. Of course, that isn't his fault but the pain I felt after was crippling. So crippling I thought about ending it. This guy in front of me brought me back. The opening lines to the song pull at my heartstrings.

Baby, I know you are hurting

Right now you feel like you could never love again

Now all I ask is for a chance

To prove that I love you

While the lyrics of the songs are talking about a heartbreak and being quick to judge, I can't help thinking about how much this song pertains to my relationship with Jeremy. I've never judged him. Well maybe after the coffee shop incident when he ignored me. I did think he was just a typical football player. But once I got to know him, I never judged him. He was just Jeremy, my boyfriend's older brother and my best friend. Now he's seeping in, trying to break through my heart to be more.

He's been begging me for a chance. He may not have said the words but I know how he feels. I can feel it anytime he's near me. I can hear it in his words. I know it when he pushes me to conquer my fears.

How do I let him in? The ice around my heart is slowly thawing but I'm scared.

As the song ends, Jeremy whispers the last few lines in my ear.

I'll never break your heart

I'll never make you cry

I'd rather die than live without you

My heart thaws a tiny bit more. I don't dare look up at him. I know we'll kiss and then it'll be happily ever after. I'm not ready for that.

A faster song comes on and I'm thankful to be out of that heavy moment. Was Jeremy thinking the same thing as me?

I shake my head. It doesn't matter.

Jeremy spins me. I laugh and we dance together more. Everything with him flows so easily. He can pull me out of my head without saying a word. Take earlier for example when he kissed me and pulled me out of a panic attack, or just now when he simply spun me.

Several songs later, it's hot despite the temperature outside. We get some water and I grab my jacket I left on the chair as we head out.

We take a walk down on the boardwalk running along the lake. The moon reflects off the water lighting up the night sky.

We take a seat on one of the benches and stare up at the night sky. Being in the city, we can't see a ton of stars but there are still a ton that twinkle above.

Jeremy breaks the silence. "I probably shouldn't say this because I don't want to cause another panic attack, but you know Logan is up there watching over you."

"It's okay. He once told me that the stars are people we have lost looking down on us. If we're ever feeling sad, we can look at the stars above and know that every time a star twinkles, it's them smiling down."

"It's true." He squints at the sky like he's looking for something. He points above us. "See the big dipper?"

"Yes?" I question him.

"Now see the star just below and to the left?"

"Yes."

"That star is Logan."

"What're you talking about?"

Jeremy pulls out a piece of paper.

At the top it reads the star registry with coordinates, a name, and message.

αγάπη μου

"*When we love someone, we look to the stars. With each twinkle is a smile from above.*"

I'm confused. This looks like someone named a star. "What is this?"

"I found that in Logan's backpack that they pulled from the car. I'm assuming it was going to be a Christmas present. He named a star for you."

"Is that Greek?"

"Yeah, I translated it to see what it means. It's a Greek translation for 'My Love'."

"And it's that star right there?"

"Yep. It took me forever to figure that out. I didn't want to show you this until you were ready. With what happened today, I thought it was the right time. Emma, him and your baby are looking down on you with so much love. They want you to be happy, living your life, loving, and cherishing every moment. It's up to you to decide what that looks like."

I stay silent because I don't know what else to say.

As we drive home, I look over at Jeremy as he drives. He and Logan look so much alike. Many times people would mistake them for twins. Looks isn't what has me falling for Jeremy though. It's his heart. The way he cares about the people he loves. I know I'm one of those people, but the difference now is I think that love has shifted into more than just a friendly love. I know my thoughts are changing every day. The more he pushes me in other aspects of my life, the more I'm falling for him. Am I ready to admit it? Not even close, but I recognize it's there and it scares me.

What scares me even more is that the day when I do admit it draws closer and closer. I can feel it and I really hope when that day comes, I embrace it with everything I have.

"Thank you, Jer."

He briefly glances at me. "You're welcome Emma. I'd do anything for you. No matter how long it takes."

It's like he just read my mind. I turn my head to the window before he can see everything written across my face. I stare at the "Logan" star. As it twinkles, I imagine Logan's face and the face of our unborn baby. I imagine their faces lighting up and smiling down on me.

I whisper into the night, "Thank you Logan."

Jeremy laces his fingers with mine and gives my hand a squeeze. I continue to stare at the stars but I can't help squeezing his hand back. It's a step, albeit a small step, but a step towards my future.

Chapter Eighteen

I can't wait for tonight. My brother and Ashley are coming into town. Tyler is staying at a friend's house close by and Ashley is staying here at Jeremy's apartment. I mean my apartment. Our apartment? It doesn't matter how long I've lived here or that it feels like home, it's still weird to say "our apartment".

We're having a movie fondue night, all four of us. I hope it becomes the first of many.

I put the finishing touches on the trays for each fondue. We're doing all three courses–cheese, broth, and chocolate. I set the plastic wrapped dessert tray in the fridge for later. The stuff for the chocolate fondue is set up ready to be put into the pot.

Jeremy actually had a fondue pot specifically for chocolate. When I asked him about it, he said he thought it would be romantic for the ladies. I didn't ask how many times he's used it because I really don't want to know.

We're starting out with the first two courses. I thought since so many of the items you dip in go well with the cheese and broth, why not have them both at the same time.

I grab the other two trays, one filled with chicken and steak and the other with apples, two types of bread, cauliflower, carrots, broccoli, and potatoes. I set them on the coffee table in the living room and check on the fondues that are heating up.

This coffee table is one of the most amazing things Jeremy had in his condo when I moved in. It has sockets built in to charge your phone or in this case plug in a crockpot and fondue pot.

I open the lid of the crockpot filled with the cheese fondue. I stir it a few times. My nose is filled with a delicious aroma of sharp cheddar and bacon. I could stand here all night breathing in this scent.

"If you don't stop breathing it in, I'm afraid you're going to sniff all the yumminess out."

I drop the lid. Thankfully it lands right side up on the pot. I set the spoon down and look up to see Jeremy leaning against the doorway leading to the bedrooms. I was so focused on the fondue that I didn't hear him come in.

He's dressed in a black shirt and gray sweatpants with the Titans team logo on the side. I force myself to look away before he says something cocky about me staring at him but, as I turn away, I see him smirking.

Now what was it he said about the fondue? Something about me sniffing the yumminess out. Wait, what?

I move towards the broth to check on the temperature. This one's in an actual fondue pot so it's easier to adjust the heat and you want it hot at all times to cook the meat.

"Jeremy, that doesn't even make sense."

I go back into the kitchen to grab the plates, napkins, forks and those special stabby fondue forks. We each get a color. Blue for me. Green for Jeremy. Red for Ashley because the pack didn't come with pink. Yellow for Tyler.

With everything in my hands, I head back over to the coffee table as I hear a knock on the door. I set it on the table.

"I'll get it." He passes me but not before kissing me on the cheek and whispering in my ear. "I love when you get flustered."

Before I can show my protest he has already moved toward the door. Ashley barges in as soon as Jeremy opens the door.

"Emma, your room. Now." She doesn't stop, heading right past me to my room.

I glance at Jeremy and he shrugs, then turns back to the door as Tyler walks in.

"I'll be right back." I follow Ashley into my room. She's face down on my bed with her duffel bag thrown to the floor.

I lay on my side with my face propped in my hand. "Are you going to tell me what's wrong?"

Ashley says something but I can't understand a word she says with her face smooshed into my comforter.

"You're going to have to lift your head because I have no idea what you just said."

She lifts her head and says, "Your brother pulled up at the same time as me and before I could even get out of the car, he was opening my door. He went on to ask how I was doing and all that other dumb small talk and then he asked me if I wanted to go out to dinner with him before I left." She then drops her head back onto the bed. All this is said so quickly that if I wasn't well versed in Ashley lingo I wouldn't have caught it all.

"And... what did you say?" I hear her groan. "Ashley?"

She slowly rolls over to her back and stares at the ceiling. "I didn't say anything. I just grabbed my bag and ran to your door."

I start laughing and can't stop. Ashley glares at me but eventually joins in.

Jeremy pokes his head in. "What's going on in here?"

"Nothing. Ashley is just telling me funny stories."

"Okay, sure." He shakes his head. He knows I'll fill him in later. When it comes to the drama of Ashley and my brother, Ashley doesn't care what I tell Jeremy. She even insists because maybe he'll have advice since they're both single guys.

"Well the fondue is going to be gone if you both don't get out here soon. It smells way too good to not dig into," says Jeremy.

"We're coming." Ashley rolls off the bed and into the bathroom. Knowing her, it's to make sure she looks good before going out to where my brother is.

I link arms with Jeremy as he leads me to the living room. "Tyler?" He whispers. I nod. He doesn't need much more than that to know something happened.

In the living room, Tyler has already helped himself to fondue. "I see you just help yourself to the food without saying hi to your sister first." I prop my hands on my hips.

Tyler turns with his mouth full of bread and cheese. "Hi sis."

"You're lucky I love you." I walk over to him and give him a side hug before plopping down on the opposite couch. The living room has two couches, both angled slightly toward the TV on the wall with the square coffee table in the middle of the room. The couches are angled perfectly so everyone has some table in front of them.

Jeremy walks over to the far end of the couch to sit next to Tyler but I signal for him to come to me. I pull him down to the couch next me. He gives me a look saying "do you know what you are doing?" I shrug.

Ashley comes waltzing in like nothing has happened. She stops when she sees where the only seat left is. She glares at me as she sits next to Tyler as close to the end as she can.

"Hi Ashley," Tyler says grinning at her.

"Hi," she mumbles out as her cheeks turn pink. I always love when Ashley blushes because it's a very rare occurrence.

"I won't bite, unless you ask nicely."

She turns her glare to him. "I'm good but thanks."

"Suit yourself." He grabs another cheese dipped bread from his plate and shoves it in his mouth.

Ashley crosses her arms and sits back. I know I won't hear the end of these seating arrangements later but for now it is the best entertainment. Plus it's something she would do to me.

"What're we watching?" Tyler asks in between bites.

"I've been making Emma watch all of the Fast and Furious movies and we are currently on the fourth. I thought we could start there," Jeremy answers.

"That's the worst one." Tyler laughs.

"It is, but then the fifth is one of the best so we'll end on a good note."

"Sounds good to me, doesn't it Ashley?" He glances over at her.

She plucks an apple off his plate. "Sure does. What girl wouldn't want guys in tight shirts with big muscles driving in fast cars for the next few hours." She winks at him and takes a bite of the apple she stole.

There's the Ashley I know and love. She picks up her fondue forks and starts adding meat to the broth to cook. I follow her lead as Jeremy hits play.

As the movie goes on I can't help but notice Ashley has moved slightly closer to Tyler. I know it isn't by accident because nothing she does is by accident. She's almost in the middle of the couch at this point.

The movie ends and Jeremy calls for a short intermission. I start clearing the coffee table of all the fondue stuff so I can bring out the chocolate.

I set the crockpot bowl in the sink to soak. Tyler joins me in the kitchen with the trays, forks, and plates. "You wash, I'll dry?" I nod. "Let me grab the fondue pot."

I start rinsing off the plates and adding them to the dishwasher when he returns. We would do this all the time growing up. It's where we had our serious talks.

The silence surrounds us and I can feel his question burning through me. "Just ask the question, Ty."

"So you and Jeremy?"

I sigh knowing this was coming. "We're friends." Before he can say anything else, I add, "I needed somewhere to live so he offered his extra bedroom here."

"I think he's good for you, Em. It's nice to see you smiling again. I know he's the reason for it. Just be open to it, okay?"

"I will but Ty, we're just friends."

"Who's just friends?" Jeremy questions as his arms circle around my waist. Since I kissed him at the Olympics, he's been a lot more touchy feely with me.

I glance up at him. "Who do you think?"

He rolls his eyes as he says, "Oh right, us. My bad." He kisses my cheek. "You keep thinking that. Now hurry up, I want some chocolate fondue."

I hand him the chocolate fondue pot with the ingredients to take out to the living room and start heating the chocolate. Tyler and I finish the dishes and I can feel him smirking the whole time. Jeremy and I have been doing this push and pull for a while. My feelings are changing but I'm scared. I'll also never admit that to him so here we are.

Tyler hangs the towel back up. "Em, put the guy out of his misery and give him a chance. If you could see the way he looks at you."

"I could say the same about you, you know."

He sighs. "I'm trying."

"Just be good to her, okay. Don't make me come after you."

Tyler nods. "Now let's go eat some chocolate. Maybe that'll give you the confidence to make a move. Shouldn't be too hard in private after kissing him on national television." He runs before I can smack him.

"Tyler, get back here." I run after him as he leaps over the couch falling on Ashley. I smirk at him as I turn back to the fridge to get the tray of goodies for the chocolate. I hear Tyler whisper to Ashley, "Hey pretty lady."

I can practically feel Ashley's blush from here. I swear everything Tyler does and says makes her blush.

I set the tray on the coffee table next to the chocolate fondue plate along with plates, napkins, and forks, then take a seat.

"I didn't know you had a fancy chocolate fondue pot, Emma?" Ashley asks.

"It's Jeremy's," I tease.

"Why would Jeremy need a chocolate fondue pot? Although now that I think about it, I know of some fun you could have with chocolate." Tyler winks at Ashley as Jeremy laughs.

"Ewww," both Ashley and I scream.

"I don't even want to know how many girls you have invited over to have "fondue", I say.

"Actually, none." Jeremy gets very serious. "I bought it with someone special in mind." I feel his stare. I slowly bring my eyes to meet his. The electricity between us is undeniable and it's pulling me towards him. Just before his lips meet mine, I turn my head and clear my throat.

"We should probably start the movie." I can't face Jeremy. I can't face what I feel.

I grab a plate and start loading it up with bananas, strawberries, shortbread, and pretzels.

Jeremy hits play and the movie begins before anyone can say another word.

About halfway through the movie, the chocolate fondue is gone. I set my plate on the table. A minute later, Jeremy slips his fingers through mine. I suck in a breath.

I sneak a peek at Jeremy and can see him smirking. He knows exactly what he does to me. I look past him to Ashley and Tyler. I am surprised to see her head on his shoulder. If Ashley can get the courage to move forward with my brother, then maybe I can gain the courage to do the same with Jeremy.

I scoot a little closer, take a deep breath, and rest my head on Jeremy's shoulder.

Small steps.

I must fall asleep because when I open my eyes, the menu screen is up. I lift my head off Jeremy's shoulder to see him on his phone. Tyler and Ashley are gone.

"Where did Ash and my brother go?"

He looks up from his phone. "Tyler had to go and Ash walked him out, like ten minutes ago."

I go to get up before realizing I'm still holding Jeremy's hand. I quickly let go and book it to the front door. "I'm going to go check on them."

I take the elevator down to the parking lot. After what feels like hours later the doors open. I hear whispering as soon as I walk out. I don't mean to eavesdrop but I want to make sure everything's okay. There are benches around the corner so I assume they're seated there.

"Fine. One date," Ashley says.

"You won't regret it, cupcake." Cupcake? I haven't heard him call her that before. I'll have to ask Ashley about it.

I peer around the pillar to see Tyler lifting her chin and giving her a sweet kiss. "I'm all in. I won't hurt you," he says before pulling her into his chest, giving her a hug.

I turn back to the elevator not wanting to intrude anymore. I take it back up to the thirty-seventh floor.

Inside the condo, Jeremy is clearing the table and washing the last few dishes.

"Find them?"

"Yes, my brother was persuading Ashley to go on a date with him."

"Did it work?"

"I think so."

Ashley walks in with a dreamy look on her face. "I'll be in your room Emma."

I nod.

Jeremy flicks the towel over his shoulder and walks over to me. "Maybe one day, I'll persuade someone else to go on a date with me."

I look up at him. "Maybe," I say with a small smile.

He kisses my forehead. "Now go talk to your best friend." He starts walking back to the sink before whipping the towel in my direction.

"Hey!" I yelp and head to my room. Ashley isn't the only one that's nervous about her feelings. Jeremy has me so upside down.

I find Ashley asleep in my bed already so I quickly change and brush my teeth before slipping in next to her. Girl talk can wait till tomorrow.

I'm sure I'll be busy dreaming of a certain brown hair, blue eyed football player.

Chapter Nineteen

I walk into the restaurant looking around for my brother. He's heading home tomorrow but has a date with Ashley tonight. I want to talk to him before it happens and let him know he better not hurt my best friend.

I find him smiling at a waitress at a table towards the back. *How dare he.*

I stomp over to the table and sit across from him, glaring.

The waitress must see the look on my face because she quickly excuses herself.

"Someone got up on the wrong side of the bed this morning," Tyler says.

"No. I'm mad at you."

"What'd I do?"

I glance back to the waitress. "Does Ashley, my best friend, ring a bell?"

"Umm I'm confused. What does Ashley have to do with our waitress that you're currently staring daggers at?"

I sigh. "The fact that you have to ask that is why I'm mad."

"Again, I'm confused."

"Are you or are you not currently dating Ashley?"

"Yes, we are. We have our first date tonight."

"And does she know that you plan on dating other girls?"

"No..."

"You better tell her before--"

"Hold up. I don't plan on dating any other girls. Where would you get that idea?"

"You were flirting with our waitress when I walked in."

"Her?" He points to our waitress. She sees him and heads our way. "We were just catching up. She graduated with me and was telling me a funny story. She asked about grabbing dinner right before you walked up. I didn't get a chance to tell her no."

"Why do I not believe you?" He looked like he was being way too flirty.

"Hi Tyler," says our waitress in a very flirty tone.

"Hey Shelley. So about dinner, I can't go with you. I'm dating an amazing girl, and I don't want to mess it up."

"Can't or won't?" She replied.

"Won't."

"If you change your mind, you know where to find me." Tyler simply nodded.

"I think we're ready to order."

"What can I get you both?"

I've always believed my brother and he's never lied to me. However, he's always been flirty like Jeremy. I really hope this time he isn't lying because if he breaks my best friend's heart, I might have to strangle him, brother or not.

We place our orders and she walks away to put them in.

"Do you believe me now?"

"I want to, but don't think I won't kick your butt if you hurt Ashley."

"I wouldn't dream of it."

I give him a look that says I hope so.

"I'm serious. I know it's brand new but I really do like her. I think I always have, but it's taken a while to get over the whole sister's best friend part."

"I love you both, and I want you to be happy."

"Love you too sis. I'm happy with her and I don't plan on hurting her. It's why I want to take things slow and get to know this side of her, rather than just knowing her as your friend."

"I think that's good but make sure she knows how you feel."

"I will. I'm taking her to the new Thai place you were talking about. Ashley's face lit up when you mentioned it last night."

"She'll love that!"

"I know and then I thought we'd grab some ice cream and stroll on the boardwalk."

"Sounds perfect. Don't forget about the dance club on the roof. They play different music every night. And Ty..."

"Yeah?"

"Just be honest with her about everything. It's no secret she's liked you forever."

"I will. Now enough about me. Let's talk about a certain football player."

I groan. Thankfully a server, not our waitress from before, brings us our food so I don't have to answer for a minute.

"Uh uh. You don't get to accuse me of cheating on Ashley and then get away with not answering some questions."

"Fine. Lay them on me. Doesn't mean I'm going to answer."

"What's up with you and Mr. Quarterback? We didn't have time last night to really talk." He would go right for the big question first.

"Nothing. We're friends."

"Still going with that? I saw you both last night. Why do I not believe that?"

"You can believe whatever you want."

"If you're friends, then why do you keep kissing each other?"

How does he know? Well he would know about the one at the Olympics since he was there. Does he know about the other? No he couldn't.

He must see the question on my face because he says, "Jeremy is my best friend. He wasn't breaking your trust but he told me he kissed you by the boathouse on New Year's."

I'm speechless. When I started dating Logan, Jeremy and Tyler got close, especially going to Florida State together.

"Then you kissed him at the Olympics."

"That was a thank you kiss," I reply.

"A thank you kiss on national TV after winning a gold medal. Really, Em?"

"Yes," I squeak.

"You keep thinking that. All I'm saying is that I think he'd be good for you. I know you're good for him."

"I'm good for him?"

"Yes. You keep him grounded but on his toes at the same time. His life is so routine and sure he gets challenges on the field during games. Outside of that though, he doesn't get much to challenge him except for you. You challenge him and push him to be better."

"Oh..." I'm surprised at how much Tyler has paid attention. We've always been close as siblings but the past few years we've been living in different places. Then again he has always been good at reading the room and people. It's what will make him such a great lawyer.

"It's okay to be scared. Believe me, I know all about that. Take my advice and go for it. It might just be the best thing you do." He has a dreamy look in his eye. I'm so glad he finally got over his fear, as he calls it, and started pursuing Ashley. Maybe one day, I'll get over my fear and do the same.

He continues. "Logan wants you to be happy, not afraid to move forward."

"Thanks Ty."

"Of course. What're big brothers for?"

I really did get lucky with him. I got lucky with all the people in my life.

We finish our lunch and pay at the front.

"Want to grab coffee next door?" asks Tyler.

"Now you're speaking my language." I smile and link arms with my brother.

Chapter Twenty

"What do I do?" There are multiple papers spread out in front me. "These are all offer letters but I don't know what to do next."

Ashley sips her coffee. "Let me see them again." She reads them as my phone rings. Ashley glances at my phone and smiles knowingly when she sees Jeremy's name. She makes a kissy face.

I answer the phone as I swat at her. "Hey. What's up?"

"Hey! So I was working with the physical therapist team here at the Titans training facility. We got to talking and they're looking for a new hire to work with the physical training department. Pretty much keep us players on track with any therapy we might need. Anyway long story short, they'd love to bring you in for an interview. They know your story and think you'd be a great fit. Plus you get to see me all the time."

"That sounds awesome–the job part, not the seeing you all the time part. Not that that wouldn't be good, just..." I know I'm rambling and can hear Jeremy laughing on the other line. "I'd love to meet with them. Just let me know the details."

He continues to laugh. "Sounds good. Hey are you doing anything--"

I cut him off before he can finish. I know he wants to talk about us and take me on an actual date. I've been kind of avoiding him which hasn't been too hard even though we live together. "Hey... I'm going to have to call you back. I'm right in the middle of something."

"Okay talk to you later." He hangs up and Ash crosses her arms smirking at me.

"What?"

"You have it so bad and you don't even know it."

"No I don't but even if I do I need to focus on finding a job."

"It sounds like he just offered you the perfect job."

"He's setting up an interview for me, not a job." I pick up the offer letters and fan them out on the table. "These are actual jobs right here and I need to make a decision." I flip through the pages. "This one's working with future Olympic teams, this one is for a full time position at Vanderbilt working with the sports teams, this one is a swim coach, the list goes on... ughh why can't I make a decision. I just don't know what to do." I rest my head in my hands.

Ashley scoots her chair over. "Hey, we'll figure this out. I've known you my entire life. You've always had control of every-thing in your life. This is the first time you haven't had anything on your plate and it scares you. I get that."

"I wish I could talk to Logan. He'd know what to do." He always had the best advice and ideas. He was the one to come up with the idea of me going to school for physical therapy and that basically saved my life these last few years.

"You know what he'd tell you?" I look at her. "He'd tell you to follow your heart and do what you want to do." She pushes the papers to the side. "I think before you make a decision about a job, you need to make another decision about a certain someone."

"Ash I...I can't." I know she's talking about Jeremy but I can't go there now. Or maybe ever.

"Why, because you're scared? Scared of what Logan would think? Scared of what other people will think? Why not do something that no one expects you to do? Go out on a limb and tell him how you feel. Until you can be honest with yourself, you won't be able to move forward."

She always knows exactly how I feel. Logan is the only other person that could do that. I guess that's why they were the two closest people in my life until Jeremy came along. He wiggled his way in. Now he can read me just as well.

"Ash, it's his brother. I can't fall in love with his brother. There're rules against that."

"Rules? What is this, teen drama?" Ash laughs. "Remember prom, our junior year? He trusted Jeremy to make sure you had a good time, when he wasn't able to go. Remember your freshman year, he trusted Jeremy yet again to watch out for you while he was away at a different school. Emma, I'm pretty sure if you were to move on with anyone, Logan would want it to be his brother. Before you say anything... people aren't going to think you weren't faithful to Logan, and if they do then they are clearly blind. I've never seen a more epic love than what you and Logan had. But babe, it's been years. You need to move on."

"I know, but that doesn't make it easier." Everything she says makes sense but I still hate the situation.

"Just because you move on doesn't mean you'll forget about Logan. He'll always live within you and Jeremy. Plus from that kiss I saw after you won your last gold medal, I'd say you have done a good job of moving on whether you realize it or not."

"That was a thank you kiss, for your information."

Why does no one believe me?

Ashley eyes me from across the table, still not believing me. "What is a thank you kiss?" I shrug, not wanting to admit it was anything else. "That was one thank you kiss."

"Fine, I'll talk to him and maybe tell him how I feel." I avoid eye contact because I know she'll see right through me. Then again she probably already knows that unless that conversation is forced upon me, I won't be looking for it. I haven't built up the courage like my brother has. Speaking of which...

"Now tell me about your date last night?"

She covers her face with her hands, embarrassed. "How did I know you would bring that up?"

"Because you know me well, and I heard his plans at lunch yesterday. Now tell me, was my brother a gentleman?"

"Em, he was such a gentleman and we had so much fun. He took me to the new Thai place that opened up. We talked, laughed, and danced. I didn't want the night to end."

"I feel a *but* coming on..."

"But... I don't know how it will work. I'm just starting my business. He'll be done with school this year and I don't see him leaving New York City."

"Have you talked to him about it?"

"We kind of avoided the heavy topics but I don't think we could do long distance."

"Why not?" I know my brother has never been one to settle down, but I've seen the way he looks at Ashley when she isn't watching. I know after our lunch yesterday he had been biding his time and working up the courage to ask her out.

"As much as I think he likes me, I don't see him ready for a serious relationship. He's about to graduate law school and will be busy with a new job. Plus he will be a hot shot lawyer in New York City. Why would he want to have a long distance relationship when he could be going out on a date with a new woman every night?"

"Maybe you should talk to him about it before making any conclusions. I've seen the way he looks at you. He has never looked at anyone else like that before."

"I know you're just saying that." She shakes her head again as if she really doesn't believe me.

"Ash, I wouldn't say it unless it was true. After my lunch with him yesterday, I know he's serious about you. He really likes you, but he's scared to mess things up."

"He won't know if he doesn't try."

"I told him the same thing. So when are you going to see him again?"

"We decided to just take it slow and date, not put any labels on anything. He's had a few law firms approach him about a job when he graduates and I want him to decide what he wants without factoring me in."

"That's very noble of you but you know he's going to still factor you in."

"That's what I am hoping for." She winks.

"You sneaky girl."

"It'll tell me how serious he is without forcing the subject. I know we'll have to talk about the serious stuff later, but right now we can have some fun."

"I think that's good. It'll let you all try out the long distance without too much pressure. Just don't wait too long for that conversation."

"I won't. Speaking of conversations, when are you going to have a talk with a certain someone?"

I glare at her. "Eventually."

"I was once told, don't wait too long. Oh and you won't know unless you try." She sticks her tongue at me. I stick my tongue back at her.

"I think I need a new best friend."

"You wouldn't know what to do without me."

We stand up from the table and I link my arm with hers as we head outside. I put my sunglasses on and pull her into one of the stores nearby.

"You're right. Your fashion advice is the real reason I've kept you around. I really need your help picking a new outfit for my interview with all these hot football players."

Her mouth drops open. "Think I could shadow you during the interview?"

"Now what would my brother have to say about that?"

She laughs. "You're right. Lawyers are so much better than football players anyway. The way he kissed me last night..."

"Ewww." I cover my ears.

"You asked about my date."

"I wanted to know about the date. Not how my brother kisses. You can date him but I don't want those details."

She waggles her eyebrows at me. I open the door to the shop before she can continue.

"Maybe my new best friend can help me pick out clothes," I say back to her.

"No, you need me. I'm the best."

She's right. She's the bestest friend I could ever ask for and I wouldn't trade her for anything.

Chapter Twenty-one

A few days later, I wake up to the smell of... is that bacon? Why do I smell bacon? I usually do all the cooking.

I throw on my robe and head to the kitchen. The sight I see is something I could get used to while making it that much harder to resist Jeremy.

Jeremy stands in the middle of the kitchen, shirtless with gray sweatpants. He's leaning over the stove sautéing veggies. A bowl of whipped eggs sits next to the stove.

"I thought you couldn't cook?" He doesn't have to turn for me to know he has a giant smirk on his face. He reaches for a coffee mug on the counter and fills it with coffee. He then stirs in a splash of cream and sets the mug in front of me on the island, pushing it towards my awaiting hand.

"I may have watched some cooking videos. I just never have time to do the actual cooking. I might have to still practice making meatloaf, though."

I shake my head at him as he goes back to the stove. I inhale the vanilla aroma. He started buying this vanilla flavored coffee. It adds a hint of vanilla to the taste but doesn't have all the sugar you would get from vanilla creamer. I take a sip and let out a moan.

"Now that I know you can cook, I might just make you share the cooking responsibilities." I wink at him and start walking back toward the hallway. "Let me know when breakfast is ready. I have this interview to get ready for." I hear his laughter as I enter the bathroom.

I set my three-quarters of the way empty coffee mug on the counter and turn on the shower to heat up. I strip off my robe and pajamas and finish off my coffee.

I hop in the shower and let the hot water cascade down my back. I have my interview with the Titans Physical Training team today. For some reason, I'm really nervous about this interview. My short time at Vanderbilt was a dream come true. This job with the Titans will be similar, but on a much bigger scale and my all-time dream job.

There's already talk of the Titans going all the way to the Super Bowl this year.

I quickly wash and condition my hair, knowing breakfast will be ready pretty soon. I turn the water off and grab my towel.

I have to say, one of the best things about living with Jeremy is all the luxury things he has. It's all top notch, like these towels. They're huge and soft and amazing.

I step out of the shower onto the fluffiest bath mat ever. I hear Jeremy shout that breakfast will be ready in five minutes.

I wrap my hair in the towel and grab my makeup bag. Lately, I've been doing more makeup than I used to. I add eyeliner, eyeshadow and mascara to give myself a light natural looking smokey eye. I then add a touch of blush to my cheeks and I'm done. I have Ashley to thank for teaching me quick makeup tricks.

I brush my hair, opting for it to air dry. I go into my room and put on the clothes I laid out last night.

I decided on a black pencil skirt, blue button up blouse and short black heels. I take one last look in the mirror and go into the kitchen room. Jeremy is setting plates on the island breakfast bar. We only ever eat at the table if more people are with us.

I sit down and I'm instantly impressed with the perfect looking omelet and strips of bacon in front of me. To think how far he's come from flipping already burnt bacon.

There's a giant bowl of fruit. We always have cut-up fruit ready to go in the fridge. My coffee cup is filled with coffee. Wait, how is my coffee cup filled with coffee? I thought I left it in the bathroom.

Before I can say anything, Jeremy reads my mind. "I snuck in while you were in the shower to top it off. Don't worry I didn't peek."

I laugh because he would add that last part. "This looks delicious." I take a bite of the omelet and decide that Jeremy is officially cooking more in the future. It's filled with gooey cheese, onions, peppers, spinach, and something else.

"What's the seasoning in this?"

"Chives."

"It's even more delicious tasting than it smells. What's the occasion?"

"I know you have the interview today with the Titans and I wanted you to be able to relax before it."

Is he not the sweetest? Why can't I just say yes and move forward with him. I have such a hard time getting my head to agree with my heart in moving forward.

"You know what this means, right?"

"That you'll go out with me."

I gulp. I may have just been thinking something along those lines but I'm not ready to have that conversation. "Umm no. That I was serious about sharing cooking responsibilities. I want to know what else you can make. I know not meatloaf." I laugh, trying to steer the conversation elsewhere.

"Only if you agree to one date."

"Jeremy…"

"I'm serious Emma. Can't you feel this pull between us? We don't even have to go anywhere. We can stay here and I'll cook for you."

"I'll think about it."

"That's fine. I know I'll wear you down since I'll be seeing you every day."

It takes me a second to realize what he's talking about. "I still have to get the job. Today is only an interview."

"Yeah, but I have no doubt that you'll get the job."

"I hope so. It's even more of a dream job than the one I had at Vanderbilt."

"Speaking of your interview, what time is it at?"

"Nine, but I was thinking about getting there early and looking around."

"I have to leave in fifteen minutes if you want to ride with me. You'll be there about an hour early."

"Sounds perfect." I finish off my last strip of bacon and my coffee. "You go get dressed, and I can finish these dishes."

"You don't have to do that. I just have to throw on a shirt and shorts. All my gear is already at the stadium."

I shoo him away. "It's fine. You cooked and I can clean."

He nods and stands up to head to his room.

Jeremy has already done most of the cleaning. The bacon tray and egg pan are washed and drying on the rack. I rinse off our plates and cups and put them in the dishwasher. I cover the fruit bowl and place it back in the fridge. Jeremy has already put all the veggies and omelette fix-ins back in so I wipe the counter. I finish just as Jeremy comes sauntering back in the room.

"Ready to go?"

"Yes. Let me grab my bag and we can head out."

In my room, I grab my bag and my phone. As I walk back into the living room where Jeremy is waiting, I notice a text from Ashley.

Ashley: *Good luck today! Feel free to send me pictures of the weight room ;)*

I laugh because I know the weight room is code for all the shirtless football players.

"What's so funny?"

I show him the text and he grins. "You know we could start pictures now." He pulls up his shirt showing off the firm lines of muscle on his six...eight pack? Did he add more muscle? Emma, stop drooling. You shouldn't know how much muscle he has.

I glance at his face to see him grinning even wider. He knew I was checking him out and that is exactly what he was trying to get me to do.

I push him towards the front door. "Let's go Mr. Ego!"

As he passes me, he leans down to whisper, "You don't have to use Ashley to get photos. All you have to do is ask."

Thankfully he has already passed me and can't see the blush creeping onto my cheeks. This guy and his ego. I'm in so much trouble if I get this job. Living with him is one thing because I can usually avoid him if I need to. Seeing him every day, working out, all sweaty... I gulp. Someone help me.

I sit down with the department head, Mr. Brown, and he asks me the typical interview questions such as why do you want this job or what qualities will you bring to the job.

By the end of the interview, I'm loving everything about the job and feel I could make an impact.

He gives me a tour of the facilities and I'm amazed at what it offers.

We head to the weight room where the team is working out. It smells of sweat and bleach which is a weird combination. At least I know they clean everything.

I look around at all the different machines and the sweaty guys everywhere. If Ashley could see me now with a gym full of hot, chiseled, half naked guys, she'd be freaking out. I'm almost tempted to take pictures for her like she asked, but then my brother would probably kill me.

We walk through the room, as Jeremy comes over. His shirt is off and his abs are sweaty from his workout. He has a sweat rag wrapped around his shoulders. I gulp as I feel his strong arm drop over my shoulders.

"How's the interview going?"

"Grr...Great." I nod, not able to articulate my words. And now I sound like Tony the Tiger.

Mr. Brown joins us. "Jeremy, how's your shoulder holding up?"

He removes his arm and rotates his shoulder. "Doing good. A little stiff still, but nothing you therapists can't help me work out." When Mr. Brown turns to one of the other players, Jeremy winks at me. "Emma, what do you think I should do?"

"Uhhh... well muscles need heat to help them relax. After that I'd say a massage to work it out."

"Something like this?" He massages my shoulders and I let out a sigh.

"Yeah... something like that." I gulp again and lean into his touch. I can't help myself. I need to get away now. Ashley's right.

I like him more than I want to admit and I don't know what to think at this point. "I'm going to grab some water."

Mr. Brown points to the water fountain across the room. "Okay I'll be right over and we can head back to my office."

I glance at Jeremy who's smirking at me. I practically run to the fountain.

Jeremy is still smirking when I look in his direction. He knows exactly what he does to me. I feel a hand on my arm and see Mr. Brown. "You ready?" I nod and follow him back to his office.

He grabs a folder, pushes it towards me and then crosses his hands on his desk. "This is what we're offering you."

I pick up the folder and gasp. "Wow. I'm not sure I understand."

"We'd love to have you here as the Director of Sports Medicine. We need someone to work with the other trainers. You'd go with the team to away games, home games, and training, anything like that. You'll be with the team 24/7 making sure they get the therapy they need after long hours of work on the field."

"May I be so bold as to ask if Jeremy or the fact that we have the same last name have anything to do with me getting this job? I mean you already had the offer letter ready."

"Mrs. Anderson."

"Miss," I correct him.

"Sorry, Miss Anderson. We're offering you this job on your outstanding marks in school and recommendations. You're also already an American Board Physical Training Sports Certified Specialist. Plus we're really impressed with your story, the accident, and how you used your schooling to get yourself back into training for the Olympics. I will admit that Jeremy did put you on our radar, but you speak for yourself with everything else. Take some time to think about it and let us know. I can give you till the end of next week."

"Okay, I'll do that. Thank you so much." I'm still shocked that they know so much about me.

Mr. Brown stands to shake my hand. "Please let us know if you have any questions. We look forward to hearing your decision."

"Yes, sir. I'll be in touch." I walk out of the training center. I open the folder again and read what they are offering. They'll be paying enough that I could easily pay for Jeremy's ridiculous apartment rent twice. Maybe even three times.

I close the folder and think about how closely I'd be working with the team, including a certain shirtless quarterback. I pull out my phone and call Ashley. I need help deciding not only a job but certain feelings that are becoming harder and harder to hide.

Chapter Twenty-two

I drive through our small town of Marshall Creek and see all the homecoming banners. It's the reason I'm back. I've only been home a handful of times. It gets easier every time I do but I still avoid it when I can.

Jeremy and I drove in last night. Tyler gets here tonight and Ashley tomorrow. The big game is tomorrow night. Jeremy was asked to present an award at the game as well as announce the Homecoming King and Queen at the dance. Somehow he persuaded me to attend both.

I'm excited to be back at my high school and I've always loved football. My dad is still the coach. I don't know if he'll ever retire. I think he'll still be coaching when my kids are in high school even if he is old, gray, and in a wheelchair.

I'm headed to the Anderson's house for dinner. It'll be good to see them after clearing the air. I thought they blamed me for Logan's death but they never did. They were only giving me space but never far away.

I drive by the park and pull into the small parking lot. I won't get out but I let the memories fill my mind for a few minutes.

I've said my goodbyes to Logan. I'll say my other goodbye soon. Now it's time to leave the past in the past.

Logan will always be a part of me. Logan was my first love, the easy love. Everything was easy with him. Things with Jeremy are more complicated. He pushes me and I push back. The sparks are undeniable, have been since the beginning. I loved Logan and would have forever. The day I met him, all other feelings were pushed aside. Logan was the one I wanted. Now...like I said, it's more complicated. It's getting harder to ignore these sparks that have always been here. These sparks between Jeremy and me.

As I pull out of the parking lot, I can't help the tears that fall. It truly feels like I am leaving him behind and driving towards my future.

In the driveway, I fix my makeup and walk to the front door. Mrs. Anderson opens the door and immediately pulls me into a hug.

"Emma. We've missed you." The last time I was here was when they showed me the video of the crash. Just like the rest of the town, this house holds too many memories.

"I've missed you," I say as I hug her back. I make a mental note, to try to visit more often. I want to make new memories while soaking in the past.

Knowing I need a moment, she says, "Jeremy will be right down. We're eating out back if you want to go out there and wait."

I nod. She leaves toward the kitchen. I pass under the balcony toward the french doors in the back. I always thought their house was so intimidating but the more time I spent here, the more comfortable I felt.

Outside, I take a breath of fresh air. The water calls to me. I take the path down to the dock. I pass by the treehouse and pause to look up at it. That's one place that is filled with too many memories.

I continue down the path. I kick my boots and socks off, roll up my jeans and dangle my feet in the water. It's cold but I welcome it. The weather is turning from the nice crisp fall air to the cold winter air. I want to soak in the water and weather before it gets too cold.

I close my eyes, soaking in the setting sun.

I feel him sit next to me. We are quiet for a few minutes.

"Are you trying to freeze out here?"

"I just wanted to soak in the sun while I can. The sun is just about set."

"My mom wanted me to let you know dinner is about ready.

He stands and gives me his hand. "Come let's get you warm under the heaters." During the summer, they keep the heaters stored away but now that it's getting chilly again, they pulled them out so everyone can enjoy the outside.

I take his hand and he helps me up at the same time I leap up. The momentum causes me to crash into his chest. I don't immediately back away even though I should. I lean my head back to look at Jeremy.

He brushes a hair out of my face and smiles at me. "You know what this spot is, right?"

I don't have to look around to know. I back away before he can do anything.

"Very soon, I'll be kissing you again Emma. I would wait for you forever, but I know I'm wearing you down and you'll give in to this thing between us."

I gulp. I know he's right. I know, it's only a matter of time. If he kisses me, I'll probably fall then.

He tosses my socks in my boots, grabbing them in one hand and taking my hand with the other.

We walk up to the deck where Jeremy's mom is bringing out dinner. It smells delicious.

She sees us and glances at our linked hands. She gives Jeremy a knowing grin before heading back in the house.

"Let me get you a towel to dry your feet off so you can put your boots back on."

Several minutes later we sit down to eat, enjoying the warmth from the heaters surrounding the table, basking in the purples and pinks of the dusk sky, and filling our bellies with yummy food.

The crowd cheers as our team scores another touchdown. The stands are filled with bright red, the color of the Marshall Creek Grizzlies fans.

I'm sitting with my mom, brother, Ashley, and the Andersons. My dad and Jeremy are down with the team. There's a minute left of the game.

At halftime, Jeremy presented the angel award to a player on the team. It's an award dedicated to Logan for the person that displays the most team spirit. Logan may not have been on the football team but no matter what he did, he always showed team spirit and was there to help everyone else. He was the first to be there and the last to leave.

Each sport now gives the award out at different points of the season. Football gives it out during the homecoming game. It was a special moment to see.

Jeremy asked me beforehand if I wanted to help present it with him. I said no. Maybe one day. I've been saying that a lot lately but it all feels too soon.

The game ends and we win. We head down to the field to celebrate with the team.

My dad sees us and spins my mom around like when they were young. I love seeing them like that.

Jeremy is talking with the quarterback, probably giving him feedback on the game. He sees me and smiles, holding up a finger.

I turn around taking in the field. I grew up on a football field with my dad coaching. It's my home away from home.

I feel arms snake around my waist.

"I missed you down here."

I turn around in his arms, taking a slight step back so his arms drop. He has been getting bolder and bolder, almost as if he knows my defenses are dropping.

"I'm never down here."

"But you will be when you accept the position at the Titans."

"If I accept it." I still have time to decide, even though I already know in my heart what my decision is.

"You seem to always forget that I know you. You may not have signed a piece of paper yet, but you've already agreed. It's your dream job. Why would you say no?"

Of course, he's right.

"We'll see." I turn on my heel heading towards Ashley and Tyler standing on the sidelines. I don't have to look back to know he's smirking at me.

Ugh. Annoying, ego, man.

We all head out to dinner and then back to the Andersons for a movie night. The movie ends and my parents head home and Jeremy's parents retreat to their room. Ashley, Tyler, Jeremy, and I turn on another movie. We all end up falling asleep in the comfy, leather lounge chairs.

The next morning Ashley drags me to the local spa for the whole treatment before the dance tonight. It may not be our Homecoming, but we're still attending.

After manicures, pedicures, and massages, we go to a local boutique to buy dresses. I find a simple strapless black with a line of sequins at the top. I pay at the front and wait for Ashley to make her selection. As she pays, I leave my bag at the front and go to the bathroom. I come back out and we go to my house to get ready.

It's deja vu as we walk down the stairs of my house, only Logan isn't at the bottom with Jeremy. Instead it's my brother, and his eyes are locked onto Ashley.

I lock eyes with Jeremy and it takes my breath away. He and Logan always looked like twins, but Jeremy has a more chiseled jawline and is much broader in the shoulders.

He's dressed head to toe in a black tux with a red tie that matches my dress. I bought the black one but while I was in the bathroom, Ashley switched it out for the same exact dress–only in red.

He reaches out a hand towards me and I take it when I reach the bottom of the stairs. He gives me a twirl.

"Bold choice with the red. I like it."

I blush. "That would be Ashley."

"I know. She told me to get a red tie."

"Of course she did." I glance over at her. Her and my brother are staring deeply at each other. They've been together since our movie night. It's long distance and there are no labels but they're exclusive. I'm so happy they finally stopped being stubborn with their feelings. I really hope it works out for them because I plan on having both of them in my life forever. Ashley's basically my sister already.

Outside is a limo. Inside we each have a glass of champagne. I'm going to need courage for tonight. Last time I went to a dance with Jeremy, I was dating Logan. Now things have changed and my feelings are complicated.

At the school, we enter the gymnasium that's been transformed with lights.

There's a DJ in the corner and a stage is against the far wall. The entire court has been sanctioned as the dance floor. Several couples are already dancing in the center of the gym floor on top of the giant Grizzly bear school logo.

We walk over to where the chaperones have congregated. We aren't chaperones but I sure feel old next to the kids dancing—even though I'm not actually much older. We're here to support Jeremy as he gets to make the announcement about Homecoming King and Queen.

We dance a little and the time for the announcement comes. Jeremy makes his way to the stage to introduce the full Homecoming Court to the stage.

Ashley and I are helping out. In everyone's hands we put a rose. Red for the king and queen, and white for the rest. We figured the boys could give them to their dates.

On the count of three, everyone reveals their flower from behind their back.

A cute brunette I noticed in the stands just below us from last night and the quarterback have red roses. I see the brunette blush as her king takes her hand.

They walk down the stairs of the stage and to the middle of the dance floor. Jeremy walks over to me. "He has a huge crush on her."

"How do you know that?" I ask.

"He told me last night. He seemed really nervous and I asked him why. He mentioned a girl was in the stands and pointed her out to me."

"Well I think she likes him too."

"It's the night of crushes' dreams coming true."

"It is." I stare at them dreamily. I glance back at Jeremy and he's staring at me.

"Would you like to dance, Emma?"

"Sure." I take his hand as he leads me down the stairs and to the dance floor.

A new song comes on, one I recognize from our Prom when we did the waltz.

I look at Jeremy and he's smiling mischievously. Of course he asked them to play this song.

"Do you remember the move?"

"Yeah, but I highly doubt I can do them in this dress." I look down at my dress. It's short with not much give in it.

"Instead of lifting you up with your leg extended, I'll just lift you straight up and then down."

I follow his lead like last time and we dance around the floor. It feels natural, just like last time. Only now, I don't have any-thing stopping me from feeling something. Not that I wanted to last time. I was happy with Logan and if I could get him back, I would. I know Jeremy would in a heartbeat too, but the past is the past. I need to remember that and look at what the future holds.

That might just be what's in front of me. If I can get my heart to stop racing so fast and breathe.

The song ends and like last time, he dips me–only this time he doesn't pause before kissing me. He leans down and gives me a short sweet kiss on the lips.

I don't pull away. I softly kiss him back but only for a second before he lifts me back up.

We dance some more with Ashley and Tyler joining in. They're so cute together. I can't stop watching them.

On the way home, we're all silent, thinking about the night.

My head is on Jeremy's shoulder. I figured this would be the best way to not talk about what happened tonight.

The limo stops in front of my house and Tyler and Ashley get out, going inside. Ashley is staying with us and sleeping in my room since her parents aren't home. She may live next door, but she didn't want to be all alone.

Jeremy gets out first and then helps me out. He walks me to the front door and my heart starts racing again.

We reach the front door and I turn to him.

Why am I so nervous?

He grips my chin. "Emma, breathe."

I laugh because he always knows what's going through my head.

"I promise I won't kiss you again. I kissed you. You kissed me. I kissed you tonight. Now it's in your hands."

I nod because what else am I supposed to say?

"I'll see you tomorrow. Pick you up at 11 a.m. and we can head out."

"Sounds good," I say, finally finding my voice.

"I know I told you earlier but you look absolutely gorgeous tonight. I was the luckiest guy there."

I blush. He leans in and kisses me on the cheek.

"Good night, Emma."

He turns to head back to the limo.

"Good night, Jeremy. Thank you for tonight."

He looks back at me. "Anytime. You just say the word."

I enter my house knowing he won't leave until I do. The door closes behind me and I can't help wondering about tonight. We never really said if it was a date or not.

Do I want it to be? Maybe

Am I ready? I don't know.

I want to so much but I'm scared. I'll never admit it out loud. Eventually I'll have to learn to take that risk. As Ashley always said, "the best moments in life are from the biggest risks."

The real question I should be asking myself is, am I ready to risk my heart, once again?

Chapter Twenty-three

Homecoming last night was a blast and I still get chills thinking about it. Now I'm preparing myself for something that has been a long time coming. I force myself out of my car, grabbing the box in the passenger seat.

I slowly walk down the path taking in the crisp autumn air. It's getting chilly. Thankfully I have on jeans and a light sweater.

I come to the end of the path, and instead of going into the gazebo, like I do most times I come here, I go to the tree Jeremy planted.

I still remember the day Jeremy showed me the tree with the plaque next to it, "Logan Anderson - when life gives you apples, take a bite and enjoy the sweet life."

I miss him so much. I miss his smile and the way he always knew how to cheer me up. I could go on and on but it's not the day for that. I've said my goodbyes to Logan. Today is about saying goodbye to someone else just as special.

Using my hand, I dig out a small section next to Logan's plaque.

I open the box next to me and take out the plaque from inside.

I place it down in the small hole I just made, filling it in on the sides. I softly press it down so it fits in the dirt.

It reads: "I never felt your hand but I feel you in my heart and your presence from above. We love you, Mom and Dad. Give Daddy a hug for me".

We never found out if our baby was a girl or boy. It was too early with an ultrasound. I'm sure they could have found out when they removed the baby, but I didn't want to know. Especially back then. I didn't care about anything.

It still doesn't matter now. I'll always love our baby no matter what. I hope Logan and our baby are dancing around in heaven together.

I run my fingers over the inscription. The tears start to come before I can stop them. Losing Logan was one of the hardest things of my life. More than the possibility of not walking. More than losing my Olympic dreams. But losing my baby on top of Logan, was by far the worst.

I could've dealt with losing our baby if I had Logan to get me through it. Or I could've had a piece of Logan if just our baby survived. Instead I lost both of them, and it sent me into the worst kind of depression.

For so long I was numb. I didn't want to live. I wanted to end it all.

Jeremy was the only one that could have pulled me out. Everyone tried. My parents. The Andersons. Ashley. Tyler. But Jeremy's voice was the only one that came through the fog. It scared me for the longest time, and it's why it has taken me so long to give in to him. I've been fighting my feelings for him.

I've said my goodbyes to Logan but in order to fully move on, I need to move forward. For so long, I thought it was my fault. Our argument leading to the accident, but I've come to realize I can't blame myself. Seeing that video was incredibly hard, but it helped heal my heart.

Putting the plaque for our baby was the first step in releasing that hold and guilt I've been holding.

I look down at the two plaques side-by-side.

"Logan, you once told me if anything ever happened to you, turn to your brother. I laughed it off because I never thought it would happen. Now I somehow fell for him. Everyone keeps telling me that no one will ever doubt my love for you. While I believe them, I need you to know too. I will always love you! So now I'll ask you for your permission to move forward with him. Give me a sign that it's okay. I'll never forget you, but I need to know this is still what you want."

A breeze blows through the trees. I look up to see the sun piercing through the leaves. I'm blinded for a second but as the leaves rustle I notice about halfway up, two apples blooming right next to each other. One is big and the other mini. The mini apple rests slightly on the top of the larger apple, like it's being carried.

The dam bursts and the tears don't stop. Several minutes later, I look back at the apples to make sure I wasn't imagining them. They're still there.

Is this my sign? Maybe the signs were always there and I chose not to see them. New tears form because I know in my heart that this is truly my goodbye.

I'll be back to the park but no more heavy goodbyes. From here on out, only lighter and happy visits.

"Thank you Logan. Hold on tight to our baby."

As much as I wish at least one of them was here with me, I'm glad they have each other.

I eventually stand up, brushing the dirt off my knees, and lift the empty box.

As I turn to leave, I notice several figures sitting in the gazebo.

I walk over to them and Ashley stands to give me a hug. Several tears run down my face. I thought I was cried out but they never seem to stop.

She leads me to the bench and Jeremy wraps a blanket around my shoulders. I rest my head on Ashley's shoulders. Jeremy wraps his arm around me and Tyler does the same with Ashley.

It was a rough visit, but a huge part of my support system is never far. They knew I needed to do this on my own, but they still showed up in case I needed them.

I take in the mountains and the color changing trees.

I casually glance at Jeremy. He's been my rock. He pushed me to get out of the hospital bed and to walk. Then he pushed me to return to school, to train again, and have confidence in myself. Now it's time for the last thing on his list of moving forward.

Learning to love...again.

I've avoided it because I was scared. Scared of what was right in front of me. A love so strong I pushed it away. He's been so patient with me.

I reach my hand out and he instantly winds his fingers through mine with the hand that isn't around my shoulders. He smiles at me. He knows what today meant. He knows I had to come here before we could officially have a date. He knows that by coming here today, I'm ready to move forward.

We leave the park to head back to the Anderson house for a cookout. We have to leave later today to head home but figured one last home cooked meal would be delicious. With me starting a new job and Jeremy's season starting, who knows when we'll have time to come back here.

As always, the Andersons go all out even with it just being our families. My dad is at the grill with Blake and my mom is with Victoria, placing bowls of food on the outside table.

Tyler and Jeremy head to the grill to see what needs to be done.

I walk over to my mom.

"Do you need help with anything?"

"No sweetie. Go relax. We've got it. Victoria has become quite the cook."

"She has the best teacher." My mom is one of the best cooks and bakers I know. Probably the reason why she has one of the top food blogs.

Mrs. Anderson walks over. "Your mom is the best teacher. If they hadn't become our family, I would have to fire our chef."

They laugh. I try to join in but I'm still drained from the park.

My mom notices. "How was the park?"

They both know why I went there. They both know about the feelings Jeremy and I have for each other.

"Good," is all I can manage.

"Logan would be so proud of everything you have accomplished since the accident," Mrs. Anderson says to me. "Right after you all got engaged, he told me he had no idea how a girl like you fell for him. He loved you so much, just as you loved him. In the past year, I've seen the way my other son looks at you and the way you look back. Logan won't love you any less because you move on, even with Jeremy. He wants you to smile and be happy. I know you're scared, but no one will think any less of you if you decide to pursue something with Jeremy."

She pulls me into a hug and I wrap my arms around her. "I may be a little biased because I don't want to lose you as my daughter-in-law but no matter what happens with you and Jeremy, you'll always have a place here."

Despite me trying not to cry, a few tears escape.

"Thank you," I say as I pull back.

She gives my hand a squeeze. My mom moves to my side and gives me a hug. "Your baby is up there loving every time you smile, so keep doing it. Now go get Ashley. She's looking lonely and keeps looking over at you know who."

Sure enough when I glance at Ashley, she is staring longingly at Tyler who's helping Jeremy move the heaters. They are moving them to different spots from the last time we were here.

"Dinner will be ready shortly. The ribs should be just about done."

I head over to Ashley.

"He'll figure out his feelings for you one day and you can actually put a label on your relationship."

"I don't know about that. There are days when he's so sweet like today and others, well most days he treats me like a little sister."

"Have you ever thought the reason he treats you like a little sister is because he's just simply comfortable with you?"

"Maybe, but he could also stop treating me like this precious little thing and show me that he actually cares. It might be the long distance." She sighs.

"Come here," I say, pulling her into a hug. Over her shoulder I make eye contact with Tyler. I point to Ashley and give him a firm look. He nods and walks over.

"Can I steal Ashley?" My brother asks.

"Sure."

Ashley pulls away. I squeeze her hand and push her towards Tyler.

"Hey Pretty Girl. Walk with me."

She takes his hand and they set off towards the water.

I see them stop at the water's edge and he pulls her in for a kiss.

I look away as Jeremy walks up to me.

"Are you ready to eat?"

"Yes. I'm starving."

"Where did Ashley and Tyler go?"

I point down to the water. They look to be in a serious conversation.

"Let's go help get everything ready to eat. They'll join us when they're ready."

Each of our dads are setting a tray of ribs on the table with all the other food. Our moms went all out. They made caprese salad skewers, broccoli salad, potato salad, corn on the cob, and a fruit platter. With the amount of food, I'm surprised no one else is coming. At least we only live a few hours and can take some home with us.

A few minutes later, Ashley and Tyler join us and we fill our plates. The ladies start and take our seats at the table on the deck.

"Quickly before the boys get over here, tell me what happened."

"He asked me to come to New York for Christmas." She has the biggest grin on her face.

"I'm excited for you."

"What're you beautiful ladies talking about?" Jeremy asks.

"Just that all this food looks so yummy and the boys need to hurry up so we can dig in." I wink at him.

Tyler sits next to Ashley and gives her a kiss on the cheek.

Her face lights up even more than I thought was possible.

We enjoy the delicious meal and help clean up. Afterward, I walk down to the boathouse to enjoy some quiet time before we have to leave.

I have no idea how long I've been down here when I feel arms wrap around me. I don't have to look back to know who it is.

"Is it time to go?"

"Yes, I want to head out before traffic gets bad."

"Okay. Let's go." I turn to face him. The sunlight is shining on my face and I can barely see.

"You look beautiful," Jeremy says.

"Thank you?" I ask.

"Why is that a question? You always look beautiful, so much that you take my breath away. You have your ready-to-swim look before you dive into the pool, and then the wet-from-the-pool, I-just-won-a-gold-medal look. Next there's the dressed-up-for-a-dance or dinner look, and the morning look when your hair is everywhere, your clothes are disheveled, and you're still half asleep getting your coffee. But my absolute favorite is at night when you're in pajamas, makeup off, and relaxed on the couch with a glass of wine."

"You notice all that?" I ask shocked. Most of those I don't think I look good at all but the fact that he notices makes my walls fall a little more.

He nods. Before I can say anything else, he gives me the softest peck on the lips.

Isn't it my turn to kiss him? Then again, the kiss was so soft, I don't know if it actually happened or I imagined it. I don't have time to think because Jeremy is pulling me back towards the house to say goodbyes before we head home.

I'm so done for!

Chapter Twenty-four

I accept the position working with the Tennessee Titans as the Director of Sports Medicine. I've been working for about a month and it's been hard work. I've gotten to know all the players and their positions, plus any current or past injuries. It's my job to be aware of it all so we can create the right program for each player.

Despite the hard work, I've never felt more at home. This is similar to what I was doing at Vanderbilt only on a bigger scale since it's a professional team.

Tonight is my date with Jeremy. I've avoided the topic for a month but just like he said, he's been wearing me down. I finally agreed so he'd stop, not that I didn't like the attention. He's cooking dinner at home but won't tell me what. He said he wants it to be a surprise.

I know the ball is in my hands. I just have to be brave enough to make the play. The first step was accepting the date.

Today at work, I'm working with the offense to show them some new stretches they can do at home. It should be a pretty busy day which will keep my mind off later tonight.

First up are the wide receivers and running backs. I show them how to stretch their legs to keep from cramping when they go home to relax. We work through a few other stretches and I pull out my clipboard to see who's next.

I have one on one time with the quarterbacks. Jeremy is the first to show up. "I'm ready to get all my muscles stretched out, my shrink."

I roll my eyes at him. "Okay Mr. Hot Shot. First off, I'm not that kind of therapist. I don't think I could listen to you all whine about your problems. Give me muscles and joints any day. Second, we have two others we're waiting on before we begin."

"Oh you didn't hear? They won't be coming. Our third string is home sick and the second string is working on some passes. Since we're killing it this season, we thought we might give him some playing time."

I gulp. What's a little alone time with Jeremy? I live with him so we have plenty of alone time, but this feels different. We're on the verge of reaching the end zone and I don't know if I'm ready. I spoke to Ashley about what I'd say to Jeremy but so far I've chickened out.

"Okay, let's get started then." I move to the resistance bands I set up on the wall to work his arms. I feel him come up behind me as he grabs the bands on either side of me, caging me in.

"I love the resistance bands," he whispers in my ear. I spin to face him, remove the bands from his hands and push him away.

"Yes, well we're going to work one arm at a time." I hand him one of the bands and he starts pulling, working out his arm like I showed him in previous sessions. I position his arm out a little.

As I touch his arm, I feel the sparks and let go as soon as I can. The sparks have been getting more consistent. Probably because I'm trying to ignore them and it makes me more aware. Or maybe they've always been there but I subconsciously ignored them.

After he works the other arm, we move to the floor. He lays down and I hold his feet for him to do sit ups. Not that he needs me to hold his feet but it gives him some resistance. He does a few and stops at the top. "So when are we going to talk about this thing between us?"

I push him back down. "What thing?"

In between sit ups, he says, "Oh you know, the fact that I kissed you and you kissed me and then I kissed you again."

I stand up and walk over to grab a foam roller for the next exercise. "Yeah, under each circumstance, they didn't mean anything. Now come lay on this mat and I'll show you the next exercise."

I lay down on my stomach on the mat and grab the foam roller so I can show him what I want him to do. "Okay the first is working the front of your thighs. Place it right in the middle and roll back and forth like this."

He takes my place and starts to roll. I stand to check his form. I make sure to keep my distance and not touch him. We do a few more exercises on the foam roller.

The last one I show him is rolling out the side of his thighs. I lay on the mat again to show him. He comes up behind me on the same foam roller. I jump up so fast. "What're you doing?"

"I know you feel it when we touch." He takes my hand which I immediately pull away.

"I don't know what you are talking about," I mumble, walking over to where my notes are to see what the next stretch is.

Jeremy stands behind me. He moves my hair, softly kisses my neck, and whispers, "Why are you resisting?"

The goosebumps move up my arms. I step out of the way and grab a lightweight. "Take this and stand here. I want you to put your arm in an "L" shape and move it up and down like this."

He does as he's told and I grab my iPad to check out the scan I took of his muscles. I also need a minute to control my breathing.

I tell him to stop and touch his shoulder blade. I push a little. "Does this hurt?" He shakes his head. I move my hand below his shoulder blade and push. "How about this?" He spins around and grabs my hand that was just on his shoulder.

"No, Emma. It doesn't hurt, but this does." He puts my hand on his heart. "This does."

I back away. "Jeremy, I just can't."

He steps towards me. "Give me one good reason."

"Logan."

He shakes his head.

"I wasn't done. He was your brother and people will talk."

"Let them talk!" He steps closer and I take another step back.

"Aren't you worried people will think something happened before Logan died?"

"If people think that then they didn't know you or my brother."

"That's what Ashley said. So did everyone else." I say that last part under my breath as I go to step back again but I feel the wall press up against me. I try to step to the side but Jeremy is quicker. He places his hands on either side of me, trapping me.

"She always was a smart girl. And everyone else already knows you were loyal to Logan. Now are there any other reasons why this can't work between us, or can I kiss you? It's in your hands so I won't just kiss you again unless you say I can."

"Umm well... how about the fact that you travel around all the time for games?"

"I seem to remember you having a job where you travel with that so-called team for all those games."

I try to think of any other excuse but my mind is blank. All I can think is if I don't come up with something, he's going to kiss me. Not that I would mind, but then it'll be all over. We will kiss, fall for each other, and live happily ever after. Am I ready for that? I've been fighting it but maybe it's time to let him in. I'm tired of fighting my feelings. I've said my goodbyes and told myself to move forward. There's still something stopping me. I know what it is but I can't admit it so I think of another excuse.

"Okay, what about how we have nothing in common?"

"Nothing in common other than us both competing in professional sports, being super hot," I punch him in the shoulder, "and a whole list of other things."

"Fine. There is...is...is..." I know there are a billion other reasons but with him this close I can't think straight. My mind is officially mush.

"When you're done thinking of another lame excuse let me know so I can kiss you."

"Jeremy I just don't think it's a good idea." I place my hands on his chest and try to push him away but my hands fall to his abs. I suck in a breath and quickly lower my hands to my sides.

"Look at me," he says. I slowly raise my head. "Now tell me the real reason." He knows! He always knows when I'm hiding something. No use trying to lie to him. He'll see right through me.

"I'm scared," I reply, not making eye contact. I slide down the wall until I'm seated.

He slides down next to me. "What're you scared of?"

"I'm scared to fall again. I loved Logan more than anything and look where that got me. He left me."

"What happened to my brother was a terrible accident and one that will live with us forever. You both had an epic love but that doesn't mean it can't happen again. It also doesn't mean that the lucky guy you fall for is going to drop dead."

"It doesn't make it any less scary."

Jeremy takes my hand in his. "I promise to never leave you."

I glance at our entwined hands. "That's nice, but you can't make that promise."

He draws a heart on the top of my hand with his thumb. "Okay, how about this, what if I promise to always fight for you, even on my deathbed?"

I sigh. I know Logan would have fought for me if he could. I also know that sometimes in life, things happen out of your control. The question is what are you going to do about it? I've been fighting that question since the accident and I'm done fighting.

"Okay, I'll give this a shot. Please don't hurt me."

"Never." He turns my chin towards him. "Now can I kiss you so we can go home and I wow you with my amazing cooking skills?"

I nod knowing this moment will change everything. There's no going back. I raise my eyes to his and the emotion there surprises me.

He kisses me. It takes me a second but I kiss him back as he deepens the kiss. I may be sitting but I feel the kiss all the way to my toes. Something I haven't felt in a long time.

Chapter Twenty-five

I'm currently sitting on my bed in my towel, fresh out of the shower. We've been home for about an hour. I'm freaking out about what to wear tonight and possibly the kiss we shared at training.

We're having dinner at home so I don't have to dress up, but I also don't want to just wear sweats and a t-shirt. I want to look somewhat nice.

Ashley's not texting me back. I keep getting a whiff of garlic and something sweet. It's making my mouth water and my stomach rumble. My phone vibrates on my bed.

"Ashley!" I yell into the phone in a panic.

"What's wrong?" She immediately says.

"I don't know what to wear. Jeremy's out there cooking and I've been in here forever."

"First, just breathe. Second, I can't believe he finally persuaded you to have dinner."

I haven't told her what happened earlier with the kiss.

"Among other things..." I say more to myself than her but she still hears.

"What exactly do you mean other things?"

"We may have kissed again."

I pull the phone away as Ashley screams, "Finally."

"I'll tell you all about it tomorrow. First tell me what to wear."

"Okay, put on a pair of black leggings and your teal long sleeve tunic. Leave your hair down. You'll look comfy for at home but the tunic will give you a little bit of a dress up feel."

I love how she knows all of my clothes and doesn't have to be here to help me pick out something to wear.

"You're amazing. Now I have to go before Jeremy comes looking for me and sees me sitting in a towel."

"I'm sure he wouldn't complain."

"Ashley!"

"I'm kidding. Well...kinda. On second thought, just go out in the towel."

"I'm hanging up now."

"You better call me tomorrow and tell me everything."

"I will." I hang up before she has any other ideas. I go into my closet and get the clothes she mentioned. I put them on and debate about grabbing some fluffy socks. My feet always get cold so I love wearing them but they don't really go with this look. I opt for not wearing them.

I didn't wash my hair in the shower so it's still dry. I run a brush through it and take a look in the mirror.

Ashley really is a genius with clothes. I look comfy and casual while also a little fancy for dinner.

I take a deep breath. I can do this. Channel my inner Ashley, except when it comes to my brother. That's the only time she gets shy.

I head toward the amazing smell in the kitchen. "What smells yummy?"

Jeremy comes around the counter and grabs me by the waist. "Your dinner for the evening madam." He kisses me. "I was just about to come get you. Go sit down at the table and I'll bring you a glass of wine."

I'm very glad I put my clothes on fast or he really would've found me in a towel.

I make my way to the table and notice the set up. There are candles lining the middle with rose petals scattered throughout. It's a romantic and very beautiful centerpiece.

I sit down and Jeremy produces a glass of wine. He sets the wine bottle in a chilling bucket on the table.

I take a sip, hoping it'll calm my nerves. I know we agreed to officially date, but it doesn't stop the nerves from bubbling up. If anything they're worse because I know this is it. I know that by deciding to date, we'll fall in love and live happily ever after. I had that with Logan and then when he was gone it hurt worse than anything. I don't know if I can handle that again.

Jeremy interrupts my thoughts as he sets a plate down in front of me. He sits across from me with his plate. He pours himself a glass and looks at me. "Dig in."

I pick up my utensils and cut off a piece of chicken. I let out a moan the moment it hits my tongue. It's sweet and not dry at all. It practically melts in my mouth. "What is this?"

"Bourbon pecan chicken." He smiles as he takes a bite of his.

I take another bite. This is a definite recipe that will be on repeat. In addition to the chicken, he also made garlic potatoes and a vegetable medley with broccoli, cauliflower, and carrots topped with lemon sauce. He's come so far in his cooking.

"This is all really good. You need to cook more often. Are there any other skills of yours that I should know about?"

I realize my mistake as soon as the words leave my mouth. Jeremy grins wide. "I mean like cooking. Not those skills. I'm sure you're great, seeing all the girls that are on your arm." I shut my mouth before I babble anymore.

"The only girl I want on my arm and to experience those skills now is sitting across from me." He reaches across the table for my hand. "Emma, you have no idea how happy I am that you decided to give us a chance. I promise that I'm not going anywhere, and I can't wait for what our future holds."

"Just be patient with me. I like you a lot and it scares me because there hasn't been anyone since Logan."

"I know, and I'm going to enjoy every moment I have with you." Time is something I cherish because you never know how much you actually have. The accident was proof of that.

He squeezes my hand and goes back to eating his food.

"So now that we're dating, am I going to get hate mail or mean glares from all the women you dated? I mean "The Jeremy Anderson" is now off the market."

"I like the sound of that." My jaw drops. He wants me to get hate mail. He chuckles. "I meant the off the market part, not the hate mail. That's for my PR team to deal with if it comes to that."

I know he has a really good public relations team for the Titans and even for his personal affairs. After all, I know her. We spoke briefly when I was in the Olympics and she helped me out. I guess now she will be covering me again as Jeremy's girlfriend. I wouldn't want anyone else.

"And Emma, you know that most of those girls were just arm candy. I've really only dated, slept with-whatever you want to call it with a handful of girls."

"I figured a lot of them weren't real but I didn't want to assume. After all you are Mr. Ego."

"Yeah I am!" he exclaims. I laugh because some things will never change.

I finish the last of my food on my plate and stand to take it to the kitchen.

"Here, let me."

He takes my plate for me and his as well and sets them in the sink.

"You cooked so I should clean."

"No, tonight is about you relaxing."

He refills my wine glass. "Why don't you go sit on the couch and I'll bring over dessert." He kisses my temple before ushering me towards the living room.

As I head over to the couch, I see Jeremy open the oven. My nose is instantly filled with chocolate. Whatever he made for dessert smells amazing.

I grab the remote and turn on the show we've been watching. I couldn't even tell you the name. It was Jeremy's turn to pick the show. It's some sci-fi space show. It's pretty good but I won't admit that to him.

Jeremy joins me on the couch with two plates of what looks to be a brownie.

He hands me one of the plates with a fork. I take a bite and my taste buds explode. This is not a normal brownie. Is it some sort of cream or cheesecake?

"What's in this?" I question him.

"It's a cheesecake brownie. Cheesecake is your favorite and brownies are mine, so I thought why not combine them."

"You did good. This is one of the best desserts I've ever had."

I take another bite, not able to keep in the moan that leaves my mouth. It's a good thing I'm not training anymore or I'd be in the pool all day to work off this dessert.

I eat the last bite and place my plate on the table, grabbing my wine glass. I sit back, eyes fixed on the TV. I feel Jeremy's eyes on me. I keep focusing on the TV.

Eventually I glance at him. He raises his arm, ushering me over to him.

I slowly scoot over to him, laying awkwardly against his side. He wraps his arm around my shoulders and pulls me closer, adjusting me so I'm leaning against his chest.

He whispers in my ear, "You have no idea how happy I am to have you in my arms and be able to call you mine. Now relax and let's watch the show."

His words give me a sense of calm and I sink into his chest, letting myself relax. I finish my wine and set my glass on the table, cuddling back into Jeremy.

We watch a few episodes before I am yawning. Jeremy takes the remote and turns off the TV.

"Why don't you get ready for bed and I'll wash these dishes."

I don't have the energy to fight him so I just nod. I walk to my room and change into my pajamas. In the bathroom, I brush my teeth and wash my face.

As I enter my room, Jeremy is sitting on my bed. I know he wants to sleep in here but I'm not ready for that. I know he won't push me for anything but the only guy I've shared a bed with is Logan.

He must see the turmoil in my head because he says, "I'm just saying goodnight. I would love to cuddle with you all night but I know you aren't ready."

I nod, moving over to him. "Thank you for understanding. For dinner and dessert. It was amazing. Just thank you for every-thing."

He leans down to kiss me. He pulls away and whispers in my ear, "Get some sleep. I'll see you in the morning."

Once he leaves, I climb into bed. He makes me so nervous, yet so calm at the same time. I'm glad I finally decided to give us a chance. It feels right just like it did with Logan years before. After he died, I never thought I'd fall for someone again. Jeremy broke through the walls around my heart and I couldn't be happier.

I drift off to sleep with thoughts of brownie cheesecake and Jeremy kisses.

Chapter Twenty-six

I'm falling for Jeremy more and more every day. It still scares me, but I'm so thankful for him.

Our parents are coming to our condo for Christmas dinner. They're checking into their hotel and then heading over later. I'm a little nervous because this is the first time I've ever hosted a meal and done all the cooking.

Logan and I were planning on buying a house after we both finished school and couldn't wait to host a holiday meal. This night will be bittersweet.

When Jeremy and I started dating, I told him that I had to move out. He'd looked at me confused and I said I couldn't live with someone I was dating. After much back and forth, I agreed to stay but we'd still be living in separate bedrooms. He promised to be good and so far he has, although he doesn't make it easy.

Like now for instance, I just put the ham in the oven and I'm working on the potatoes when he walks into the room, shirtless. "Have you seen my green button down shirt?"

I try not to look at his taut stomach or the way his chiseled biceps look. I take a sip of wine trying to hide my blush and distract myself. "Umm... I think the laundry room. Although not sure why you're getting changed now. We still have hours till they get here."

"I know, I was just going to iron to make sure there are no wrinkles."

"Okay. Then throw on a shirt and come help me in the kitchen."

He stands right in front of me. "Why do I have to put a shirt on? Can't I help cook like this?"

"You can, but then nothing would ever get done." I squeeze past him to check on the veggies cooking on the stove.

I feel him behind me. "Maybe I don't want to get anything done."

"Jer. You're making this so hard. I still have so much to do before they get here. You know I love you but..." I realize what I just said. I mentally try not to freak out since we haven't said those words yet. I walk over to the potatoes and continue cutting them up hoping he didn't hear me. "But you like to distract me when I'm in the kitchen."

"I love you too."

I whip around and he's still standing at the stove.

"I...I...It just kinda came out and..." I keep my head down.

"Did you mean it?" He walks towards me and I can feel his stare burning into my face.

I make eye contact because I shouldn't be ashamed of my feelings.

"Yes, I meant it. I've felt it for a while now but we've only been dating for three months and I thought it was too soon."

"It's never too soon. I'm pretty sure I've loved you since you spilled coffee on me that day in the coffee shop." He kisses me. As the kiss deepens, he lifts me up on the counter and I wrap my legs around him. I feel his abs under my hands before wrapping them around his back and pulling him close. We make out for a few minutes but I pull away before things go further.

"Jer, we need to stop," I say in a labored breath.

He rests his forehead against mine. "I know. Doesn't mean I can't kiss you."

He leans down to kiss me again before pulling away. "Let me go grab a shirt and I'll help you with the rest of the food."

I grasp the edge of the counter. This whole living together is a lot harder than I thought. Logan was the only man I'd ever slept with and I wanted to wait for someone special again. Maybe even marriage if I ever did get married again. Jer is sure making it hard, but I have to be strong.

I hop off the counter and take another swig of my wine hoping it'll calm me down a bit.

"So what're we making?" Jeremy wraps his arms around my waist and places feather light kisses down my neck.

I remove his hands and drag him towards the counter on the other side of the kitchen. "You're going to work over here, mixing the ingredients for the pie while I finish cutting the potatoes."

He pouts. "Oh I see, putting me on the other side of the kitchen."

A few minutes later, I finish the potatoes and mix them with some olive oil and seasonings. I move on to the veggies, rinse them and drain the water before adding them to the bowl of potatoes.

I then lay them out on a baking sheet and cover it with foil to go in once the ham is done.

The only thing left is the pies which Jeremy is making a mess of.

I glance at Jeremy and just watch him. He's concentrating so hard trying to mix the ingredients but everything keeps going out the side of the bowl. I walk next to him and point to the bowl. "The ingredients are supposed to go in the bowl, not all over the counter."

"Oh is that so?" He takes a bit of the apple mixture on his finger and wipes it on my nose.

"Oh no you don't." I take some flour and blow it in his face.

"So this is how we are going to play." He presses his body against mine so my back is to the counter and I'm stuck. He then begins to wipe the pumpkin mixture down my cheek and neck.

Minutes later, the kitchen is a mess and we're covered in flour, pumpkin pie and apple pie filling. We sit down on the floor of the kitchen laughing. "This place is a mess. So you get to clean this up and I'm going to shower." I start to get up but Jeremy pulls me back down and I fall on his lap.

"Not so fast." He kisses me and before I know it we're making out, once again. Things get heated fast as he lays me on the floor. Hands start to wander when the oven timer goes off.

"Saved by the bell," I exhale.

"Probably a good thing." He gives me a quick peck before pushing himself up and helping me up too. He pushes my hair out of my face, getting pie filling in it in the process. "I love you Emma and I'm so happy with you."

"Oh stop with all the mushy stuff. The ham needs the glaze and this kitchen needs to be cleaned." I wink and walk toward my bedroom.

"Fine, you go clean yourself up while I clean the kitchen. Maybe if I work fast I can join you." He winks.

"Don't you wish!" I get to the hallway leading to my room before turning around. "Don't forget the glaze on the ham and then put it back in the oven for an hour." I pause. "I love you, too." It feels so good to have that out there and to be able to love again. I didn't think it would happen after Logan but I am so glad it did.

Our parents show up as I take out the rolls from the oven where they were keeping warm. I scoop them into a basket and bring it out to the table. I hug my parents and my mom asks if I need help with anything. I shake my head. "I just need to get the last platter and we're good to eat."

We sit down and enjoy our time together. Jeremy did a good job glazing the ham. The vegetables are crisp and the rolls fill the air with a sweet aroma.

As happy as I am, I still feel like someone is missing. It's times like this when I miss Logan the most and know he's smiling down from heaven.

After we finish dinner, our parents make themselves comfortable in front of the fire. Jeremy grabs the pies while I get the plates and a knife. We dish out the pie and I sit back on the couch watching our families laugh.

I love times when we can all get together. Even only living a few hours away from home, between Jeremy's NFL career and my traveling to all away games and events, we don't get together much. The next time we'll all see each other is if the Titans make it to the Super Bowl. It's definitely looking like a possibility.

Once our parents leave, I sit back down on the couch with a glass of wine.

Jeremy puts his arm around me and I cuddle in next to him. "You were very quiet tonight." He kisses my temple.

I sigh. "Holidays are always hard, you know?"

He takes my wine and sets it on the coffee table. "I miss him too. It's especially hard that every time I look at you, I think of him and can't help but be glad he's gone."

"What?" I pull back.

"That came out wrong. I meant if he hadn't died, I would never be here with you. I always thought you were an amazing girl but I missed my chance because I was stubborn. Then you were my little brother's girl and off limits. Don't get me wrong, I miss my brother so much every day and wish he was still here, but then I wouldn't be able to do this." He kisses me lightly on the lips.

"I get it. I feel the same way sometimes and it makes me sick. He was my first love and I'll never forget him. I'd do anything to have him back but at the same time I'm glad we're here."

I'm glad that Jeremy and I can talk about his brother. He meant so much to both of us. We love reminiscing on the times we had with him, and Jeremy tells me plenty of stories from when they were younger. Some new ones and some I've heard hundreds of times that I can't wait to hear again.

"I would too but he'll always live on in our memories. Now enough of this sad talk." He hands me back my wine. "Come here. I want some cuddle time." I chuckle. "And if you tell any of the guys I said cuddle time, I'll deny it forever."

I take a sip and lean against him. He rests his head on mine as we gaze into the fire. It may have been a rough, sad road getting here but we're more than content. I'll never forget my first love but I know he'd want me to be happy and move forward. I've never been better since the accident.

Chapter Twenty-seven

"They're on their way. Ashley sounded in a good mood which means my brother must not be annoying her too much yet."

Tyler and Ashley are coming to our condo for New Year's. They both flew in around the same time and are currently driving from the airport in the car service Jeremy sent.

They're still casually dating long distance.

Tyler is living in New York City working as an entertainment lawyer for Andertainment.

Ashley is back home after finishing her master's and is still working on creating her own business helping to plan marriage proposals. She's still deciding where she wants to start it up.

I keep pushing for Nashville but I know she's leaning towards New York. She's hoping that my brother officially asks her to be his girlfriend and not this casual nonsense.

All the Christmas lights are still up around the city so the next few days we're going exploring and having some fun.

A few days later is New Year's Eve. We decide to stay in and watch the ball drop.

We also came up with a fun activity. We all had to come up with a dessert recipe that can be made in under thirty minutes with only three ingredients.

The instructions and the exact ingredients must be wrapped up in a bag and put in the middle of the table. If the ingredient needs to be refrigerated, then a picture of the item can be included while the actual ingredient stays in the fridge.

We all gather our recipe bags and set them in the middle of the table. We pick teams. Since Tyler and I both know how to bake, we're on opposite teams. We choose to go with couples.

We all pick numbers to decide who goes first. It's similar to white elephant, only we have ingredients that we have to bake with.

We aren't allowed to open the bag until everyone has picked.

Ashley's up first and she picks a sparkly silver bag.

"This is heavy," she exclaims. I laugh because I know what's in the bag. It's my recipe.

Next is me. I pick a very badly wrapped green bag.

Next is Tyler and he picks a bag with a picture of Santa on it.

Last is Jeremy and he takes the remaining bag that is red with green polka dots. I'm almost positive that it's Ashley's bag. She always wraps in the crazy polka dot and striped bags.

We open our bags and pull out the ingredients.

I have powdered sugar and a picture of both cream cheese and whipping cream with a note:

Cheesecake Dip. Tyler.

Jeremy pulls out cinnamon, sugar and a picture of puff pastry with a note:

You're making Cinnamon and Sugar Chips. Enjoy, Ashley.

I'm already thinking how great the cinnamon twists are going to taste dipped in the cheesecake dip.

Next Ashley unwraps her bag of chocolate chips, condensed milk, and vanilla extract with a note:

Make some delicious chocolate fudge. Bon appetit, Emma.

Lastly, Tyler opens his bag to find cocoa powder, marshmallows, and a picture of milk.

Every dessert needs hot chocolate. Jeremy.

"Let's get baking. We have thirty minutes. Ready, set, go!" I shout as we all race toward the kitchen. Thankfully the kitchen is big so we have plenty of room to work.

I take out the cream cheese and whipping cream from the fridge and grab a mixing bowl to whip up the cheesecake dip. It doesn't take long to make and I notice Jeremy has made a mess with the cinnamon and sugar.

"Do you need some help?" I ask him.

He shrugs. I reach over to open the puff pastry and we spread it out on the cutting board. Jeremy cuts them into triangles while I mix the cinnamon and sugar in a large ziploc bag.

We add the triangle dough pieces to the bag, shake it up covering the pieces, then add them to a cookie sheet to bake.

I glance at Tyler and Ashley to find them flirting with chocolate. Tyler smears some chocolate on her cheek and she giggles. It's actually really cute.

The timer for the chips goes off and we have two minutes to spare.

We all finish in time and spread the food out on the coffee table to enjoy.

We still have almost two hours before midnight so we put on the movie New Year's Eve because it is, after all, New Year's Eve.

We laugh, eat, and enjoy the company.

When it gets close to midnight, we switch over to the celebration in New York City, waiting for the ball to drop.

As the countdown from a minute starts, I can't help glancing over at Ashley and Tyler. They're staring at each other very intently. I can't help swooning. All I want is for them to be happy.

Jeremy gently grips my chin, turning my head towards him.

"Hi," he says.

"Hi," I reply.

"I love you."

"I love you too."

"I'm going to kiss you now."

All I can do is nod.

I faintly hear "3, 2, 1" in the background but Jeremy's already kissing me. I lean into the kiss as he deepens it.

It took a long time to get here but I really am happy.

We break apart and stare into each other's eyes for I have no idea how long. It could've been hours but in reality it was probably only a few minutes.

When I finally come out of my trance, I notice Ashley and Tyler are still making out.

I may want them to be happy but there's only so much I want to see and hear about.

I nudge Jeremy and we quickly get up grabbing the trays of food to clean off.

Ashley must hear because she breaks away from Tyler. She instantly blushes when she realizes they were caught.

"Sorry. We got carried away."

"Carry on. We were just going to bed. Don't do anything in my bed." I wink. "See you in the morning." Ashley laughs but nods.

Now that they're dating, sharing my room won't be awkward like it would've been last time when they weren't together yet. Jeremy was fine with them both staying because he actually gets to cuddle me all night. I told him no funny business though. He laughed but agreed.

I told Ashley the same thing, when they first got here, since it's my bed but a reminder never hurts. Plus she's dating my brother. That's just gross to think about even if I know they aren't at that point in their relationship. Ashley wants to wait and I think it's a great decision. It's what I'm doing too.

In the kitchen, Jeremy is washing the last tray before he grabs my hand and pulls me to his bedroom.

I already moved a few things to his bathroom for the nights they are here. I brush my teeth and get in bed cuddling into

Jeremy's side. He pulls me close and I lay my head on his chest. He's out pretty quickly.

As I listen to his slow breaths, I think about the past year.

So much has happened. I started my dream job, I earned several gold medals at the Olympics, and I fell in love. That last one is something I never thought would happen again.

I have the man next to me to thank for all those things.

My mind wanders to the next year. I get to continue my dream job. Jeremy has playoffs and potentially the Super Bowl if they make it.

I may not have any more gold medals in my future, but I still swim when I get the chance. It's nice to be able to just enjoy the water and not focus only on training. Maybe one day, I can look into coaching and sharing my love of swimming.

Falling in love with Jeremy is as easy as breathing and I wouldn't change a thing.

There's so much to look forward to and I can't wait for the next adventure.

Chapter Twenty-eight

If I have to pick up another dirty sock or jersey, I'm going to scream. Jeremy walks into the kitchen dressed in workout clothes. He grabs water and I throw the sock at him.

"Hey," he says. "Why're you throwing a dirty sock at me?"

"It's your sock. We have a laundry room for a reason. Use it." I turn back to the counter where I set down groceries for dinner after tripping over the clothes on the ground. "Logan never left dirty clothes everywhere," I say under my breath.

"What did you just say?" Jeremy asks.

I thought he'd already left the room.

"Nothing."

"No, tell me what you just said."

"I said Logan never left dirty clothes everywhere. In fact he actually did laundry."

"That's what I have a housekeeper for."

I snort. "Yeah, she only comes once a week. That doesn't mean you get to leave your clothes all over the floor for her to clean up."

"Why not?" he asks.

"The fact that you're even asking that question makes me realize how much of a spoiled rich boy you are." As soon as the words come out of my mouth, I regret them.

"I didn't mean that." I step toward him.

"You sure? Why don't you tell me how you really feel?"

"That's not how I feel. I'm just sick of picking up all of your clothes all the time. We have a laundry basket in the laundry room to put it in. Please just put it in there on your way to your room."

"Fine. Anything for Emma. Wouldn't want to disrupt your manic organization."

"Logan liked it."

"Why're you even with me then? Clearly Logan was Mr. Perfect and I can't even manage to put my socks away. Maybe you should go find someone more like him."

"Jer, that's not what I meant." I step towards him.

"Don't. I'm going for a run before I say something else I'll regret."

Before I can say another word, he grabs his wallet from the table by the door and leaves.

What just happened?

I watch the door for several minutes, hoping Jeremy comes back. When he doesn't, I distract myself with putting the groceries away and prepping dinner.

Two hours have passed and Jeremy still isn't back. I start to get worried so I text him. I hear the ding of his phone and realize he left it on the kitchen table.

What have I done? Did I just ruin something that was going well?

I slide down the kitchen cabinets. I pull my knees into my chest and the tears fall. I wasn't trying to compare Jeremy to his brother. It just came out. The hard part is, this isn't the first time I've made a comment like that. Normally it's in a joking manner. I feel awful.

What if Jeremy doesn't want to be with me anymore? What if he thinks I'm not worth it?

I'm so lost in my thoughts and tears, I don't feel him slide next to me.

It takes me a few minutes to calm down. Eventually I look over at him and see he's soaked.

"What happened to you?" I say wiping the tears away.

"Went for a run and got caught in the rain."

I nod not knowing what else to say. We sit in silence for several more minutes.

"I'm sorry..." we both say at the same time. I nod for him to continue.

"Emma, I shouldn't have left like I did. I just needed a minute to think before I said anything else."

"And I shouldn't have compared you to your brother."

He sighs. "It's not that. I just..." He rakes his hands through his hair. "I just hate myself for being with you."

What? Well... okay then. Guess I know how he really feels. I go to stand up.

Jeremy grabs my hand before I can. He links our fingers.

"This is coming out wrong. I hate that my brother is dead and I'm here with you. I feel so guilty all the time. Every time I get to kiss you, or make dinner with you, or cuddle on the couch. Emma, you have no idea how much I love you and how happy I am to be able to do all those things. To be able to call you mine. I have wanted to for so long even before my brother died and I hate myself for that. I never would have done anything and eventually I would've found someone else but now I'm here. I don't want to take any of it for granted. I want to spend all my time with you."

"Jer..." he shakes his head.

"Let me get all this out. I've been holding this in because I didn't want you to think I wasn't happy or that my fears were the same as yours. I want you to know that if I could do anything to bring my brother back or switch places with him, I would. I would Emma, in a heartbeat."

He buries his face in his hands. I pull him into me so his head rests on my lap. I run my fingers through his hair.

"Jer, I love you. I'm so happy to be with you too. As much as I wish Logan could come back, I wouldn't change our time for anything. That might sound horrible but I get where you're coming from. We can be guilty together even if we aren't actually guilty of anything. A wise man once told me, "It isn't being guilty, it's living your life.""

Jeremy snorts. He told me that before we got together when I was fighting my feelings for him after Logan died. I felt guilty falling for someone else, especially Jeremy.

"When I was still fighting what was between us, you told me that Logan would want me to live my life and not look back. So I'll tell you the same. Jer, look forward not back. Let's be thankful for these moments. As much as we both want your brother back, he's gone. We can reminisce in the past memories but live our lives in the present while looking toward the future. I think that's what Logan would want."

Jer stares up at me for a while. "How the tables have turned." He smiles up at me. "Think we can do it?"

"I do."

"Good, because I'm not letting you go." He leans up to capture my lips in his. It's a slow kiss that shows me how much he does love me. I try to pour my love back into my kiss. We kiss for a while until I feel Jeremy shaking.

I pull back and tell Jeremy he needs to go shower to warm up.

As he goes to leave, I stop him.

"I promise I'll do my best to stop comparing you to Logan, but please will you pick up your clothes?"

"I'll do my best to pick up my clothes. And I don't mind you comparing me to him. I get it. You loved him and I never want to take that away from you. Maybe just stop with the hiding if you don't like something I do. Just tell me and don't use Logan as a way to hide it."

"I can do that."

"Good. I love you Emma."

"I love you too."

After he leaves to take a shower, I set the oven to preheat.

As I wait, I take a deep breath. We've always fought like brother and sister but now it's different. We're in a romantic relationship and those little comments are taken more seriously.

Our relationship has always been a push and pull. Jeremy pushes me to be better while I pull back because of nerves. I push him even when he's being stubborn and he pulls back because he always knows how much I can handle.

Just like every relationship, we have things to work on. Jeremy is worth every fight and hard time to come. I finally let myself fall and there's no going back.

The timer dings letting me know the oven is preheated. I put the casserole I made in the oven.

Fifteen minutes later, it's done and Jeremy walks back into the kitchen.

He comes up behind me as I take the casserole out of the oven and set it on the stove. He slowly kisses up my neck.

"Jer, you are going to make me burn myself."

I turn around to face him and he captures my lips again. I lean into the kiss. After a minute, he pulls back.

"No more fighting."

"Deal."

"Now what're we eating? It smells delicious."

"Just a simple broccoli chicken curry casserole. We serve ourselves big helpings and sit at the table. We laugh and enjoy the meal.

No matter what comes our way, we'll get through it. We both have insecurities especially with the start of our relationship, but

I can't help thinking that Logan is smiling down at us, happy that we're happy and continuing to move forward.

Chapter Twenty-nine

"This place is crazy," I say looking around at the flashing lights and feel myself wanting to dance to the crazy 80s music playing. We find the table with a few guys from Jeremy's team. They all have their wives and girlfriends with them. Even Danielle and Connor are here. Danielle and I have hung out when our schedules allow us. She and Ashley hit it off too and I swear they're so similar sometimes.

Last time we hung out, I asked her what was going on with her and Connor. I have seen their lingering glances at each other. She says they're just friends. She did admit that they got really drunk one night and kissed but both decided to forget about it. It doesn't stop them from checking each other out all night or sitting super close in the booth like they are now.

We slide in next to them. I say hi to everyone and the waiter comes to take our drink and appetizer orders. Instead of getting separate entrees, we go for a ton of appetizers to share family style. When I say a ton, I mean it. They order everything from chips with salsa, guacamole, queso to lettuce wraps to fried mac and cheese, fried pickles, and buffalo wings.

When she brings them out to the table, I would think there are hundreds of people eating, not just the ten people surrounding the table. I guess when half the people at the table are professional football players, all the food makes sense. They are celebrating after their last win which put them in the Superbowl. It's a huge accomplishment! They have a few weeks before the big game so here we are.

One of the wives, Amy, asks the question I've been wondering myself. "Can someone explain to me how this place works?"

The restaurant has major Dave and Buster's vibes but instead of new games, it has all old school retro games. It has some of the new popular games as well. There's a whole virtual reality area, go kart track, and a rollerblade rink.

Oliver, one of the running backs, answers, "It's simple. We play all the games we want. Then at any point we reserve a round of "Take Your Shot". Instead of tokens for prizes, we get points. Those points turn into ammo for the game."

This sounds super intense. "Do all the games count towards points?" I ask.

Jeremy jumps in. "Yes," as if reading my mind. "Including go-karts and rollerblading." I must look confused because he continues. "You get points in the go-karts for what place you come in. The rollerblading has different contests like dance contests or obstacle courses they set up in the arena that you go through on your blades. We get bracelets that store the points."

This place keeps getting more and more insane. Insane in a good way. I can't wait to start getting points. I love that there are many different options to get points. That way everyone has a chance.

Later in the night we all meet back up at the "Take Your Shot" for our time slot. We decided to do one long epic game instead of shorter games throughout.

One of the workers comes out to greet us and explain the rules. "Hi everyone. My name is Tom and I'll be your guide. Welcome to "Take Your Shot". You'll be selecting a theme and we will randomly put you into two teams. Each team will fight till the end. Whoever has the most players left standing or less injured will win. You'll each need to scan your card with your points and enter your name. Once everyone has entered their name, you'll have the ability to transfer points to another player. Keep in mind, this is done before the teams are selected so you may just be transferring points to the enemy. Once the teams are selected, you'll not be able to transfer points. If you follow me through this door, we can get started and I can answer any questions."

We enter a room with several computer screens. We all add our names and a few point transfers are made. I kept all my points. Call me selfish but I want to survive and this has brought out my competitive nature. I killed it at Ms. PacMan earlier and built up a ton of points. I almost beat Jeremy at Go-Karts too. I really hope we're on separate teams so I can get back at him.

Next, we select our theme. They have a ton of great ones from a war theme, to aliens vs. predators, even a Disney villain vs. hero theme. We chose zombies vs. survivors because what else would we choose?

Tom hits a button and all of our names appear on the screen either in the left or right based on the team we're on. I'm a Zombie! I'm so excited. Jeremy is a survivor along with a mix of players from his team and significant others. I have Danielle, Connor, Oliver, and Amy on my team. Oliver's girlfriend and Amy's husband are survivors. Most of the couples were split which will make it that much crazier.

I look over at Jeremy and he winks. I stick my tongue out. This is going to be fun. He's going down.

Next to him, one of his teammates is telling Oliver's girlfriend to take off her six inch heels or she's going to get caught. She complains that she doesn't have other shoes and doesn't want to catch a foot fungus. I have to stop myself from rolling my eyes. I catch Jeremy's eyes again and he hides a laugh.

Tom overhears and says they have optional boots if you don't have the right footwear. They're thoroughly cleaned in between games.

She finally gives in and agrees to wear the boots. There's a collective sigh on their team when she agrees.

"Before we enter the changing rooms, a few more things to note. Each team will enter rooms on opposite sides. Once inside you'll put on the jumpsuits and grab your guns. You'll touch your point bracelets to the top of the gun to activate it. Your name and points will appear on the screen. These points are your ammo. Once you're out of points, you're out of ammo.

This does not mean you're out of the game. You can no longer shoot people but they can still shoot you. The jumpsuits are specially designed so you can see exactly where you've been hit, just like in paintball where the paint would've exploded, only we use laser technology so all the paintball fun but without the pain. The last thing is, there are puzzles throughout that you can play to earn back some points but these are in very dangerous areas. They are filled with traps and may alert the other team to exactly where you are. Some puzzles are easy and some are harder. Does anyone have any questions?"

Danielle asks, "Are the games the only way to get points back?"

"Yes. There are tons of them in there. If one is too hard, try another. If you get hit in the head or the chest, you'll automatically die. However, you don't die permanently. You'll be required to find a checkpoint to come back to life. Once you enter through the checkpoint, you'll be back in the game. Each time you die, you lose five points. That may not sound like a lot but it adds up quickly if you keep dying. There are five checkpoints set up throughout the maze, in the corners, and one in the very middle. Keep in mind that when trying to find a checkpoint, you can still be shot and killed again. If you're killed again before reaching a checkpoint, you'll have to find two separate checkpoints before you're considered alive again."

"How will we know when we get hit?" asks Connor.

"Great question, and that brings me to the last point. When you're hit, that spot will light up purple for zombies and red for survivors. It'll stay lit, but it's not very bright so it doesn't alert anyone else. It'll vibrate in that spot and your gun that's synced to your suit will flash 'hit'. After ten hits, you die and will need to find a checkpoint. In the case that it's a kill shot, it will vibrate three times and your gun will say 'died, find checkpoint'. You'll not be able to shoot anyone until you find that checkpoint. When you hit the opposite team, your gun will say 'enemy hit' or 'enemy kill'."

"Any other questions?"

We shake our heads. "Very well. If the survivors could move to the doors on my left and the zombies to the doors on my right.

We enter the room to the right. Along the wall is a row of black suits in all different sizes. I find one that looks like my size and put it on. They're made of a material similar to spandex but thicker and not as tight. There's a head piece that protect your head and forehead.

On the other side of the room are the laser guns. They definitely look more like paintball guns though. He helps us sync our suits and we tap our point bracelets to the guns.

The clock over the entrance to the maze starts counting down from sixty seconds. We take our places.

When the clock hits zero, the doors open and we enter.

Everything is super dark. As I turn a corner, I notice what looks to be a run-down city, almost like a zombie apocalypse. I run down another path and see bright neon signs blinking with the words checkpoint on top.

Good to know where one of them is. In the middle of the room I see what looks to be a giant building of some sort. I head for it. It would be the perfect place to snipe people as they run by.

Just as I get to the door at the bottom, I feel a shiver run up my spine. Not a bad shiver but a good shiver that feels like lava. I know Jeremy is nearby. I quickly open the door and go inside. The second I enter the room, Jeremy is in front of me.

"You make a very cute zombie. If this were real life, I'd say turn me and we could live together forever but since it's not I'll have to kill you. Love you!" He shoots me in the chest and I feel a series of vibrations. Before I can say a word, he takes off running.

I'm so going to get him back. I head up the winding stairs to the top where I assume a checkpoint is. This is the middle of the maze so there should be a checkpoint somewhere.

At the top, there's a large room with desks and cubicles at each window. It looks like an office. I see on the other side a sign blinking checkpoint above a door. I sneak over to the door and peer in. I don't see anyone inside so I quickly run through and my gun comes back to life. I take a look around and see what looks to be the boss office with a giant desk in front of a large window. There's a small couch off to the side and a bookcase opposite with tons of fake books.

They really went crazy with the different decor for this maze. I leave knowing I've wasted enough time already. I run to a room next door where I find a cubicle to hide in. I have the perfect position for anyone that comes up to this checkpoint as well as anyone that runs past down below.

At that moment I see a survivor run past and I shoot, hitting him in the leg. Another minute later, I see Jeremy creep by and I aim for his head. I fire and a red light appears on the back of his head.

Bullseye!

He looks up towards my window and I immediately crouch down. When I look back down, he's disappeared. I hear someone running up the stairs. I make sure I'm hidden but I have a slight view of the checkpoint across the room, enough to see Jeremy run through the checkpoint office doors. He comes out and does a quick sweep of the cubicles. He doesn't see me and I don't want to give up my spot so I stay quiet. Soon, he leaves back down the stairs.

Time passes and I get some great shots in. Anytime one of the survivors comes up to this checkpoint, I stay quiet and hidden. Eventually I get bored of my spot and venture out. I see a giant tree over in the other corner. I head in that direction and find some of my team planning an ambush. I guess the survivors have been hiding in the opposite corner doing something similar to what I was doing in the office building.

We make a plan and all spread out in different paths to get to the opposite corner where there are several houses in a row.

As I get closer, I see several guns pointed my way and they all shoot. A few hit me but none hit my head or chest. I take cover behind one of the houses.

I see Amy ahead of me and together we enter the house and shoot at whoever is inside. Amy's husband and two other survivors are inside. We hit them a few times. Amy manages to kill her husband and as he runs past, she blows him a kiss.

I hear him whisper, "Be ready for a punishment later." He winks and disappears through the door.

Amy blushes. Just as we turn our guns back to the others, our guns start blinking and our suits start vibrating. That must mean the end of the game. I look at my gun and it says 'return home'.

We head back to the locker rooms and remove our suits, putting away our guns. We throw our headpieces and suits into a big laundry bin. Good to know they wash those in-between games.

Back in the lobby area, we wait for everyone to finish changing. Jeremy comes over to me. "Was that you that killed me from the office building?"

I smirk. "Maybe."

"I knew it! You were the only one that killed me."

"Well you're the only one that killed me."

"We're a perfect match." He kisses me. Before it turns into some crazy show, Tom enters the room.

"Alright everyone, we have the results."

"The winners were the zombies but only by one point. This is the closest game we've ever had. Congrats everyone and I hope you'll come back soon. On your way out you can each collect a sheet that shows how you performed individually, detailing who you hit or killed and who shot or killed you. See you next time."

"This was so fun!" I exclaim.

"It was. Now let's go see who won that bet," Jeremy says.

"My team won."

"But it has to be you specifically."

We grab our sheets and of course, he won. We both only died once at the hands of each other but I got hit nine times whereas Jeremy only got hit three times.

"How did you only get hit three times?"

"I'm just that good."

"Fine, you can pick the next movie night but I still think I should get a shortened foot massage since my team did win overall."

"Deal, but only five minutes a foot. I think I'm in the mood for a horror movie."

"No. Please, anything else," I beg. He winks at me.

He's lucky he doesn't have practice tomorrow because he won't have any feeling in his hand by the time the movie's over.

Did I mention I get really scared?

Chapter Thirty

We stop at the light on our way home. It was nice to go out and have some fun, celebrating the win that puts them into the Super Bowl.

The light turns green and Jeremy hits the gas. He reaches over to grasp my hand, kissing my fingers.

"Tonight was fun," I say. "Amy is hilarious."

"Well she'd have to be to keep up with Thomas."

Thomas is one of the linebackers on the team. He's a huge guy and Amy's so tiny. They've been married for a year and are adorable together. Their banter is next level and I couldn't stop laughing.

I lean back in my seat and squeeze Jeremy's hand. I look over at him scanning his features. He's been my rock these past couple of years. We've been dating for several months now.

At first I was scared more because of how people might look at me dating him when in reality no one cares. They're so supportive and never once thought it was happening when I was with Logan.

Logan made everything easy. He never pushed me more than I could handle. He was the calm in my storm. He was my best friend and my true love. He will always hold my heart, but Jeremy is the fire that burns in my heart and my soulmate. He was there from the beginning, being the friend I needed, and when the time came for more, he pushed me when he knew I was ready. He helped me move forward after the accident; pushing me to finish school, to get in the pool, and to win another gold medal.

I will never forget Logan and the love we shared, but Jeremy is my future. I have to remember that.

We stop at another red light. I continue to take in his long jawline, the angle of his nose and his messy brown hair from constantly running his fingers through it.

The light turns green and he hits the gas. A flash of light shines on us as a car comes barreling from the left, clearly in a hurry and running the red light.

It's deja vu all over again. This can't be happening.

I close my eyes and brace for the impact.

Jeremy must slam the brakes because I feel the car lurch forward. Instead of stopping, the car slides.

We must have hit ice.

I open my eyes and see we are in fact sliding through the intersection towards a giant parking lot. Thankfully!

Jeremy keeps the steering wheel in the same direction.

I know if you turn your steering wheel in the opposite direction, it could cause you to spin.

We hit a curb forcing the car to stop. Jeremy immediately unbuckles my seatbelt and pulls me onto his lap. He wraps his arms around me tight and I bury my head into his shoulder.

I hadn't realized I'd been shaking or crying. The instant his arms come around me, I feel safe. The tears continue but now they're more of relief tears than tears of fear.

"Emma, I got you. We're safe and I promised I wouldn't leave you. I'm sticking to that promise. Now look at me."

I lift my head. He searches my eyes looking for I'm sure something that tells him I'm not about to go into a panic attack.

"I'm okay," I say, more trying to reassure myself than him.

He rests his forehead against mine. "I'm so sorry. I should have seen that car not slowing down after the light turned red."

"It's okay. We're safe. No injuries. Even the car seems to be in one piece."

Jeremy kisses me, slowly pouring every emotion into it. Relief that we're okay. Reassurance that he isn't going anywhere. Love because that's what this is.

"Are you okay to sit back in your seat and we drive home?"

"Yes." We're still about fifteen minutes away and the only other alternative is walking. That's not happening.

The snow is coming down hard now. I have this pit in my stomach anytime I'm in the car and there's ice or snow. I have a good reason especially after what could've happened tonight. Thankfully, Tennessee doesn't get a crazy amount of snow. It's enough to enjoy but not too much that I have to worry about driving in it every day for months on end. I love it here too much to move, so I'll deal with the small amount of snow.

Jeremy carefully pulls out of the parking lot. I've never been happier than when we finally pull into our parking spot in the garage at the condo.

We get out and take the elevator up to the condo. This night was a blast, but I'm ready for it to be over. I want to climb into bed and fall asleep.

Jeremy must sense this because he kisses me goodnight before giving me a push towards my room.

I get ready for bed and fall into bed. I close my eyes, hoping tomorrow is a better day.

I'm driving down the road with Jeremy next to me. The snow is lightly falling, and all I can think is how I can't wait for winter to be over. We come to a light and I look over at Jeremy. He smiles at me. He takes my right hand and intertwines our fingers.

The light turns green and I hit the gas. Lights flash from the side then I feel the impact. A sense of dread fills my stomach. I look over at Jeremy but find Logan sitting there covered in blood and blank eyes.

I blink trying to stop the images. I glance back at Logan to find Jeremy with some sort of metal piercing his side. I can see his chest moving up and down so I know he's still alive.

Where did that metal come from?

I look out the front windshield and find my answer. The truck that hit us has a ton of metal rods on the roof rack on his car. It hit us in the front right corner and the windshield shattered. One must have come loose and flown through piercing him.

"Jeremy. Jeremy wake up." I shake him, careful not to jostle him too much. He slowly comes around.

"What happened?" He says groggily.

"We were in an accident." He goes to move before realizing he has a metal rod in his stomach.

He reaches for my hand. "We'll be okay. I won't leave you." He gives me what I'm sure he hopes is reassuring but I see right through him. He's nervous. I can see how much blood he has lost.

"I can't reach my phone." I also can't feel my legs but I don't mention that right now.

I hear an engine start and notice the truck that hit us move.

Wait, where are they going?

Just as I'm about to say something another metal rod comes flying through the windshield and pierces Jeremy right in the chest. His hand in mine goes slack.

I let out a scream. This can't be happening again. I close my eyes. When I open them again I'm in the hospital surrounded by my family and Jeremy's.

I open my mouth to say something but it's hard to talk. "Jer..?" I manage to get out.

My mom shakes her head. No! This can't be happening. Not again.

She takes my hand in hers.

"Emma, we need to talk about something else."

My dad jumps in. "I think we should wait."

"What is it?" I need to know whatever it is.

"Your legs got crushed in the accident. You damaged the nerves so badly that you won't ever be able to walk again."

First Logan. Then Jeremy. Now me. I wish I was dead. I try to take a breath but I can't get oxygen to my lungs. I squeeze my eyes shut. This has to be a dream. I let out a scream.

"Emma. Emma wake up." That sounds like Jeremy. Wait, I thought he was dead.

"Emma." I feel pressure on my shoulders. I open my eyes and only see pitch black. I blink a few times and then see Jeremy above me.

"Emma, are you okay?" He looks extremely worried.

"What happened? I thought you were dead?"

"Dead? You had a nightmare. I heard you screaming and came in here to see what was wrong. Do you remember what happened?"

"We were in an accident and you were pierced by a metal rod twice. The second one killed you. There was so much blood and then I was in the hospital and I was told you died and I would never walk again," I blurt out in a frantic flurry of words.

"Come here." He pulls back the cover, takes my hand, and helps me stand. I take a few steps. "See? You can walk."

I nod.

I know it was a dream and it was probably caused after we slid on the ice and almost crashed last night.

After the accident with Logan, I had trouble sleeping for months. Jeremy helped me through the nightmares along with Ashley. I haven't had one in years though.

"Now get back in bed. I'm going to get you some tea."

I get back under the covers but refuse to close my eyes. I don't want to have another nightmare.

Jeremy comes back a few minutes later with a mug. He slides under the covers with me and wraps his arm around me. He hands me the mug and I cuddle into his side.

I sip on my tea. Chamomile with a little bit of honey.

"From now on, I'm sleeping in here until you fall asleep." I go to argue but he puts a finger over my mouth.

"We'll be getting married soon and I want to keep the nightmares at bay. You need to know I'm not going anywhere. Now drink your tea and go back to sleep. I won't be leaving you."

I sip at my tea some more. Married? I never really thought about it. Sure I was married to Logan, but I never thought it was in the cards for me again.

Until Jeremy...that is. Even then, I thought it'd be a long way off.

"We're getting married? Did I miss the proposal?"

Jeremy chuckles. "No, but I knew from the moment you agreed to go out with me that I'd ask. Even before that, but I didn't want to scare you away when I had just gotten you. Don't worry, you'll know when I propose."

I take another sip so I don't have to respond. I could see myself marrying Jeremy. We've known each other for a long time now and he's my rock. I love him with all my heart. Logan may have had my heart first and still have a piece of it, but Jeremy is the one that keeps my heart beating.

Jeremy knows that though. I think a part of Logan will always be missing from his brother too.

I finish my tea and he takes it from me, setting it on the bedside table. I lay my head on his chest and take a few breaths. I hear his heart beating.

He's alive.

It was just a dream.

My eyes close and I fall asleep to the steady beat of his heart keeping the nightmares away.

Chapter Thirty-one

"I still can't believe Jeremy made it to the Super Bowl." I give her a look. "Okay. I can believe it but it's just so cool," Ashley says.

"I'm so excited to be on the sidelines," I say.

"I'm excited for NSYNC to perform. Do you think we'll get to meet them?"

"Probably not. I don't think I'll even get to watch them. I'll most likely be in the locker room helping with any injuries."

"Boo. I'll have to talk to Jer."

I glance at all the colors. I normally get a french manicure or simple color but maybe this time I'll get something bolder. I grab a red and a navy, both colors for the Tennessee Titans.

Since I've been dating Jeremy, I have been getting bolder but I don't think I am ready for red nail polish. I set it back on the shelf. Ashley quickly swipes the navy from my hands and switches it with the red I was just holding.

"Do it." I must look skeptical because she continues. "You're planning on wearing your red coat, right?" I nod. "Then it'll match great."

"Fine." I take the red and sit back down in the seat.

I was lucky to get the day off work to have a girls day with Ashley. I'm pretty sure Jeremy had something to do with it. So while he's off sweating on the field, I'm here relaxing and getting pampered. Have I mentioned I love him?

A few minutes later, our names are called.

We sit down side by side in the chairs and soak our feet in the hot water.

"Pedicures are the best." I relax back into the seat after selecting my massage cycle.

Ashley does the same thing. "They are."

We're quiet for a few minutes before Ashley blurts out, "do you think you and Jer will get married?"

I practically choke on the cucumber water I just took a sip of.

"What? We haven't even been dating that long."

"I know I know, but if he were to ask. Would you say yes?"

"Of course, but I doubt he's planning that anytime soon."

"Okay." She relaxes back in the chair.

"Where did that come from?" I ask.

"Umm...I was just thinking of Tyler and me. He's been acting weird."

"It's probably his job. He's been working non-stop."

"Yeah... I don't know what to do. I love where I'm at and my small business I've created. I've thought about moving up there to expand it and where better than New York City but--"

"But you want him to ask you to move up there?" I say, finishing her sentence.

"Yeah." She sighs.

"Just give him time."

We're quiet after that as our feet are pampered. I know they'll work it out or at least I really hope they do. My brother is stubborn and doesn't always show what he's feeling. Ashley wears her heart on her sleeve but she's very good at hiding her emotions when she wants to. I'm scared of what it'll do to her if they don't work out.

The nail tech starts on the nail polish and with the first swipe of red, I think of the accident. I remind myself to breathe. I'm here now.

My phone dings alerting me of a text. I take one more deep breath and pick up my phone.

Jeremy: *Just thinking about you. I hope you're having an awesome time with Ashley! I love you <3*

Somehow Jeremy always seems to know what to say. I really would marry him tomorrow if he asked. Like I told Ash, we've only been dating a short time but I love him. There won't be anyone else. I know that in my heart. Logan was my best friend and the love of my life. Jeremy is my soulmate. I know it deep within me. It's why I struggled so much in the beginning coming to terms with my feelings for Jeremy.

I feel pressure on my hand and look down to see Ashley squeezing it.

"You okay?"

"Yeah. The red freaked me out for a second but then Jer texted me and pulled me out of it. I don't know how he always knows when I need a text from him."

"He's your soulmate, babe. You're connected."

My toes are finished and I walk to the table to get my hands done.

Ashley follows and sits at the table next to me. We get our nails done and head to the Mexican restaurant next door.

We order margaritas because every girls day needs them. We settle on splitting a quesadilla and super nachos which are pretty much nachos with everything on them.

"Emma?"

"Yeah?"

"Do you think your brother is cheating on me in New York?"

I pause before answering. "Honestly, no. He's been so busy with work that I don't think he's doing much socializing, unless it's with coworkers or clients."

"I thought so. I hoped being with me would prevent him too."

"Ash, that's a given. He's so lucky to be with you even if you'll refuse to put a label on it. You're already exclusive and he wouldn't jeopardize that."

"Whenever we're together in person, he's the perfect gentleman, but then when we're doing the long distance thing, I feel like we're complete strangers. I don't want to text him all the time and be the clingy girlfriend but when he cancels our weekly calls more often than not, it's hard."

"I'm sorry Ash. It's not an excuse but like I said work keeps him busy. We had lunch when he was down here last time and he's loving his job, but he's been throwing all his time into it."

"I know and that's why I've been trying not to bug him, but I like him so much and I just want to know how he's doing. I don't know how much longer I can keep doing this long distance with no official labels. At least if we had a label, it would help me feel more confident that he was in this with me. Right now, I feel like he could do anything and get away with it and there's nothing I can do."

"Just talk to him. I know how much he loves you. He may not have said those words but I have known you both my entire life. Next time he comes down, talk to him and tell him what you're worried about. He might be stubborn, but I know he has a heart."

"I'm just scared of what he might say."

"Don't be. If you don't get the answer you want, then he isn't the guy for you and I'll send Jer and some of his buddies on him."

"Don't hurt him," Ashley says jokingly.

"Of course not. They can just rough him up a bit." I wink. "I'd never hurt my brother but I will if he breaks my best friend's heart."

Ashley sighs. "I hate relationships. Or in this case, it's a non-relationship or a relationship with no title. Or I don't know. Whatever we have sucks."

"Relationships are confusing."

"You have the perfect relationship. First Logan, who was perfect for you! He was the perfect best friend who would go to the ends of the Earth to give you the world. Now Jeremy, who again is perfect for you. Yet, with how many similarities you'll have, you couldn't be more different. He pushes you to do more than you're capable of and doesn't let you give up yet knows when enough is enough."

"I know. They're both so different but fill a piece of my heart. There are days when I think back to the accident and imagine Logan living. Ash, I don't think we would have made it, if he lived."

"Why?" she asks although she seems to already know what I'm about to say.

"Nothing to do with Jeremy. We never would've gotten together if Logan was still alive." Ashley nods. "As horrible as it sounds, I don't think Logan could've gotten me out of the depression and loneliness I was in. No, I wouldn't have lost him but I would've lost our baby and had my same injuries. Even though I know now, back then I blamed myself for killing them both. That would've been no different. Logan had a heart of gold and he would have gone along with anything I asked. 'I don't want to do therapy today.' 'Okay, we can try tomorrow.' Or cue a baby crying, 'I can't be here with a baby crying.' 'Let's go home and we'll go to the store another day.' Jeremy pushed me more even when I wanted to give up. I love Logan and miss him every day, but I don't think he would have been strong enough to push me through it. Does that make me a horrible person?"

Ashley reaches across the table and squeezes my hand. "You couldn't be farther from a horrible person. I get what you're saying. Logan was kind and all he wanted to do was make you happy but I think he could've brought you out. It would've just been in a different way and I think it would've had its challenges too. Don't ever think that just because you have doubts about the accident, that you're selfish for continuing your life. Logan would want you to continue living your life, and he's probably looking down thankful that his brother was there to bring you back to life."

"We're both a mess. Want to run away with me and forget these boys?"

"Always! First, we need to finish these margaritas and nachos, then we're going to the stadium to catch the end of practice. You need to put a smile back on your face and I know a certain someone that might just do that."

As she says that, a small smile works its way onto my face.

"There it is."

Chapter Thirty-two

February is chilly and I can't wait to head south where it'll be at least a little warmer.

We're headed to New Orleans for the Super Bowl. NSYNC is playing in the halftime show and I'm freaking out. I loved them when I was little, so to see them perform is going to be a dream come true. It does help that my boyfriend also happens to be the starting quarterback in the Super Bowl.

Our parents are meeting us there on Saturday and they're even flying in Ashley and Tyler. Ty is working for Andertainment in New York City. I keep trying to persuade him to transfer to the Nashville office. After all, I have some pull with the CEO who happens to be Jeremy's dad. He loves it in the city though. Maybe one day, I'll wear him down or a certain best friend of mine will. Either way, I'm so proud of him.

Ashley, thankfully, is a lot closer in Chattanooga where she's using both her History and English degrees to create a sort of "help plan the perfect engagement" firm. It's actually pretty interesting. I've been trying to persuade her to move up to Nashville too but she seems to have her eye on New York. I think her eye is more on a certain someone rather than the actual city of dreams. They're still doing the exclusive, no titles, long distance thing which I tried to get Ashley to talk to him about at our girl's day. Maybe one day.

Sunday morning, I wake up to a knock on my door. I throw on a robe and open the door to find Jeremy holding a tray with breakfast and a bouquet of roses. I put my hand on my hip. "Shouldn't I be bringing you breakfast? It is after all your big day."

"You know that's right. Here, take this." He hands me the tray. "I'll be in my room. Just come on down."

I watch as he walks down the hall. "Jer… Jeremy…" He keeps walking. "Jeremy Cooper Anderson get your sexy butt back here right now."

He looks over his shoulder giving me his signature Anderson smirk. He runs back and grabs the tray for me. He sets it on the table and before I even know what's happening he has scooped me up. He carries me over to the bed and drops me. He crawls on top of me. "So I have a sexy butt huh?"

"Maybe." I giggle. He has a way of always surprising me.

He leans down to kiss me and I flip him over on his back. "Well this morning is turning out to be better than I planned."

"Oh don't get your hopes up. I just needed a way to get the bacon first." I hop off of him and grab a piece of turkey bacon.

Jeremy takes a bite of the piece I just picked up. "Yum."

"Hey!" I push him back on the bed.

We sit down and enjoy our egg white omelets and fresh squeezed grapefruit juice. I try to eat healthy with Jeremy because of his strict diet, plus it seems weird not to after training for the Olympics for so long. It's nice to let loose sometimes and eat whatever I want since I couldn't for the longest time.

As Jeremy finishes, I admire the bouquet of flowers and inhale the wonderful scent. I notice one of them looks almost waxy. I pick it out of the rest. "Hey Jer, why's this flower fake?"

I see him smiling. "Just a reminder about how much I love you. I know it's cheesy but I'll love you till the last flower dies."

"You're right that is cheesy, but I love cheesy and I love you." I give him a quick peck. "Guess I better keep these in a safe place."

Our time is soon up because he has to meet the team for some last minute meetings and strategy sessions. He kisses me and heads for the door. He leaves but then sticks his head back in the room. "I still don't see why we have separate rooms?"

"Because you need sleep before the big game and I don't want you staying up super late worrying about me and my nightmares." I haven't had any since that one over a month ago but he insists on making sure I'm okay. I just think he wants to cuddle every night which I'm not complaining about.

"I'll change your mind soon enough." He winks. "I'll see you at warm ups."

I clean up the breakfast and get ready for the game. In honor of the Titans playing today, I wear my red peacoat to keep me warm. Underneath, I have my black leather boots, black skinny jeans, and a navy long sleeve Titans shirt. I put my hair half up and half down, completing the look with a navy headband. I have to show off my team spirit and support for my boyfriend.

When Ashley and I had gotten a mani/pedi earlier this week, she reminded me that I needed to look my best because cameras would be everywhere since it was after all the Super Bowl. I had shaken my head at her because I don't care about that stuff, but know I should at least try to look decent.

Once I'm ready, I head downstairs to meet with the rest of the physical therapy team before we walk over to the stadium.

As we walk into the stadium, I'm amazed. I've always watched the Super Bowl on the TV and never attended in person but it's like nothing I've ever experienced. The crowds are filled with an excited energy and it makes me pumped.

We make our way onto the field where the team is already warming up. I make sure everyone's good to go. I'm going to be on the sidelines the whole game.

About an hour before the game, Jer and I head over to our families who've taken their seats at the 50-yard line. They wish us luck, mainly Jeremy. Ashley is talking to Ty and they look very close. They stop talking as soon as I walk over. "So you took my advice and made sure you looked hot for the game, huh?"

"Yeah, yeah." I look over at Jeremy who motions to go back down to the team. "I'll see you after the game when we celebrate the Titans win."

"Yes we'll have a lot to celebrate." Ashley winks at Jeremy.

"Right. Well, I'll see you then." I have no idea why she's winking at Jeremy but I don't dwell on it. They're always joking around which makes me happy. I wave to my parents.

Soon the guys are headed into the locker room before they're announced. The Titans kick off to Indianapolis and the game begins.

Football has always been my favorite sport behind swimming. I don't get to watch the game as much as I want but every now and then I get a glimpse of what's happening on the field.

As the offense and defense each run off the field throughout the game, my team and I are checking the players. We make sure they're ready to get back on the field. We try to prevent any cramping and tend to minor injuries that always happen.

There are a few minutes left in the half and the offense is about to go back on.

I'm rubbing Jeremy's shoulder working through the muscles. "Find Ashley at halftime." I'm confused because normally we're super busy during the half wrapping up ankles, wrists, etc... "You'll be in the crowd watching the halftime show." I glance at my PT team. "I already checked and you're covered." He gives me a quick kiss and runs back onto the field.

By the end of the half, we're up 17-10. The teams are quickly ushered into the locker rooms and Jeremy blows me a kiss. I blow him one back before making my way over to Ashley.

People are setting up the stage for the halftime show. It's a weird shape and I can't tell what it is from here.

Ashley, Ty, and I make our way to the stage. As I get closer, I see it's in the shape of an infinity symbol with a heart in the middle. This will be interesting to see with the dancing. It seems like they'll have to really pay attention to where they're going.

Ashley shows them some sort of pass and they let us into the front section. I look up at the stage, psyched that I'll be this close to NSYNC.

When NSYNC comes on the stage, Ashley and I revert into our old high school fangirl selves. I can see out of the corner of my eye, Tyler rolling his eyes at us.

They play all the classics from "Bye, Bye, Bye" to "Tearin' Up My Heart"." Throughout the songs, the lights flash onto the stage making it look like the infinity sign is moving around the heart in the middle.

Before they play their last song, they announce one lucky girl will be brought onstage. A security guard comes over to me. "Come with me ma'am".

I look at him surprised. "Are you talking to me?" He nods. My first thought is 'what did I do' and then I feel Ashley give me a little shove.

Still confused, I follow him as he leads me onto the stage. They place a chair in the center of the heart and tell me to sit down. Justin Timberlake asks me my name. "Emma." I'm so freaked out because one Justin Timberlake just asked my name and two, why in the world was I brought up here?

Why did they single me out in the first place?

There are plenty of girls in the audience with giant signs and crazy glitter shirts with messages for NSYNC. I've gotten better with being in front of crowds but this is intense. At least I don't have to speak.

"Well Emma, we have a special treat for you tonight." They begin singing "I Promise You".

"Oh, oh

When the visions around you

Bring tears to your eyes"

I love this song and sing along to the chorus. The band takes turns singing to me. They keep me so involved, I almost forget I'm on a stage in front of thousands of people and on live TV. I can't believe this is actually happening.

As they sing the next verse, I can't help but think how the lyrics pertain to my relationship with Jeremy after Logan died.

"I've loved you forever

In lifetimes before

And I promise you never

Will you hurt anymore

I give you my word

I give you my heart

This is a battle we've won

And with this vow

Forever has now begun"

The song goes on and I look out to see Ashley and Ty. They give me a thumbs up and I smile. Before the next chorus, the band continues singing but back up to the side. As the chorus begins, they part and Jeremy walks through the center with a single white rose. He's still in his uniform and his hair is tousled from playing. I can see dirt smudged on his cheek.

"And I will take you in my arms (I will take you in my arms)
And hold you right where you belong (right where you belong)
Til' the day my life is through
This I promise you, babe"

He walks over to me and takes my hand, urging me to stand up.

"Just close your eyes each loving day (each loving day)
And know this feeling won't go away (no)"

He hands me the rose and I realize it's the fake one from this morning.

"Every word I say is true
This I promise you"

He gets down on one knee before pulling out a ring box and opens it. My hands fly to my mouth as I gasp.

"Every word I say is true
This I promise you"

I hear him whisper, "Will you marry me?" I nod. He jumps up, puts the ring on my finger, and spins me around kissing me.

"Ooh, I promise you"

As the song finishes, I look at him amazed at how he pulled this off. He plays his heart out on the field, managed to plan this, and just being the great guy he is. I never thought I'd move on after his brother died but as the song says, *"And I promise you never, Will you hurt anymore, I give you my word, I give you my heart, This is a battle we've won, And with this vow, Forever has now begun"*.

We truly have been through a long journey but we made it through and every day hurts less. I'm lucky to have an incredible guy standing in front of me who I can now call mine forever.

Chapter Thirty-three

3 months later

A tear falls down my cheek as I take in my appearance in the mirror. I'm in a white dress with a sweetheart neckline and a skirt that flows like water.

"No crying or you're going to smudge your makeup," Ashley warns me as she appears in the mirror next to me.

"Okay," I say as I wipe the tear from my cheek. Today is bittersweet. Don't get me wrong, I'm so excited for what the day holds but I never thought I would be here again. When I married Logan, it was the best day of my life. Now I'm getting married again–to his brother who I love just as much. I want it to be the best day of my life but that thought makes me sad.

Ashley turns my head towards her. "It's okay to think of him but don't let him take over today. Today is about moving forward toward the future. Your groom has not stopped smiling today. He told me to give you this."

She hands me a rectangular box. I take it from her. "How would you know how smiley he's been?"

"I...I...I was in there talking to him."

"Oh really? You were talking to Jeremy? My Jeremy?"

"Yep," her voice squeaks out at the end.

"Sure you were."

"Fine, I was talking to your brother. We haven't seen each other since the Super Bowl."

I laugh because they are still as obsessed as ever but are both too stubborn to be exclusive.

I look down to the jewelry box she handed me. I slowly open it and gasp. Inside is a star shaped charm at the end of a silver chain. In the middle of the star is a white pearl that sparkles in the light.

"Flip it over," Ashley says.

On the back is an inscription, "Love Moves Forward".

Another tear appears in the corner of my eye.

"What did I say about crying?"

"I can't help it." I half laugh and sniffle. "This necklace…"

"I know."

To anyone else this might be a star shaped necklace with a saying on the back. To me it's my past, present, and future.

Logan is in my past, but he will always be with me. It's evident every time I look at the night sky and see his star shining down on me.

The baby we lost is represented by the pearl in the middle. I know our baby is in Logan's arms watching over me.

The inscription on the back is my present and future colliding. Logan once told Jeremy to look after me if anything ever happened to him. These past few years he has done nothing less. I know Logan wants me to love again. It's taken a long time to get here but I am and I couldn't be more excited to move forward.

"Let's put it on." Ashley's voice breaks through my thoughts. She takes the necklace from my hands and clasps it around my neck.

"It's beautiful," my mom says from behind me. I hadn't noticed her or Mrs. Anderson enter the room. I had asked them all to give me a few minutes.

She comes forward, wiping my tear-stained cheek. Thanks to the waterproof makeup, you can't even tell but she does. She is after all my mother.

I pull her into a hug. As we pull apart, she takes a bracelet from her purse. "You have the necklace as your new, but this is for your borrowed." I look down to see a silver charm bracelet. It's the bracelet my dad got her on one of their anniversaries in college. It shows their relationship. I've always admired it and love that I get to wear a piece of their love on my wrist.

Victoria steps forward and hands me a silver barrette lined with sapphires.

"This was my mother's and her mother's before that. She passed it down to me on my wedding day. Now I would like to do the same for you as your old and blue. I didn't give it to you before, because your mother had given you something old. I figured I'd give it to you on another occasion but now I have the chance."

"Thank you. It's beautiful."

I turn around so she can put it in my hair. I went with a simple half up, half down hairstyle with the ends curled. I passed on a veil this time around.

I look at myself once again in the mirror, surrounded by the three woman who mean the world to me.

We stand there in silence for a minute when the door bursts open behind us and the fourth important woman in my life shouts, "Who's ready to get married?"

I burst out laughing because leave it to Danielle to burst the sadness bubble in the room.

"I'm ready."

"Good, because there are some very handsome men out here. I might need to snag one of them."

I walk toward the door with Ashley, my mom, and Victoria behind me. "As long as you don't take the QB, he's mine."

"Or the lawyer," Ashley adds next to me.

"Nah. I got my eye on the tall, dark, and handsome one." She and Connor have been on several dates but things are very casual. They both travel a lot with work.

My mom goes ahead of me to find my dad and make sure the boys head down to the docks where the ceremony is taking place.

Mrs. Anderson takes my hand. "Emma, I want you to know how glad I am to continue to call you my daughter. You made not just one, but two of my boys happy. I want to thank you for that."

"Thank you for letting me and for being the best second mom a girl could ask for." She gives me a hug and then follows my mom.

My dad appears in the hallway.

"Emma. My baby girl," he says.

Ashley and Danielle leave the room giving my dad and me a few minutes alone before the ceremony.

"Hi Dad."

"Are you ready?"

I nod.

"First I have to ask, are you sure you want to marry the quarterback?"

I laugh. All my life, I've been surrounded by football players and he always told me one day I could marry the wide receiver, like he was. I told him I wanted to marry the quarterback instead. It was a running joke with us. Then my crush on Jeremy happened, and the day I'll never forget in the coffee shop. After that day, he ignored me and I told myself I'd never marry the quarterback. I even told my mom and dad as much.

"I'm sure. He's one of the good ones." I smile thinking about everything he's done for me.

"I agree. He came and asked my permission before he proposed, and we had a long talk. I thanked him for everything he has helped you with these past few years. I loved Logan like a son, and I've never seen you happier than when you were with him. But Jeremy ignites something in you that pushes you to be better and more confident. I am so proud of the woman you are growing into. I love you."

I run a finger under my eye to catch the tear that has gathered in the corner. "Thanks Dad. I love you too."

"Now let's go marry you off to the quarterback."

We head into the hallway and down the stairs to the back patio. Ashley is waiting by the doors to outside.

"The coast is clear. The boys just ushered your mom and Jeremy's parents to their seats. Everyone else is seated."

We walk outside and I see Jeremy standing in the distance. We pass the pool and take our places at the end of the path down to the docks. The trees block us now so we can't be seen.

We hear the music start for Danielle and Ashley to make their way down the aisle.

Ashley is my maid of honor and Danielle is my bridesmaid. Jeremy chose Tyler as his best man and Connor as his grooms-man.

We kept the wedding small with a few of my friends from work and a few of his teammates.

I couldn't have asked for a better day. The sun is warm and shining bright, reflecting off the lake in the background. The sky is blue with not a cloud in sight.

The wedding march starts. My dad squeezes my hand and then links our arms.

"Time for the winning play?" he asks.

I laugh because he always uses football phrases when he can. "Always."

We start walking. Jeremy comes into view as we round the corner. I have to remind myself to breathe. I've seen him in a tux plenty of times, but this is all for me.

I know the second he sees me because his face lights up like a kid on Christmas morning. That smile could kill someone but in the best way possible.

I seem to float down the aisle and before I know it, we've reached the end. My dad places my hand in Jeremy's and kisses my cheek. He goes to sit next to my mom.

The same pastor that married Logan and me is here to marry me to Jeremy. He gives a beautiful speech about loss and finding the light to bring happiness. It's very fitting.

We prepared our own vows. I've been getting better at public speaking, but I still don't like it. Today is the first time I want to say something. I asked to go first, because I know Jeremy's vows are going to make me a blubbery mess.

"Jeremy Anderson. Where do I even begin? You completely turned my life around. From my first crush to my first heartbreak when you ignored me. Then I fell in love with your brother and you became my best friend. You became one of the few people I could always turn to. You always made me laugh with your flirty comments. You protected me without me realizing. Then we experienced one of the worst things a person can experience in their lifetime: a loss that hurt deep within us. A loss that almost made me end it. But you were the voice that kept whispering in my ear. The voice that pulled me from the darkness. The voice that I would not be here today without.

You pushed me to go back to school so I could have a career I love. You gave me the confidence to swim again. Lastly, you taught me how to learn to love again. I stand here today vowing to be your best friend, confidant, shoulder to cry on, battleship partner, and number one fan. I love you so much and I can't wait to be your wife."

I see a tear slip down Jeremy's cheek. I run my finger over it and then place my hand back in his.

Jeremy begins his vows, "Wow, okay. I don't know how to follow that." The audience laughs. "Emma Collins Anderson. My beautiful bride. I once told you that you make the most beautiful bride. But never in a million years did I think you would be standing across from me. I missed my chance when I didn't say anything that day in the coffee shop. Honestly, I was scared to death of your dad." His voice gets quiet. "I still kind of am." He quickly glances to my dad who smiles and nods at him. He looks back to me and continues. "When Logan asked me at the Olympics to take care of you if anything ever happened to him, I didn't even think twice before agreeing. After the accident, my heart broke twice. I lost my brother, and I lost you. No one could help you. We all tried until one day it was like something clicked inside you. I don't even remember what I said to you but you looked up at me like I was your hero. From that day forward, I vowed to keep my promise to Logan and do whatever I needed to do in order to protect you. Today I vow to love and cherish you, to push you past your boundaries, to be the man that you deserve, and be that hero that you saw me as. I love you, and I can't wait to be your husband."

The tears are running down my face. I gave up trying to stop them. I lean up to give him a quick peck. I look over to the pastor and thankfully, he's smiling.

"Sorry. I couldn't help it."

He laughs. "Let's get these rings on so then I can pronounce you officially." We exchange rings and then he pronounces us husband and wife. "You may kiss the bride."

Jeremy places a hand under my upper back and dips me. He then kisses me until I hear cat calls.

Jeremy lifts me back up, raising my hand above us. The audience cheers as we make our way down the aisle to the tables set up in the yard.

The rest of the day we enjoy dancing, delicious food prepared by my mom and Jeremy's, a bourbon apple cake with apples from the apple tree Jeremy planted at the park, and a gorgeous sunset over the lake.

I can't help noticing Ashley's smile the entire night. I saw her and Tyler in a very serious conversation and ever since then, the smile has not left her face. I'll have to ask her about it.

As the night ends, Jeremy and I sit on the dock looking out at the lake. The stars twinkle above us. I can't help thinking that one star in particular shines brighter than the rest.

"What are you thinking about, wife?"

"How much I love hearing that!" I say laying my head on his shoulder. We stay silent for a few minutes before I answer his question. "I was thinking about the stars."

"The stars are bright tonight. Especially that one." He points at a particular star. "It seems to be shining down, watching over us, and never far from our hearts."

"That it is, husband."

"I will never get tired of hearing that."

"I love you, Jeremy Anderson."

"I love you, Emma Anderson."

Epilogue

4 and a half years later

"Mommy, are we leaving?" Christopher asks me. He's three years old and already forming complete sentences. His sister, Sophia is two years old and right behind him. Jeremy says it's all my brain but he's just as smart.

"Yes, baby in five minutes. I'm just waiting for daddy and we'll be off." I kiss the top of his head. I gather their toys and other things we'll need.

"Daddy!" Sophia reaches up for Jeremy. He picks her up and spins her around. She's a total daddy's girl and I love watching them together.

I make eye contact with Jeremy and he winks.

"Did you grab your football?" Jeremy asks Christopher.

"No, I'll go get it." He runs into his room and comes back out with the football in his hand. Jeremy had gotten the game ball after his second Super Bowl win and the whole Titans team signed it. Christopher loves showing it off to his grandparents. They act surprised every time he shows them.

"Okay time to go." I grab my purse and the kids' bag. I take Christopher's hand and we walk out to the car.

When we get to Jeremy's parents' house, my parents' car is already in the driveway. They all come running outside.

Sophia runs over to our moms and attempts to give them both hugs at the same time. "Grammies," they chuckle.

Inside the house, it smells like all my favorite Thanksgiving dishes. My mouth is already watering.

Ashley and Ty are sitting on opposite couches, completely ignoring each other. They finally admitted their true feelings at Jeremy and I's wedding. They dated exclusively with titles for a few years, but a few months ago, they called it quits for good. Neither of them will tell me what happened but I know I'll get it out of Ashley eventually.

I say hi to both of them and Christopher runs up to Ty. "I brought my football." He lifts up the football. "You're going to play right?"

"Yeah buddy, but only if I can be on your team?" Christopher nods enthusiastically before running over to Jeremy asking when they can go outside.

I ask my mom if she needs any help with Thanksgiving dinner. "No. We pretty much have everything prepped and as soon as the turkey is done, we'll throw everything else in to cook."

"Okay."

"I think it's time for our annual Thanksgiving football game." My dad walks up kissing my mom.

"I have the ball." Christopher holds up his football before running outside.

We all laugh and follow him to the backyard. I pick up Sophia and we sit down in a chair on the deck to watch the game. It's a gorgeous sunny day, not a cloud in the sky, and surprisingly warm. Well, if you count the sixties being warm.

My mom and Victoria sit down next to me.

Christopher runs over to me. "Mommy, aren't you going to play?"

"No, I'm going to sit here and catch up with the girls but you go play and I'll watch."

"Okay. Daddy said to give this to you." He hands me the signed football. He loves to bring it everywhere with him but they prefer to play football with a ball without sentimental value.

I hear my dad ask Christopher if I'm playing and he says, "No she's catching up with the girls." Jeremy gives me a knowing smile. I wink at him.

Ashley plops down in the chair next to me. I ask her, "Are you ever going to tell me what happened with my brother?"

She shrugs. "The long distance was just getting to us, and too many hot girls for him to flirt with in New York." I know that's all I'll get for now. I also know not to push her. She'll tell me when she's ready. We're similar in that way. "Now where's my Sophia? Your Auntie Ashley has been dying to see you."

Sophia jumps in her lap and they start playing with the doll in her hand.

I turn to my mom and Mrs. Anderson. "So no football today, Emma?"

"No, some days I just like to watch." They both look at me and then each other. When they look back at me, they both have knowing smiles. I shrug and turn to the game.

It's my dad and Blake against Ty and Christopher. Jeremy's the all-around quarterback like always.

After his proposal at the Super Bowl, he went on to beat the Colts. Two years later, they went to the Super Bowl again and won against the Patriots. He retired a little over a year ago, thankful for the two Super Bowls he won as that was more than most—unless you're Tom Brady and then you have to have one on every finger.

Jeremy now works with his father at Andertainment heading up the Sports division. One day he'll take over the whole company but he loves the sports side right now.

Ty still works in their New York office as an entertainment lawyer and loves it. I was hoping I could persuade him to move closer but I don't think he ever will. I wonder if that's one of the reasons Ashley and him called it quits. I know she wanted to move back here. In fact, since the breakup she has. I love having her close again but it makes me sad that my brother is being stubborn.

When I had Christopher, I switched to part time with the Titans and now work on a more freelance basis. I'm hoping when the kids get a little older to open my own Physical Therapy practice.

We bought a house about twenty minutes away from both our parents to be closer. It's actually on the other side of the lake from Jeremy's parents' house. The lake is so massive that it takes a full twenty minutes to go around. I wonder if it would be faster by boat. We'll have to time it one day.

We have a huge back yard overlooking the lake and Jeremy just built a swing set for Christopher. There's a huge wrap-around porch and I made sure Jeremy added a swing that we can rock on. I love sitting on the swing watching the kids play or cuddling under a blanket with Jeremy watching the moon rise over the lake.

I look back at all my boys as they play the game we all love. I look over at Ashley playing with Sophia and then over at my mom and Victoria talking. All of my favorite people are here and I couldn't be happier. There are still times when I think of Logan, especially when everyone is together, but I truly believe he's looking down from Heaven smiling at us.

After dinner, our parents watch the kids so Jeremy and I can take a walk before dessert. We stand on the dock looking out at the water.

As the moon casts a glow across the lake, I think back to our wedding day. We got married three months after Jeremy proposed since we didn't see the need to wait. We got married right here at the Anderson house. It was a magical and warm summer day.

I rest my head on Jeremy's shoulder. "So many memories and so much to be thankful for."

He gazes down at me. "Yes. And you know what I'm most thankful for?" I shake my head. "You, Emma. You've always been there, from a crush to a friend and then sister-in-law and then friend again. You became my support and then the love of my life. Now you're my wife and the mother of my children. I love you so much."

"I love you too." We gaze out at the lake.

"Are you ready to tell them?"

"Yep. I thought we could tell them at dessert, although I think my mom and your mom already know."

"Probably, I mean this is after all the third time." He laughs at me.

"Yes and the last. I love our kids but I think three will be enough."

He wraps his arms around my waist resting his hands on my stomach. We both look at my slightly growing stomach. I'm three months pregnant and you can see a slight bulge. We wanted to wait till we were all together, in person, before we told anyone which is why we've waited till now. It's why I suspect our moms already know.

"We can never have enough because I'll never have enough of you Emma. Plus, practicing is fun." He winks.

I punch him in the arm. "And I'll never have enough of you." He kisses me and we turn back to the vast open lake. This is where it all began many years ago, and I can't wait for the many more to come.

A Note from Kaitlyn

You made it to the end. You either hate me for killing off Logan, or you're happy (sounds awful) because you're team Jeremy. Whichever it is, thank you for sticking around.

When I first started writing Emma's story, I always knew it would be Jeremy. I never wanted to kill off Logan, but sometimes when writing a story, things happen, and you just have to go with it. Writing this book was emotional. It's the reason it took so long, because I had to take a second to get over what was on the page. Emma did a lot of growing in this book, and I'm proud of who she became.

Emma and Jeremy's love story may be over, but their story is far from over. You'll see plenty more of them in the future with the next-generation series. But first, we need to see if Ashley and Tyler will ever figure out their love story. Are they destined for each other, or is it actually quits for good? Find out in the Learning to Love series book 3.

Thanks again for picking up "Love Moves Forward"! If you have a chance, please leave a review.

Love,

Kaitlyn Calicott

Acknowledgments

A special thanks to:

My husband, Lloyd, for encouraging me to keep writing and make millions (maybe one day – what every author dreams of)!

My sister, Kelsey, for sticking with me since the beginning and giving me tons of feedback.

Lynne, for helping me create the blurb. You always have a way with words.

My mom and dad for always supporting my dreams and reading my book.

To Jess and Ashley for being the best beta readers and giving me some good ideas.

My editor, Jessie for fixing grammar, making sure everything lined up with the first, and encouraging me to add a special wedding chapter.

To my fellow NHC teachers, you know who you are, for inspiring me to add more boy bands. Gotta love the NSYNC and Backstreet Boys references.

About the Author

Kaitlyn Calicott writes romances with a guaranteed happily ever after; sometimes, it just takes a while to get there. When she isn't writing, she loves reading and getting lost in the world of books with a glass of wine. She also loves spending time with her husband and two boys, cuddling on the couch watching movies, playing with their chickens, boating, and baking delicious treats. For upcoming releases, spoilers, and so much more, check out her Facebook Group or website at Kaitlyncalicott.com.

Also By Kaitlyn Calicott

Learning to Love Series

Book One – I Will Always Love You

Free Bonus Chapter – Logan's POV

Book Two – Love Moves Forward

Book Three – Ashley's story